Praise for

THE SISTERS GRIMM SERIES:

Today Show Kids Book Club Pick
New York Times Bestseller
Book Sense Pick
Oppenheim Toy Portfolio Platinum Award
Kirkus Reviews Best Fantasy Book
A *Real Simple* magazine "Must-Have"
New York Public Library 100 Titles for
    Reading and Sharing Selection

"Why didn't I think of *The Sisters Grimm*?
What a great concept!" —Jane Yolen

"A very fun series . . ." —*Chicago Parent*

★ "The twists and turns of the plot, the clever
humor, and the behind-the-scenes glimpses
of Everafters we think we know will appeal to
many readers." —*Kliatt*, starred review

ALSO BY MICHAEL BUCKLEY:

In the *Sisters Grimm* series:

BOOK ONE: THE FAIRY-TALE DETECTIVES

BOOK TWO: THE UNUSUAL SUSPECTS

BOOK THREE: THE PROBLEM CHILD

BOOK FOUR: ONCE UPON A CRIME

BOOK FIVE: MAGIC AND OTHER MISDEMEANORS

BOOK SIX: TALES FROM THE HOOD

BOOK SEVEN: THE EVERAFTER WAR

BOOK EIGHT: THE INSIDE STORY

In the *NERDS* series:

**NERDS: NATIONAL ESPIONAGE, RESCUE,
AND DEFENSE SOCIETY**

The Library of Congress has cataloged the harcover edition of this book as follows:

Buckley, Michael.
The Everafter War / by Michael Buckley ; pictures by Peter Ferguson.
p. cm. — (The Sisters Grimm ; bk. 7)
Summary: After their parents awake from a sleeping spell, Daphne and Sabrina become caught in the middle of a war between the Scarlet Hand and Prince Charming's Everafter army and learn a shocking secret about a deadly enemy.
ISBN 978-0-8109-8355-7
[1. Characters in literature—Fiction. 2. Sisters—Fiction. 3. Magic—Fiction. 4. War—Fiction. 5. Mystery and detective stories.] I. Ferguson, Peter, 1968– ill. II. Title.

PZ7.B882323Ev 2009
[Fic]—dc22
2008045924

Paperback ISBN 978-0-8109-8429-5

Originally published in hardcover by Amulet Books in 2009
Text copyright © 2009 Michael Buckley
Illustrations copyright © 2009 Peter Ferguson

Printed and bound in U.S.A.
10 9 8 7 6 5 4 3 2 1

Amulet Books are available at special discounts when purchased in quantity for premiums and promotions as well as fundraising or educational use. Special editions can also be created to specification. For details, contact specialmarkets@abramsbooks.com or the address below.

ABRAMS
THE ART OF BOOKS SINCE 1949

115 West 18th Street
New York, NY 10011
www.abramsbooks.com

THE SISTERS GRIMM

· BOOK SEVEN ·

❖ THE EVERAFTER WAR ❖

MICHAEL BUCKLEY

PICTURES BY PETER FERGUSON

AMULET BOOKS

New York

ACKNOWLEDGMENTS

These books benefit from the amazing editing of Susan Van Metre and Maggie Lehrman, who not only correct my bad grammar but encourage me to navigate down roads I would never have known to take. The books also owe greatly to the tireless efforts of Jason Wells, who sings their praises near and far (even on weekends). Thanks to everyone at Amulet/Abrams who works so hard to make such beautiful books.

I owe a great deal of thanks to my literary agent, Alison Fargis, as well as her team at Stonesong Press, and, as always, my good friend Joe Deasy, who eagerly reads and rereads each manuscript.

Much thanks to Lucie Plaisimon, Caroline Hochberg, Ayshia Levy, and Zakiya Casey for their friendly smiles. But mostly thanks to Alison, who gave me Finn, who gives my aimless life an explanation.

THE SISTERS GRIMM

BOOK SEVEN

THE EVERAFTER WAR

SABRINA STOOD AGHAST, *shocked from the discovery she had just made and the wave of emotions that accompanied it. Terror, betrayal, and disgust filled her head, sending mixed signals to every part of her body. One moment she wanted to run—to put as much distance between her and the figure standing before her as possible. The next she wanted to snatch him by the collar and shake him in anger until he explained himself.*

"You? You're the Master? You're the leader of the Scarlet Hand?"

"Yes," he said calmly.

"But you—" Daphne said, trembling.

"But I was your friend? Is that what you were going to say?"

"Yes! I trusted you. We all trusted you!" Sabrina cried.

"Then I'm afraid you've made a terrible mistake."

1

SIX DAYS EARLIER

abrina Grimm's life was a collection of odd events. But sitting in her grandmother's living room with three massive brown bears might have been the oddest of them all.

The bears had arrived in the company of a curly-haired blond woman with dazzling eyes. Her face was round and tanned, with dimples in her cheeks and a dainty nose sprinkled with golden freckles. Her name was Goldilocks. Yes, *the* Goldilocks, only twenty years older and overflowing with a nervous energy that kept her rushing around the living room rearranging furniture to her liking. She moved lamps and rugs, switched chairs with tables, and even took down family portraits and rehung them on different walls. When she moved something, she would step back and look at it, mutter something incomprehensible to herself, stick her tongue out, and then move it again. If she liked where it landed she would beam with pride and say, "Just right."

Sabrina sat uncomfortably in a loveseat across from the group. Her sister, Daphne, sat next to her, chewing on her palm—a quirky habit she had when she was very excited or happy. The only other witness to Sabrina's strange company was the family's two-hundred-pound Great Dane, Elvis. He seemed just as nervous as Sabrina; the dog's head swung back and forth from Goldilocks to the bears and then to Sabrina. He let out a soft, confused whine.

Sabrina shrugged at him. "Welcome to Ferryport Landing, Elvis." The dog let out a soft bark.

"How long are we going to wait?" Sabrina whispered to her sister.

"Granny said she'd come and get us," Daphne whispered back. "Maybe we should offer them something to drink, to be polite."

Sabrina nodded. "Would anyone like anything to drink?"

The bears grunted and huffed and the blond woman responded in a series of short grunts. When they had finished chatting, Goldilocks turned to Sabrina and informed her that the biggest of the bears liked Earl Grey tea, very hot. The second biggest would prefer hers iced. The littlest of the bears would love some chocolate milk if it wasn't too much trouble. Being from New York City, Sabrina had seen many crazy people talking to animals: She'd once seen a man discuss Napoleon's defeat at Waterloo with a one-eyed mutt and its filthy rubber chew toy. In this case, however, the woman talking to the animals wasn't crazy. Animals really did talk to her.

The girls excused themselves and went into the kitchen with Elvis in tow. There they found a little girl in red pajamas huddling in the corner. She had a sad face framed by amber curls that fell across her shoulders. Her name was Red Riding Hood. Sabrina immediately wished she had stayed in the living room with the bears. Red had been a homicidal lunatic the day before, but when she was cured Granny had invited the child to live with the Grimms.

"Are they gone yet?" Red asked. She was extremely shy.

"No," Daphne said. "But they're friends. You don't have to hide in the kitchen."

Red didn't look convinced.

Daphne went to work preparing the drinks while Sabrina spied on Goldilocks through a crack in the kitchen door. Goldilocks was still rushing around the room reorganizing the Grimms' possessions.

"She's giving me a headache," Sabrina said.

"Don't spy," Daphne scolded. "It's rude."

"I can't help myself. Aren't you curious about her? I mean, what did Dad see in her?" She studied the woman's features. Goldilocks was pretty and she seemed nice in a ditzy kind of way, but she was no Veronica Grimm. Sabrina's mother was a knockout.

"Love is weird," Daphne said. "We can't know why Dad was in love with her."

Sabrina laughed. "What do you know? You're only—" She stopped herself when her sister flashed her an angry look. She was already treading on thin ice with Daphne. She didn't need to make their relationship any worse. "Yeah, that's true. We can't know."

"Red, are you going to join us?" Daphne asked the little girl.

Red shook her head vigorously and sank back into her hiding space.

The girls left her there and returned to the living room with the drinks. Sabrina found the three bears sitting on the couch, shaking the last few gumdrops out of a jar Granny Relda kept on a coffee table for guests. The biggest bear gestured toward the jar as if to say "MORE!" It made Sabrina uncomfortable. She hated when she saw animals behaving like people. Animals

shouldn't eat gumdrops! They shouldn't drink tea or chocolate milk, either.

"This is a bad idea," Goldilocks fretted, sitting on an ottoman, then jumping back up to move a vase. "I shouldn't have come."

"No, you did the right thing. We've tried everything to wake them up. You're our last hope," Sabrina said, nearly panicked that the woman might turn and walk out of their lives. They had been searching for her for so long.

"Have some tea," Daphne said.

Goldilocks ignored the offer and went to work rearranging the books in the family's huge bookshelf. "Your dad told me he didn't want to see me anymore and I tried to respect that. I moved to New York City and lived there for a long time. I had a nice little apartment in the East Village close to where CBGB's used to be. Then I heard he and Veronica had moved to Manhattan. I never went to see him. It was the only way I could say I was sorry, and now, here I am. I know you need me to help him now, but when he opens his eyes and sees me standing over him I don't think he's going to be happy. And your mother! She's going to think I'm . . . I'm a harlot."

"What's *harlot* mean?" Daphne asked.

Sabrina knew and thought Goldilocks might be right. "A harlot is—"

"I asked Goldilocks, not you," Daphne snapped.

Sabrina frowned. Daphne always turned to her whenever she didn't understand a word.

"A harlot is a woman with a bad reputation," the woman explained. "A harlot is a woman who kisses another woman's husband."

"My mom will get over it," Daphne said matter-of-factly.

Goldi turned to the three musky-smelling bears. "What do you think I should do?"

They stared into the woman's eyes and shrugged at the same time.

"A lot of help the three of you are!" Goldi scolded then turned back to Daphne. "What is keeping your grandmother?"

"Same old Goldi," a voice said from across the room. Everyone turned to find a tall, handsome man with a mop of blond hair and a nose that had seen the knuckles of one too many fists. He wore a trench coat with hundreds of extra pockets sewn into it. Uncle Jake smiled at everyone. "Just as impatient as ever."

Goldilocks frowned. "Jake Grimm!"

"You ready to get this show on the road?" he asked her.

The blond beauty bit her lower lip. "Just a second," she said, then snatched a paperweight from the coffee table and set it on the bureau. She stood back and admired it, then smiled with satisfaction. "OK, let's do this."

She followed Jake up the stairs with the bears lumbering behind her. Sabrina and Daphne followed them, unfortunately downwind of the bears' special brand of funk. Elvis followed reluctantly.

"Are you coming?" Daphne said to Red, who had crept back to the couch now that everyone was leaving.

Red shook her head. "This is your family. I don't belong."

Daphne rushed back down the stairs and took the little girl's hand in her own, then pulled her to her feet. "C'mon."

At the top of the stairs, they met Granny Relda, a chubby, stout little woman with wrinkles lining most of her face. She had white hair streaked with faint traces of her old fire-engine red. These days she rolled it all into a bun on the top of her head, though wisps of it escaped through the course of a day. She had changed from her nightgown into a bright white dress and a matching hat with a sunflower appliqué in its center. She smiled and hugged Goldilocks as if she were one of her own children.

"It's good to see you, Goldi," she said in her light German accent. Granny had grown up in Berlin and moved to America when she married the girls' late grandfather, Basil.

Goldilocks smiled. "It's been a long time."

Granny led everyone into a spare bedroom furnished with a full-length mirror and a queen-size bed. Lying comfortably on the mattress were Sabrina and Daphne's parents, Henry and Veronica Grimm. Both were deeply asleep. Granny Relda sat down next to her slumbering son and took his hand in hers. For the first time since Sabrina had met her grandmother the old woman's shoulders didn't look as if they were carrying the weight of the world.

Goldi stepped over to the bed and looked down at Sabrina's parents. "Relda, I—"

Granny Relda stopped her. "I know what you're going to say and it's nonsense. There was never a need for an apology. What happened to Basil was not your fault. It wasn't anyone's fault."

Sabrina watched Uncle Jake's eyes drift to the ground.

"I'm not sure Henry feels the same way," Goldi said. Sabrina saw the expression the odd woman gave her father. It was clear that even after all the years they had been apart Goldilocks still loved him. "How long have they been like this?"

"They disappeared two years ago," Daphne explained. "They were like this when we found them about three months ago."

"We've tried everything to wake them up," Sabrina added.

"What about Prince Charming?" Goldilocks said. "He seems to have a knack for this kind of thing."

"He also has a habit of marrying the women he wakes up," Granny said. "Might be coincidence, but his kiss seems to have a power all its own. I'd rather not chance it."

"I don't want William Charming for a stepfather," Sabrina grumbled.

Uncle Jake crossed the room and patted Poppa Bear on his furry arm. "Good to see you again, old man," he said. "And the boy. He's getting big."

"You know the bears?" Goldilocks asked.

"Oh yes, Poppa and Baby Bear helped me retrieve a phantom scroll from a Romanian constable a few years back," Uncle Jake explained.

Poppa Bear let out a low grunt.

"Retrieve or steal, Jacob?" Goldilocks asked disapprovingly.

"To-may-to, to-mah-to," he replied with a sly grin. "Goldi, you and the bears have given up a lot to come here. You do realize you're trapped in Ferryport Landing? The barrier won't let you out."

Poppa Bear gave a long bark.

"He says it was time to reunite his family," Goldilocks explained. "Momma Bear was here, and Poppa and Baby Bear were not. They had all hoped the magical barrier would eventually fall down and they would be reunited, but no such luck. He says it's better to be trapped together than apart for another day."

"I don't mean to be rude," Sabrina interrupted. "But we've been waiting a long time for this. Could we get started?"

Goldilocks nodded and turned to Uncle Jake. "So, Jake, you're the expert on magic as far as I can tell. I just plant a kiss on Henry and he'll wake up?"

"That's the word on the street," Uncle Jake said. "Snow White and Briar Rose both explained what happened with them. Briar said there's no special trick to it. Just pucker up and lay one on him."

"Briar Rose said 'pucker up and lay one on him'?" Sabrina asked. She couldn't imagine such a demure woman being so . . . vulgar.

"I'm paraphrasing," Uncle Jake said sheepishly, then turned back to Goldilocks. "Just kiss him."

"What about Veronica?" Goldilocks said. "She needs a kiss from someone who loves her. I can't wake her up."

Daphne took her by the hand. "Your kiss will wake up Dad and then he'll kiss Mom."

"And all of this will be over," Sabrina added.

Just then, the full-length mirror leaning against the far wall began to shimmer and shake. Its reflective surface rippled like a bubbling brook and when it calmed, a big, bulbous head materialized in the reflection. He had deep-set eyes, thick lips, and a heavy brow. A crackling thunderstorm ignited the sky behind him.

"WHO INVADES MY SANCTUARY?" he bellowed. Red Riding Hood jumped and tried to run from the room, but Daphne held her hand tight.

"It's us, Mirror," Granny said. "No enemies here."

The lightning faded and the face brightened. "Oh, am I missing something?"

"Sorry, Mirror," Daphne said. "We were just about to call for you. Goldilocks is here. She's going to smooch my dad. We think it will wake him up!"

Mirror glanced around the room at the many guests and smiled. "Hello, Ms. G. It's nice to see you again."

Goldilocks returned the smile. "Still looking great, Mirror."

Mirror smiled. "Thanks. I owe it all to Botox and my trainer."

"Again, folks, can we do this?" Sabrina said.

"OK, here goes," Goldilocks said. She tucked her blond curls back behind her ear and leaned in close. Sabrina held her breath in all the excitement and realized everyone else was doing the same. They had all waited so long for this moment. There had been many nights when Sabrina was convinced it would never happen. But, now, finally, her family would be reunited. Things might go back to normal.

And then someone farted. Everyone turned in the direction of the horrible noise. There, standing in the doorway, was Puck, a shaggy-haired boy who, like Red Riding Hood, had been adopted by Granny Relda. He was somewhere in the range of four thousand years old, though he looked like he might be twelve. He was wearing pajamas with robots fighting monkeys all over them and had on a sleeping cap so long that the end dragged a herd of dust bunnies behind him. He scratched his backside with a wooden sword and scowled.

"You people have woken me up. I was going to come out here and complain that it sounded like there was a pack of bears running through the house and look what I find! A pack of bears!" Puck turned to Granny Relda. "I suppose you have invited them to move in, as well. You've never met anyone you didn't hand a set of keys to. I mean, after all, you've invited a murderous lunatic who only wears one color."

"I'm sorry," Red Riding Hood squeaked.

Then Puck turned to Daphne. "A chunky little monkey who eats us out of house and home."

"Hey! I'm not chunky. I'm big-boned."

"Yeah, like a brontosaurus!" Puck snorted and turned to Sabrina. "And then there's this one. A girl so ugly burn victims stare and point at her. So let's have some bears move in, too. Why not? Maybe we could invite a couple of giants while we're at it, or maybe a bunch of those idiot Munchkins from across town. We've got plenty of room! Why not turn this place into a bed-and-breakfast for every second-rate Everafter with a hard-luck story?"

"Puck, that's not very nice," Granny said. "We're sorry we woke you but Goldilocks is here. She's going to kiss Henry and wake him up."

"Who? What?" the boy said.

"Goldilocks, my father's former girlfriend," Sabrina said. "She's going to kiss him and break the magic spell that's kept him and my mother asleep for two years."

"There's a magic spell on them?" the boy said. "I thought they were just really lazy."

Sabrina growled.

"We're glad you're here, Puck," Granny Relda said.

"I'm sure you are," the boy said, letting out another fart. This one was so loud it made Elvis jump in fear. "Is there any food at this shindig?" Granny shook her head. "You people throw the lamest parties."

"Goldi, please, just kiss my dad," Sabrina cried.

Goldilocks nodded, leaned in, and nervously touched her lips to Henry's. The kiss was gentle and a little longer than Sabrina would have liked. It was clear to Sabrina that it had a big impact on Goldilocks. Her face was bright red and she looked as if she had just been caught doing something illegal. But her expression was nothing compared to the looks on the faces of Sabrina's uncle and grandmother. Both of them looked defeated.

"What? What's wrong?" Sabrina asked.

"It should have worked already," the old woman said.

"Try again," Uncle Jake urged.

Goldilocks bit her lip but did as she was told. She took a deep breath, as if it might be her last, and bent over to kiss Henry once more. When she was finished she hovered there, inches from his face, and whispered something Sabrina couldn't hear.

"Perhaps Goldilocks has fallen out of love with Henry," Mirror said. "It has been more than fifteen years since they were a couple."

Goldilocks shook her head but said nothing.

"Then what's wrong?" Sabrina cried, fighting a bubble of panic and despair rising up into her throat.

"Let's try one more time," Daphne said hopefully.

"It won't help," Uncle Jake said. "Briar said the result would be immediate."

Granny nodded sadly. "I've read accounts of these spells being broken. The moment her lips touched your father's he should have woken up. This must be some unique version of the spell. We'll just have to go back to the drawing board and find another solution."

Daphne flashed Sabrina a look that said "don't freak out," but it was too late.

"This has been a stupid wild-goose chase!" Sabrina exclaimed. "The Master and the Scarlet Hand are probably getting a big laugh out of this right now!"

"Don't give up hope, Starfish," Mirror said.

"Give up hope! I haven't had any hope in two years."

"Bummer!" Puck said. "Well, maybe whoever is pounding on the door downstairs can wake him up."

"Puck, could you answer it for me?" Granny asked.

"What am I? The butler?"

"I'll get it," Sabrina said. She needed to get out of the room. The disappointment was hanging in the air, threatening to suffocate her.

"Whoever it is, don't forget to invite them to move in with us," Puck said sarcastically. "Don't forget to show them where the towels are!"

"Freaking out isn't helping Mom and Dad," Daphne said as she raced down the stairs after Sabrina. "Everyone wanted

Goldilocks to wake up Dad. So it didn't work. Exploding in frustration every time we have a setback is, well, annoying."

Sabrina marched to the door, then turned to face her sister. "First of all, you don't even know the meaning of most of the words in that last sentence. I'll be angry and upset if I want. I have a right to be angry. My life is horrible."

Sabrina threw the door open and there, standing on the porch, was a rail-thin woman with a hooked beak of a nose and eyes like tiny black holes. She was dressed entirely in gray. Her handbag was gray. Her hair was gray. When she smiled, her teeth were gray.

"I think it's about to get a lot worse," Daphne groaned.

"Hello, girls," the woman said.

"Ms. Smirt!" Sabrina cried.

"Oh, you remember me. How it warms the heart," she said as she snatched them by the wrists and dragged them out of the house and across the lawn where a taxicab was waiting in the driveway.

"Where are you taking us?" Daphne cried, trying and failing to break free from the woman's iron talons.

"Back to the orphanage," Smirt snapped. "You don't belong here. Your grandmother is unfit. She kidnapped you from your foster father."

Sabrina remembered the last foster father Smirt had sent them to live with. Mr. Greeley was a certifiable lunatic. "He was a serial killer. He attacked us with a crowbar."

"The father-child bond needs time to develop," Smirt said as she pushed the girls into the backseat of the taxi.

"You can't send us back to him," Daphne shouted.

"Sadly, you are correct. Mr. Greeley is unavailable to take you back due to an unfortunate incarceration. But don't worry. I've already found you a new foster family. The father is an amateur knife thrower. He's eager for some new targets . . . I mean, daughters."

Smirt slammed the cab's door shut and tossed a twenty-dollar bill at the driver. "You got automatic locks in this thing?"

Suddenly, the locks on the doors were set.

"To the train station, please," Smirt said. "And there's another twenty in it if you can make the 8:14 to Grand Central."

The taxi charged out of the driveway and tires squealed as it made a beeline toward the Ferryport Landing train station.

"You can't take us back to the orphanage," Sabrina said. "We're not orphans anymore. We found our mother and father."

"Such an imagination you have, Sophie," Smirt said. "There's really nothing as unattractive in a child as an imagination."

"My name is Sabrina!"

In no time, the taxi was pulling into the train station. Ms. Smirt pinched the girls on the shoulders and hustled them onto the waiting train. The doors closed before Sabrina and Daphne could make a run for it.

"Find a seat, girls," the caseworker said as the train rolled out of the station.

"Daphne, don't worry," Sabrina whispered as she took her sister's hand and helped her into a seat. Sabrina had many talents but her greatest was the ability to devise effective escape plans. While she comforted her sister, she studied the exit doors, windows, and even the emergency brake. A daring escape was already coming together when she noticed the complete lack of worry on her little sister's face.

"I've got this one covered," Daphne said.

"You what?" Sabrina asked.

The little girl put her palm into her mouth and bit down on it.

"What's going on, Daphne?" Sabrina continued, eyeing the girl suspiciously. Daphne had never plotted an escape. Escaping had been the exclusive domain of Sabrina Grimm for almost two years. What did her little sister have in mind?

"Zip it!" Ms. Smirt snapped before Daphne could explain.

"I don't want to have to sit on this train for two hours with a couple of chatterboxes." The caseworker snatched a book out of her handbag and flipped it open. Sabrina peered at the title: *The Secret.*

"Ms. Smirt, have you ever heard of the Brothers Grimm?" Daphne said.

The caseworker scowled and set her book on her lap. "What do you want?"

"I was wondering if you have ever heard of the Brothers Grimm."

"They wrote the fairy tales," Ms. Smirt said.

Daphne shook her head. "That's what most people believe, but it's not true. The Brothers Grimm didn't write stories, they wrote down things that really happened. The fairy tales aren't made-up stories, they're warnings to the world about Everafters."

Sabrina was stunned. Daphne was spilling the family's secret to the worst possible person. They couldn't trust Smirt any further than they could throw her.

"What's an Everafter?" the caseworker snapped.

"It's what fairy-tale characters like to be called," the little girl explained. "'Fairy-tale character' is kind of a rude term. Like I was saying, the Brothers Grimm wrote about Everafters because they are real. Take Snow White. She's a real person and the story really happened—poisoned apple and all. Cinderella, Prince Charming, Beauty and the Beast, Robin Hood—they're all real people. They actually live here in Ferryport Landing. The Queen of Hearts is our mayor. Sleeping Beauty is dating our uncle."

"Debbie, you are going to look so adorable in your straitjacket," Ms. Smirt said.

"It's Daphne," the little girl said.

"Please be quiet," Sabrina whispered into her sister's ear.

"OK, kid, I'll bite. So, if fairy-tale characters are real, how come I haven't met any?" the caseworker said with a cackle.

"Because there's a magical barrier that surrounds this town that keeps the Everafters inside. Our great-great-great-great-great-grandfather Wilhelm Grimm and a witch named Baba Yaga built it to stop some evil Everafters from invading nearby towns."

"Oh, of course," Smirt said sarcastically. She slapped her knee and let out a ghastly laugh that sounded like a wounded moose. Sabrina had never seen the nasty woman laugh before and hoped she never would again. Daphne ignored Smirt. "The barrier has made people in the town angry, and a lot of the Everafters don't like us much," Daphne said. "But—"

"Daphne, stop. You've told her too much," Sabrina begged.

"Let me finish, Sabrina," Daphne said calmly. "Like I was saying, we have a lot of enemies in Ferryport Landing but we've managed to make a few friends."

Suddenly there was a tap on the window. Sabrina gazed out, expecting to see the Hudson River rushing past. Instead, what she saw nearly caused her to fall out of her seat. In the window was a familiar ragged-haired boy in robots-fighting-monkeys pajamas. Held aloft by two giant pink insect wings, he soared alongside the speeding train, grinning and sticking his tongue out at her. Sabrina had never been so happy to get a raspberry in her life.

Ms. Smirt, however, was horrified. She screamed like she had just found her name on Santa's naughty list. She tumbled onto the floor and scampered underneath her seat like a cockroach. When she mustered the bravery to take another peek, Puck had already zipped ahead and out of sight.

"Did you see that?" Ms. Smirt stammered, slowly creeping back into the aisle and then dashing to the window for a closer look. "I must be tired. I thought I saw a boy out there. Flying! Outside the window!"

Just then, there was a horrible, eardrum-blasting *clunk*, followed by the screaming of metal on metal. Something sailed past the window and Sabrina watched as it disappeared. It was part of a door, much like the one the girls had stepped through to board the train. Sabrina looked back at her sister, who was grinning from ear to ear. "Did the two of you plan this?"

"Someone's got to do the thinking in this family," Daphne replied matter-of-factly.

A moment later Puck came strolling down the aisle with his beautiful wings extended proudly. "Well, well, well. Look at me. Here I am saving you two again. You know, you're really quite helpless and pathetic. It amazes me that you can even dress yourselves in the morning."

Ms. Smirt cried out and once again fell to the floor and scooted back under the seat.

Puck turned to Sabrina. "What is she doing down there?"

"Hiding, I guess."

Puck leaned down and poked his head under the seat. "I found you."

Ms. Smirt shrieked.

Puck lifted himself to his full height and laughed. "She's fun." He leaned back down and she screamed again. "I could do this all day. Can I keep her?"

Daphne shook her head. "You know the plan."

Puck frowned. "Fine!" he snapped, then dragged the caseworker out from under the seat and to her feet.

Daphne stepped up to the trembling woman. "Ms. Smirt, I have something to say to you."

Smirt said nothing and seemed unable to take her eyes off Puck and his wings.

"We are not going back to the orphanage. Not now, not ever. We are not going back to any foster parent, either. Our family is in Ferryport Landing and we're staying. You are never going to come back to this town. You are never going to bother us again. This is good-bye, Ms. Smirt."

"Right after the merciless kicking, right?" Puck said. "We talked about the kicking."

"I vetoed the kicking, remember?" Daphne said.

Puck scowled.

Just then, the train's conductor came over the speaker system. "Next stop is Poughkeepsie, folks. Next stop, Poughkeepsie."

Suddenly, Puck's face fell and his ever-present mischievous grin melted. "Uh-oh."

"What's *uh-oh*?" Sabrina cried, looking around. Every time she heard "uh-oh" something bad happened. It usually involved running from monsters or giants.

"The barrier," Puck shouted as he spun around and ran in the opposite direction of the train's rolling. "I forgot about the barrier!"

"Uh-oh," the girls said in unison. No Everafters could pass through the barrier, and so when the train passed through it Puck was sent sailing down the aisle. He flailed helplessly.

"How do you stop this thing?" Puck cried as he was pushed by the invisible force.

Sabrina remembered the emergency brake cord hanging on the wall. She ran to it and yanked the handle as hard as she could. Brakes screamed, and the train whiplashed as it decelerated rapidly. Unfortunately, it wasn't slowing down quickly enough, and Puck was fast approaching the steel door at the end of the train car. There was no way the train would stop before he slammed into it.

Puck flopped about like a fish in the bottom of a boat. Sabrina knew what he was trying to do. If he could spin around he could trigger a metamorphosis. Besides flying, he had the ability to change his body into animals and a number of inanimate objects. Usually he changed into things that would annoy Sabrina, like a three-legged chair or a skunk, but from time to time he could transform into something useful. Sabrina could do nothing but watch his awkward effort and cheer when he finally succeeded. His arms and legs shrank to thick, treelike stumps. His body plumped up hundreds of pounds and his skin hardened into a gray armor. A hairy horn erupted from the top of his head. In a matter of moments, Puck was no longer an annoying boy in desperate need of a soapy bath, but a full-size rhinoceros. He lowered his head and his diamond-hard horn plowed into the train door, blasting it off its hinges and causing a great commotion in Sabrina's eardrums.

"He turned into a rhinoceros," Ms. Smirt said.

"He does that," Sabrina said.

While she and Smirt stood gaping at Puck, Daphne grabbed Sabrina's arm and dragged her in the direction of the blasted door. Never once had the little girl led an escape, but Sabrina was too bewildered to argue.

They saw Puck plow through the next car's door, and he was about to do the same to the one after that. Unfortunately, the train was packed tight with commuters. They cowered in their seats and hid behind their copies of the *New York Times*. No one was injured, but Sabrina suspected that many had wet their pants. She couldn't blame them. No one expects to see a charging rhino on their way to work. She and Daphne did their best to assure them that everything was under control as they ran past.

The girls reached the last car just in time to see Puck plow through its door and tumble out onto the tracks. The girls held hands and leaped to the ground below just as the train came to a stop. Once she had regained her bearings, Sabrina found that she and her sister were not alone. Uncle Jake, Granny Relda, and Elvis were waiting for them. Goldilocks hovered in the background, as did Red Riding Hood. The three bears stood at the back of the crowd with hairy arms crossed in disgust, and Puck was busy morphing back into his true form. But there were two people in the crowd that made Sabrina wonder if her mind wasn't playing tricks on her. Her parents, Henry and Veronica Grimm, stood right in front of her with arms outstretched.

"Mom? Dad?" she cried.

Henry and Veronica smiled and scooped her and Daphne into their arms. Tears fell from every eye, streamed down cheeks, and fell to the ground below. Veronica peppered them with kisses while Henry wrapped them up and squeezed.

"But Goldilocks's kiss. It didn't work," Daphne said.

"It worked," Veronica said. "But you know your father. He was always a late sleeper."

Henry stepped back and studied his daughters. "Girls, you look so different." He held Daphne's face in his hand. "You're so . . . big."

"You've been asleep a long time," Daphne said.

Henry turned to Granny Relda with questioning eyes.

"It's true. Nearly two years," the old woman said.

"Two years!" Veronica cried.

Henry looked as if someone had punched him in the belly. He stumbled back a little before righting himself. "That can't be true."

Daphne nodded. "It's true."

"But we're together now," Sabrina said, trying to shift the mood back to the happy reunion. All her worries over the last two years seemed to evaporate like dew in the summer sun. The incredible weight of being responsible for herself and Daphne lifted from her shoulders and for the first time in a long time she felt like what she was—a twelve-year-old kid.

Ms. Smirt scurried through the open train door. She pressed her bony hands across her gray suit to flatten wrinkles and struggled with a broken heel on one of her shoes. She straightened, as if mustering all of her courage. "These children are wards of the state, and they're coming with me, flying boy or no flying boy."

"Who is this woman?" Henry asked.

"She's our caseworker," Sabrina explained. "When you vanished we were sent to live in an orphanage. She placed us with foster parents."

"Horrible, evil foster parents," Daphne said. "She sent us to live with a man who was terrified of soap!"

"Don't forget the family that had a Bengal tiger living in their house!" Sabrina said.

"And the guy who rented us out as dogcatchers for his Korean restaurant."

Veronica stepped forward and snatched Smirt by the collar. "Have you been mistreating my children?"

"I did what I thought was best," Smirt sputtered as she tried to break free from Veronica's grip. Sabrina remembered how much her mother enjoyed rock climbing—she was crazy strong. Smirt squirmed like a worm on a hook.

"If I ever see you within twenty miles of my children again you'll wish you were never born," Veronica said.

"Are you threatening me?" the caseworker said.

"No," Veronica replied. "But my fist is."

Smirt squeaked and scampered back onto the train.

"We have to throw some forgetful dust on her," Sabrina said to Uncle Jake. "She knows too much. In fact, you should do the whole train."

"Do everyone but Smirt," Daphne said. Jake smiled and hopped onto the train with a handful of pink powder.

"Why not Smirt?" Sabrina demanded. "You told her everything. She'll go back to New York City and tell everyone what she knows."

"Exactly," Daphne said with a grin. "She's going to go back to the orphanage with this crazy story and they'll think she's a nutcase. They'll fire her."

Sabrina was astounded with the little girl's plan. It was almost like something she would have concocted herself. In fact, it was better.

"Henry, Veronica, we have a lot of catching up to do," Granny Relda said.

"I'll say," Veronica agreed.

"Forget it, Mom. We're leaving as soon as the girls are packed," Henry said.

"Leaving?" Granny cried.

Sabrina and Daphne eyed one another in astonishment.

Henry nodded. "We're getting out of Ferryport Landing as fast as we can."

2

ig brother, this is not one of your best ideas. You're forgetting you've been off the radar for two years," Uncle Jake said when he returned from the train. "Most people think you and Veronica are dead. Your apartment was sold. You don't have a job. You've got a mountain of paperwork to go through before you can get at any of your money, and if you were smart you'd steer clear of that caseworker and the board of child welfare until you can prove that you and Veronica are really the girls' parents. All of this will take weeks to sort out. Come back to the house—we can help."

"He makes a good point, Henry," Veronica said. "Maybe we should stay put until we get everything settled."

Henry shook his head stubbornly. "Getting out of Ferryport Landing is more important than all those details. We'll manage."

Granny Relda's face fell. She looked on the verge of tears. Sabrina had never seen her so upset. "But, Henry—"

"It's not open for discussion, Mom," he said sharply.

Sabrina's mom frowned but kept her tongue. Everyone else looked uncomfortable.

The group trudged up the embankment quietly and found the family's ancient car parked nearby. A quart of oil had leaked onto the sidewalk beneath its engine and a mysterious green fluid was seeping from the muffler. The old jalopy was a collection of ill-fitting parts from dozens of different car models and maybe a tank. Its best days were behind it—if it ever had best days. Now it looked like a wounded animal waiting for the Grim Reaper to come and put it out of its misery.

"Did you all come in this car?" Sabrina asked, looking around for another vehicle. "This old rust bucket is big, but you couldn't fit everyone and the bears inside even if you squeezed."

"That was my doing," Uncle Jake said with a grin. He reached into one of his many jacket pockets and took out a small wooden box. Inside was a green dust that spun like a tiny hurricane.

Daphne's eyes lit up with wonder. "What's that?"

"It's called stretching powder. Sprinkle a little of this on anything and you can make it as big or as small as you want. I blew a handful into the inside of the car. It's big enough for a whole forest of bears now."

"Gravy!" Daphne said, eyeing the green particles.

"Gravy?" Sabrina asked.

"It's my new word. It means something is cooler than cool," Daphne said, turning her attention back to Uncle Jake. "Where did you get it?"

"This is one of the first magical items I ever collected. Picked it up from the little old woman who lived in a shoe. She used this to get all seventy of her rug rats inside an old penny loafer."

Henry snatched the box from his brother, shut the lid, and stuffed it into one of Jake's pockets. "I'd prefer you kept your magic away from the girls. It's dangerous and I don't want them anywhere near it."

"Dad, we're old pros with the magic stuff," Daphne said. "We use it all the time."

Henry glared at his mother.

"I'm getting pretty good, too," Daphne continued, completely oblivious to Henry's rising temper. "In fact, I have my own little collection of wands and rings, just like Uncle Jake."

Henry's face turned as red as lava exploding out of a volcano. "You are five years old. You shouldn't be anywhere near magic.

You'll hand it all over to me when we get back to the house. None of this nonsense is going back to New York City with us."

"Dad, I'll be eight in two weeks," Daphne said.

Henry looked at his daughter as if she were speaking ancient Greek.

And Daphne looked like she had just been slapped. Sabrina knew firsthand how insulted her sister could be when she was treated like a baby. She herself had created a deep emotional chasm between them by not respecting Daphne. Only a few days before, she had betrayed her sister, stealing a magical item she felt Daphne was too young to possess. Now, they were barely speaking.

"Maybe we should go," Goldilocks said with a forced smile. She opened one of the rusty car doors.

Sabrina and Daphne climbed inside as an orchestra of springs and joints cried out for mercy. The stretching powder had done just what Uncle Jake claimed it would do: The interior was enormous, even bigger than Granny Relda's living room. They could have shared the car with a football team and would still have had plenty of room for everyone. Red, Goldilocks, the bears, Elvis, Puck, Granny Relda, Uncle Jake, Henry, and Veronica piled inside.

Veronica took a seat between her daughters and hugged them both. "So, what have we missed?"

Granny shifted uncomfortably. "Oh, where do we begin? Well, I've been training the girls in the art of detection and—"

"You knew I didn't want them in this town," Henry interrupted.

"I couldn't leave them in the orphanage. They've been perfectly safe," Granny said.

Sabrina laughed and the entire family turned to face her.

"You disagree?" Henry asked her.

Sabrina felt Granny's betrayed eyes on her. "No."

"Sabrina, if you have something to say I'd like to hear it," Henry demanded.

She tried to stay quiet but the truth spilled out anyway. "Well, we were attacked by Jack the Giant Killer, then nearly stomped to death by an army of giants. Rumpelstiltskin heightened my emotions then fed off the anger like I was an all-you-can-eat buffet, then he nearly blew us up in some underground tunnels but not before he sent a bunch of half-monster children to kill us. We were nearly devoured by the Little Mermaid's mutant hermit crab, almost killed by Little Red Riding Hood—"

Red seemed to sink into her seat.

"We killed the Jabberwocky—"

"It's dead?" Henry asked, bewildered.

Granny Relda nodded.

"What else, oh, I was turned into a frog and was almost eaten by Baba Yaga, we were attacked by a six-story giant robot in Times Square, nearly killed by Titania, Queen of the Fairies, sucked into a time vortex, nearly barbecued by dragons from the future, almost sliced and diced by the Sheriff of Nottingham, and just about had our heads chopped off by the Queen of Hearts and Bluebeard. I'm sure there's more but that's right off the top of my head. Oh, I was taken over by the insane rabid spirit of the Big Bad Wolf, too."

"That about covers it," Uncle Jake said sheepishly.

"Go ahead, Jake. Make a joke out of it like you always do," Henry said.

"Mom protected them every step of the way. I've been here for most of it, too," Jake said.

Elvis let out a low growl.

"The dog wants to remind everyone of his contributions," Goldilocks said.

Daphne hugged the big dog. "We all know you're our real hero."

Elvis barked.

"He says heroes deserve sausages."

"Don't even think about it," Sabrina said to the hound. Elvis plus sausages equaled a noxious smell.

"Let's not forget me," Puck said. "I've been pulling this family from the jaws of death on a daily basis and haven't seen a dime for my troubles."

Henry scowled. "If you don't mind we're having a family discussion. Who are you, anyway? Peter Pan?"

"Henry!" Granny cried. "No!"

"I AM NOT PETER PAN!" Puck bellowed as smoke blasted out of his nostrils. A moment later the top of the family car rocketed into the atmosphere, turning the old jalopy into a very crude convertible.

No one was hurt, but the outburst launched a massive, many-sided argument. Granny argued with Veronica. Henry shouted at Puck. The three bears roared and snapped at one another. Puck bellowed at everyone. The air was heavy with angry words bouncing around violently from one person to the next. All Sabrina could do was watch quietly and hope everyone didn't turn on her. When a hand slipped into hers and gave it a quick squeeze, Sabrina was elated. Finally, she and her sister were getting back to normal. But when she looked down she realized she was actually holding Red Riding Hood's hand. The little girl was trembling in fright from all the shouting. Sabrina quickly pulled her hand away. Red seemed hurt but didn't say a word.

As the argument hit a fever pitch, Granny Relda inserted two fingers into her mouth and blasted a high-pitched whistle that rattled Sabrina's brain. When everyone was quiet she turned her attention to Uncle Jake.

"Jacob, why in heavens are you driving so fast?"

Sabrina eyed the car's ancient speedometer. The red needle was pushing one hundred and ten and the engine was rattling and screeching worse than usual.

"Because we have a major problem!" Jake cried.

"What are you talking about?" Henry asked.

"Well, big brother, before you insulted the boy fairy everything was fine, but you had to go and make him angry and he blew the roof off the car. So the integrity of the interior has been compromised," he shouted over the wind.

"In English, please," Veronica said.

"The inside of the car was enchanted to fit all of you in it. Now the inside is also the outside," Jake said as he reached into his pocket and took out the little wooden box that held the powder he had used to cast the spell on the car.

"So?" Granny asked.

"So, the universe now has two choices. The exterior, which is the whole world, gets bigger to match the spell, which would be very, very bad. I'm talking earthquakes, tsunamis, insane weather. Real. Bad. Stuff."

"Then what's the other choice?" Goldilocks asked.

"The interior of the car is going to shrink back to normal, which means it's going to get cramped in here fast."

Sabrina looked around at all the people and animals in the car. There were almost a dozen passengers in the car, three of them weighing in the area of eight hundred pounds. "How fast?"

Suddenly, there was a *pop* followed by a loud hissing sound, as if someone had just stuck a balloon and let the air out. Before Sabrina knew what was happening she was pushed roughly to the center of her seat. She was practically sitting in her mother's lap.

"Very fast!" Uncle Jake floored the gas and tore down the narrow country road. The car shook and quaked, pistons screamed and gears screeched. With every mile added to the car's odometer, the interior got smaller. The passengers were squeezed closer and closer to one another. Worse, Sabrina realized she was sitting next to Puck, who was now hip to hip with her. She noticed he had mud and several plump, slippery earthworms in his hair.

"You need to go faster," Henry shouted over the wind that beat against everyone's faces. Veronica had moved onto his lap and Granny seemed destined for it, too.

"Don't tell me how to drive," Uncle Jake said.

"I'll tell you how to drive if you're driving like an old woman," Henry snapped.

"You want to drive? 'Cause I can pull over and you can show me how it's done," Uncle Jake replied.

"They sound like you two," Puck said to Sabrina and Daphne.

Both of the girls glared at him.

The shrinking increased dramatically and Sabrina found Puck's nose just an inch from her own. The car door was pushing him closer while Red and Daphne were shoving her from the other side. If the interior shrank again they would most certainly be pushed even closer together. Accidents could happen! Accidents with lips!

"I hope you brushed this morning, piggie," Puck said with a smile. He closed his eyes and puckered up for a kiss.

"Uncle Jake, drive faster!" Sabrina begged.

Looking offended, Puck scampered to his feet, using Sabrina's head as a crutch. "Fine. I'm out of here," Puck snarled as his pink fairy wings popped out of his back. He leaped into the air and allowed it to sweep him high above the car. Sabrina was relieved, but not for long. When the inside of the car shrank again she found her face buried in Poppa Bear's hairy armpit.

Uncle Jake didn't wait for the driveway. He pulled up right into the front yard, barreling through shrubbery and slamming on the brakes inches from Granny Relda's front porch. It couldn't have happened a moment too soon, as people started literally spilling out of the top of the car. Baby Bear toppled out and fell onto the ground with Goldilocks. Elvis jumped out and scurried under a bush. When Uncle Jake opened his door, he fell out with Veronica and Granny Relda. Sabrina glanced around and was startled to see Daphne was nowhere to be found.

"Daphne!" she cried. "She must have fallen out."

Momma Bear grunted and got out of her seat. There, beneath her, was Daphne, safe but a little mashed.

"I have never needed a bath so much in my entire life," the little girl groaned.

"This is exactly what I'm talking about," Henry said. "We all could have been hurt because of magic."

Uncle Jake rolled his eyes and helped everyone onto the porch. Once there, Granny went to work on unlocking the door. There were a dozen locks of all shapes and sizes keeping the house safe. When they were all open she knocked on the front door and said, "We're home!" The words deactivated a magical lock that few knew was there. It was only then that the front door could be opened.

"Veronica, take the girls upstairs and help them pack. Don't let them bring anything that can cast a spell. You know what to look for," Henry said as he picked up the phone. "I'm going to call everyone we know in New York City and let them know we're on our way."

"Henry, don't you think this is something we should discuss?" Veronica asked. Sabrina watched her father shoot her mother an angry look. She threw up her hands in frustration. "Come on, girls."

They climbed the stairs to the girls' bedroom and went inside. Veronica closed the door behind them and sat down on the bed as if she was exhausted. A moment later she snatched the girls and hugged them. Sabrina felt one of her mother's tears drip down onto her hand.

"Don't cry," Sabrina said.

"I can't help it. I can't believe how long we've been apart. You must have been so frightened."

Veronica cupped Sabrina's face in her hands. "You did a good job looking after your sister."

The words fell into Sabrina's belly and opened up into a million happy butterflies. She had tried so hard. Hearing her mother's words was like a lifetime of birthday presents rolled into one.

Veronica looked at them both closely. "And you've both gotten so pretty. My little girls—where did they go?"

"We're still here," Daphne said. "We're just bigger versions."

Veronica laughed.

"Mom, you have to talk to Dad. We can't go back to the city," Daphne said, her tone suddenly serious. "We're needed here in Ferryport Landing."

"Needed?" Veronica replied.

"Absolutely!" the little girl cried. "There's a lot of crazy shenanigans going on in this town and Granny needs help keeping the peace. There's a bunch of bad guys called the Scarlet Hand running around tormenting everyone and it seems like every time we turn around someone is on the verge of destroying the world. We can't go."

"Daphne, you don't understand. Your father has a lot of bad memories about Ferryport Landing. We should start packing."

Sabrina pulled two tiny suitcases out from under the bed. They were the same suitcases she and her sister had brought when they arrived in Ferryport Landing, though back then all they had in them were a couple of T-shirts and a pair of socks they took turns wearing. She turned to the dresser where they kept their clothes, and she noticed her sister's angry expression.

"Happy?" Daphne asked.

"Daphne, I—"

"I'm not surprised. Sabrina has hated living here since the first day. If she wants to go back, fine, but I want to stay here with

Granny Relda. I want to take on the family business. I want to be a fairy-tale detective. Besides, who would look after Elvis and Puck? And Red Riding Hood is going to need help getting adjusted."

Veronica shook her head. "Your father and I have argued on many things, from the color of paint in the bathroom to where we would send you to school, but this is one issue he won't bend on. I don't like it, and I'll do what I can, but I wouldn't get your hopes up. Daphne, if you are so eager to work with Everafters I wouldn't worry too much. You might be surprised by what you'll uncover in the Big Apple."

"Mom, we know about the Faerie," Daphne said.

"You do?"

"And about what you do for them," Sabrina said. "We went back to the city with Granny. We met Oberon and Titania. We've been to the Golden Egg and talked to Scrooge. We know all about you and the Everafter community there."

"Girls, I'd appreciate if you kept my secret life a secret," Veronica said. "Your dad doesn't know about any of it."

Henry appeared in the doorway. "There's a train in half an hour. I want to be on it."

Veronica nodded.

"Get those suitcases packed, girls," he ordered.

Sabrina was a bit surprised by her father's tone. She remembered him being so easygoing and happy. Still, the girls did as they were told, even Daphne, and with their mother's help they brought everything they owned downstairs and left it near the front door. Granny Relda and Uncle Jake were waiting for them. Henry was looking over a series of phone numbers he had scrawled on a piece of paper. Puck was lounging on the couch using his belly as a conga drum. Red Riding Hood was sitting in a dark corner. The three bears were sitting at the dining room table munching on a huge watermelon. Goldilocks was busy rearranging the rest of the bookshelves, and Elvis was lying on the floor, head resting on his paws, and moaning sadly.

"Where are we going to go?" Veronica asked her husband.

"Don't worry, we'll be fine," Henry said, ignoring her question. "Can someone give us a ride to the train station or should I call a taxi?"

"Henry, be reasonable. You can stay here," Granny Relda pleaded.

Henry shook his head. "Mom, I can't."

Granny extended her arms for a hug. The girls rushed to the old woman and hugged her with all their might. "*Lieblings*, my heart will be empty until I see you again. Look after yourselves and remember you need one another. Try not to fight. You make a great team when you put your heads together."

Daphne leaned down and kissed Elvis on the snout. He barked.

"He says he'll miss you," Goldilocks explained.

Puck stopped his drumming for a brief moment and grinned at Sabrina. "I hear they have a lot of plastic surgeons in New York City. If I were you I'd make an appointment for that face as soon as you get there," he quipped.

Sabrina scowled and shook a fist at him. "Keep it up, stinkpot, and you're going to need a plastic surgeon yourself."

Puck winked. "No need to get all mushy on me, Grimm."

Henry snatched up the girls' suitcases and stepped out the door. They followed but were quickly halted in their tracks. Sabrina was shocked to find the entire house surrounded by people— well, *people* didn't exactly describe them all. Scattered through the crowd were Cyclops, ogres, stone golems, witches, warlocks, toy soldiers, an enormous walking nutcracker, and trolls. At the front of the crowd was Mayor Heart, also known as the Queen of Hearts from *Alice's Adventures in Wonderland.* She had squeezed herself into a gaudy red dress decorated with black silk hearts. Her hair was stacked into a three-foot beehive and her makeup looked as if it had been applied by an agitated beaver. In her hand was her ever-present electronic megaphone. Standing next to her was a sour-looking man with long black hair and a goatee. The Sheriff of Nottingham, as he was known, was dressed from head to toe in leather, complete with boots, cape, and gloves. A vicious serpentine dagger hung at his waist and a grotesque purple scar ran from the tip of his eye to the corner of his mouth. He looked particularly ugly, perhaps from the frozen snarl on his face or maybe from the frightening mark on his chest: a bloodred handprint. The mark was emblazoned on the chests of the entire crowd.

"Well, as I live and breathe, it's Henry Grimm," the mayor cackled. "How was your nap?"

"Queen, I'm taking my girls and we're leaving town. We aren't looking for any trouble," Henry said.

The queen lifted her megaphone to her mouth. "Well, Henry, it appears trouble came looking for you."

Granny pushed her way onto the porch. "Now you listen to me—"

"NO!" the mayor bellowed, causing the megaphone to emit a migraine-inducing feedback whine. "You listen to me, Relda. You and your brood aren't going anywhere until you tell us what the Master wants to know."

"What are you talking about?" Uncle Jake said as he stepped onto the porch.

"Tell us the location of the traitors, Grimm. Prince Charming and the Big Bad Wolf. We know they have fled into the forest together, along with Robin Hood and his Merry Men. We want to bring them before the Master so they can face justice."

"Like that's going to happen," Daphne snarled.

Nottingham armed a crossbow with a silver arrow and hefted it onto his shoulder. He aimed it at the family. "Tell us where their camp is and your family will live through the day. As for tomorrow, well—no promises."

Uncle Jake stepped in front of his mother. "Sheriff, every time I turn around your stupid little group is making threats and every time we make you look like fools. Why don't you save yourself the humiliation and take your band of silly, washed-up misfits and get off our lawn before I—"

There was a whizzing sound in the air and then Uncle Jake let out a cry and fell to the porch. When Sabrina looked down at him she saw an arrow stuck in his right shoulder. Blood was leaking out of the wound all over his jacket and onto the porch's old wooden floorboards.

"Perhaps you didn't understand us," Nottingham said as he loaded a fresh arrow into his weapon. "Tell us where the camp is, now!"

"Girls, get into the house!" Henry shouted, snatching Sabrina and Daphne by the arms and dragging them inside to safety.

Veronica and Granny Relda followed and Henry dashed back out to drag Uncle Jake into the house. Once inside he slammed the door behind him just as an arrow crashed into the mailbox.

"House, time to lock up!" Granny shouted and Sabrina heard the tumblers turn on the front door's dozen padlocks. Open windows slammed shut and shutters closed tight. Sabrina caught a faint flash of shimmering blue light outside a window.

"OK, everyone, we're safe here. Nothing can get in now," Granny said as she turned to help her wounded son. "Daphne, I need you to run upstairs and grab a bottle of iodine out of the cabinet. It's a red bottle. Sabrina and Puck, run into the laundry room and get the white sheets out of the dryer. Rip them into bandages. Goldilocks and Red, I could use a pot of boiling water."

Everyone rushed to follow Granny's orders but Sabrina was stunned and frozen.

"Sabrina! Go!" Granny shouted as she knelt down to her wounded son.

Sabrina and Puck raced out of the room and into the pantry where they kept the dryer. She opened the lid and pulled out the fresh, clean sheets while Puck tore them with zeal.

"Nottingham really shot at us," Puck said. "I didn't see that coming."

"You sound like you're proud of him!" Sabrina exclaimed.

"Well, as a villain he has certainly stepped up his game," the fairy boy replied. "Still, he loses points for his costume. That's way over the top."

"You're hopeless," she muttered as she raced back to her family. When she arrived they were all arguing, and once again her father was at the center of the dispute.

"And this is exactly why we're going back to New York City," her father said, holding his hand tightly against his brother's wound.

"Henry, not now," Veronica begged.

"I've got the sheets," Sabrina said, hoping it would change the subject. Granny reached for them and started wrapping Jake's wound. While she was working, Daphne returned with the iodine. She gave it to the old woman and stepped back, looking shocked and scared.

"We have to get the arrow out of my arm, Mom," Uncle Jake said.

Goldilocks immediately herded the children together. "Children, I could really use everyone's help in the kitchen."

Puck stomped his foot. "No way! I've shot a few people in

my day, but I've never seen an arrow come out. This is the opportunity of a lifetime."

"Suit yourself," Goldilocks said, and she led Sabrina, Daphne, Red, and Baby Bear into the kitchen. Once there, she nervously searched the cabinets and refrigerator.

"What are you looking for?" Sabrina asked.

"Cocoa," the woman said. "Everything is better with cocoa. Oh, these cabinets. How do you find anything?"

Daphne opened a drawer and took out a box of cocoa, and Goldilocks started making some for the children.

"Why are those people attacking us?" Red Riding Hood asked.

"They want us to tell them where Charming and Mr. Canis have gone," Sabrina said.

Baby Bear growled.

"Junior wants to know why someone doesn't just tell them, then," Goldilocks said.

"Because they're our friends. Besides, we couldn't if we wanted to," Daphne said. "We don't know where they are."

There was a loud, horrible cry from the living room. Someone must have pulled the arrow from Jake's shoulder. Sabrina turned to her sister. Daphne's face was pale.

"He'll be fine," Goldilocks assured the children as she started rearranging the silverware drawer.

Puck rushed into the kitchen. He looked as if he had just gotten off a roller coaster. "That was awesome!" he cried. "The arrow coming out is totally more fun to watch than the arrow going in."

Henry and Granny Relda joined them in the kitchen.

"We need to get him to a hospital," Henry said. "That's an open wound. He's going to need stitches and antibiotics. It could get infected if it's not cleaned properly."

Granny Relda shook her head. "The hospital is deserted. All the doctors were human and Mayor Heart ran them out of town."

"We have to find someone with some medical training," Henry said as he took a glass from the cupboard. He turned the faucet on to fill it but nothing came out but a couple of brown drops. "They've turned off the pipes."

Suddenly, the lights in the house went out. "And the lights," Sabrina added.

"Nothing to worry about, folks," Puck said. "I'll run up and get my sword. Once they see that I'm armed I'm sure those losers will run for the hills."

"I don't think fighting our way out is the answer, Puck," Granny said.

"It always has been before," Puck grumbled.

"What do you have in mind?" Sabrina asked.

"Let's go ask the man with the answers," Granny said. She led everyone back into the living room, where Jake lay unconscious on the sofa. His arm was wrapped in the bandages Sabrina and Puck had made, but a small circular dot of red had appeared through the fabric and was growing rapidly. Sabrina's father lifted his brother and eased him onto Poppa Bear's back. Then everyone marched up the steps and into Mirror's room. Once inside, his foreboding face appeared in the glass.

"This place is starting to resemble Grand Central Station, Relda," Mirror said.

"You haven't seen half of the guests," Granny Relda said. "The Scarlet Hand has surrounded the house."

"Well, that's not going to help the property values," Mirror said. "Jake! He's injured!"

"We need to get him to a doctor," Henry said. "And then we need to get out of this town. Mirror, we need the slippers."

"Which slippers are you referring to, Hank?"

"Dorothy's slippers," Henry said. "Three clicks and we can teleport ourselves to safety."

"Sorry, Hankster," Mirror said. "The girls lost one of the slippers a while back."

"You lost the slippers?" Hank cried, glaring at the girls.

"A giant was chasing us," Sabrina said defensively.

"A big giant," Daphne added.

"Fine. How about the Gnome King's belt?" Henry said, turning his attention back to Mirror. "It'll do the same thing."

"Well, the girls tried that out about a month ago and they ran down the batteries. If you have forty-six size Ds then we're back in business," Mirror replied.

Henry frowned at the girls.

Sabrina shrugged. "Yeah, we've been meaning to take care of that."

Henry sighed. "For once I'm turning to magic and there's nothing available! What have we got that will zap us out of this house?"

"Well, as for zapping, we've got nothing," Granny Relda said. "But there is a way out of the house."

"There is?" Sabrina and Daphne asked.

Granny reached into her handbag and took out her set of keys. "Yes. We need to go to the Room of Reflections."

Granny stepped through the mirror and vanished. Henry and Veronica followed, then Red, Daphne, Sabrina, and Puck. Elvis was next. The three bears growled nervously but Goldilocks growled back something that seemed to calm their nerves. A moment later Poppa Bear was carrying Uncle Jake through.

Sabrina never got used to the vastness of the room hidden on the other side of the mirror's reflection. The ceiling was held aloft by marble columns taller and thicker than redwood trees. The hallway itself was as wide as Grand Central Station in Manhattan and was framed by hundreds of doors on either side. The doors were made from a countless variety of materials: Some were wood, others steel and stone, and Sabrina had seen some constructed of crystal, fire, ice, a waterfall, and even something Granny called protoplasm. All of the doors were adorned with brass plaques that explained the contents of the room on the other side.

"How come we've never heard of this Room of Reflections?" Daphne asked her grandmother.

"Because we don't use it very often and it's not exactly within walking distance," the old woman replied. "It's at the other end of the hall."

This piqued Sabrina's curiosity. She had often wondered what was at the end of the Hall of Wonders. She had tried to walk there once but after several hours she still couldn't see the end. She'd started to imagine that the hall went on forever.

Granny handed Mirror her set of keys. "I think we're going to need the trolley car."

Mirror nodded and stepped through a set of double doors to

his immediate right. A moment later Sabrina heard an engine roar and a brass bell ring, then an old-fashioned trolley car pulled out and stopped in front of the group. Sabrina had seen similar-looking trolleys on television. They were all the rage in San Francisco. Mirror was sitting in the driver's seat, wearing a short, green jacket, a black cap, and a money-changer attached to his belt. He rang a polished brass bell and shouted, "All aboard!"

The girls climbed up while Henry helped Uncle Jake and the others get settled. Henry had the unfortunate task of helping Momma Bear onto the trolley. He shoved and pushed and inch by inch she climbed aboard. Puck found the whole spectacle hilarious. Every time Henry pushed on Momma Bear's oversize rump, Puck made a farting sound. Puck laughed until tears rolled down his cheeks, leaving tracks on his grimy face.

Mirror rang the bell one final time and shouted, "Here we go!" The trolley zipped down the hall, gaining speed rapidly.

"I've always wanted to know what was at the end of the hall," Daphne said.

"I remember when your father and Jacob walked it," Granny Relda said. "We didn't have the trolley back then so they brought a tent and sleeping bags."

Henry grunted.

"What's wrong?" Sabrina asked.

"Jacob forgot to pack food. We walked almost the whole day before we noticed and had to turn around. We never did go back."

Mirror turned in his seat and addressed the passengers. "Folks, at this rate we won't get there until Thursday, so I'm going to put the pedal to the metal, as they say. So keep your hands and feet inside the vehicle at all times. Hold on to your seats, sit back, and enjoy the ride."

The trolley lurched forward. Sabrina felt the skin on her face pull back as the hallway flew by. They were going so fast everything around them turned into a blur of color and light. It was terrifying; however, Puck seemed to be having the time of his life.

"Faster!" he shouted. "It's not fun until someone wets their pants!"

When the trolley slowed and the world came back into focus Sabrina realized she had held her breath the whole way. She peered out at the unfamiliar length of hallway. The doors at this end were even more bizarre than the ones she had already seen. One looked as if it was made of a whirling blue gas with several ancient skeletons suspended in it. Another appeared to be the mouth of a huge monster, with gnashing teeth and a horrible forked tongue. Another door was constructed from the gigantic bones of a prehistoric animal.

When Mirror brought the trolley to a complete stop, Sabrina stepped off feeling light-headed. She held on to the side of the trolley until she felt better. It seemed that everyone else in the group felt the same way, except for Puck, who begged Mirror for another ride.

Once her head stopped spinning Sabrina studied her surroundings. A massive wall, much like the one at their end of the hall, stood before them. She didn't see a magical portal that led into the real world, though, just a single door made from a rough stone slab. Hieroglyphics and intricate symbols were chiseled into its surface. Sabrina had no idea what any of it meant, but the biggest of the symbols gave her a creepy feeling: It was a large sculpted eye gazing down on everyone. It moved like a real eye and studied each person intently.

"Uh, creepy?" Daphne said as she watched the eye move up and down the length of her body.

Unlike the other doors in the Hall of Wonders, the big stone door did not have a lock on it. Mirror pushed it open and led everyone inside to a circular room draped in black curtains. The floor was made of a spotless varnished pine. Twenty-five full-length mirrors were placed an equal distance from one another against the room's walls. Sabrina understood why it was called the Room of Reflections.

"Are these magic mirrors?" Veronica asked, running her hand along one's surface. The tips of her fingers disappeared in the glass and the image rippled like the surface of a pond. "Oh, they are. Aren't they?"

"Not exactly," Mirror said. "The best way to describe them is to think of them as back doors into the twenty-five magic mirrors created by Bunny Lancaster, also known as the Wicked Queen."

"Are you saying that we can go into all twenty-five magic mirrors from this room?" Goldilocks asked. "We can step right into their Halls of Wonders?"

Mirror shook his head and looked slightly offended. "There is only one Hall of Wonders. Each mirror is unique, designed specifically by the Wicked Queen for the people who purchased them. Each mirror also comes equipped with its unique guardian. I am the guardian of the Hall of Wonders."

"So, if we step through one of these portals we can go into someone else's magic mirror?" Veronica asked.

"And then we can step through its portal into the real world," Granny explained.

"Bunny created this room as a fail-safe in the case of a malfunctioning mirror or guardian. If one needed fixing, she could simply step in through this back door and make repairs.

She chose this mirror, my mirror, to be the hub, the only place where you can go to all twenty-five, making me all the more unique," Mirror said proudly.

"Gravy!" Daphne cried as she rushed to the closest mirror. "I'm going to go into this one!"

Before she could jump into the reflection, Granny Relda yanked her back. "*Liebling*, no!" She pointed to a sign hanging at the bottom of the mirror that read "Out of Service." "You can't just jump into these things. Some of them don't work."

"She's right, jitterbug," Mirror said, pointing to a few others with the same sign. "Thirteen of the mirrors have been broken beyond repair. Two more are buried beneath the earth and who knows what's crawled into them. Another is filled with a poisonous gas and yet another is, from what I can tell, at the bottom of the Atlantic Ocean. Two others have been shattered. If you were to step into them, you would be cut to ribbons. In my free time I've been removing the shards so that no one can get hurt. If there is a sign below it that reads 'out of service,' then they are off limits."

Sabrina did the math in her head. "That leaves six magic mirrors that are still working."

"Do you think one of these will lead us to a doctor?" Henry said impatiently.

"If we pick the right one and we're lucky," Granny said as she turned to Sabrina and Daphne. "And that's where you two come in."

"Us?"

"Yes. I think it would be unwise to just step into one of these mirrors, especially since we don't know who owns them, what kind of guardian might be inside, or where they might lead. You two have been in one, though, and know the guardian quite well."

"The Hotel of Wonders," Daphne exclaimed. "We were in it right after we got back from the future."

"You girls are the only people I know that have ever been inside another magic mirror," Granny said. "Do you think you can find the right mirror?"

"Sure," Daphne said.

The girls went from one portal to the next. The first two were shattered and cracked. Another reflected nothing back at them. One revealed a medieval torture chamber, complete with a stretching rack and a bubbling cauldron of what looked like tar. Another mirror showed an old-fashioned ice-cream parlor and yet another revealed a huge warehouse filled with thousands of crates and boxes. In one Sabrina saw a tacky nightclub, with a disco ball and a guardian in a polyester suit and gold chains.

Finally, Sabrina spotted a breathtaking sunset and swaying palm trees. She knew they had found the Hotel.

"Not so fast," Henry said, stepping toward the mirror. "I'll go first."

"Dad, it's perfectly safe," Daphne said. "Harry is the guardian. He's very nice."

Henry ignored Daphne as if she were babbling. It was the second time he had discounted her opinion and Sabrina noticed her frustration. Henry took a step into the mirror then, half-in and half-out, turned back to his family. "Stay here. I'll let you know when it's safe."

A second later he was gone.

"So, you want to explain this trip into the future?" Veronica asked.

"It was so cool, Mom," Daphne said, shaking off her humiliation. "We met ourselves. Sabrina was married!"

"Daphne!" Sabrina cried. No one knew the complete truth about what the girls had seen in the future. Her marriage and, most importantly, the identity of her husband, were supposed to be carefully guarded secrets. If Puck ever found out . . .

"Married?" Puck laughed. "Who would marry you? He must be blind and lack a sense of smell."

Sabrina's fists clenched. She had never had a chance to ask her older self what she saw in the smelly, annoying fairy, though she had to admit, Puck's grown-up version was very cute. Still, how did she get over all the insults, pranks, and mean-spirited jokes? Maybe there weren't any other men in the future. That could be the only explanation.

Just then, Henry's face appeared in the Hotel's portal. "Coast is clear."

Everyone piled through the portal and Sabrina found herself standing at the front desk of a very chic hotel. The floor was polished marble with beautiful Persian rugs scattered about. The walls were covered in tasteful contemporary art. Everything sparkled under the grand crystal chandelier. A bank of floor-to-ceiling windows revealed a tropical scene that looked as if it had been stolen from a postcard. Sabrina wondered if the beach was really there or if it was just a magical illusion.

Just then, a short Asian man in a Hawaiian shirt and lei appeared. He was carrying more leis in his arms and placed one around everybody's neck, except for the bears who were far too big and tall for the little man to reach. "Aloha!" he cried.

"Aloha, Harry," Daphne said.

"Sabrina! Daphne! Welcome back to the Hotel of Wonders. I wasn't aware you'd be visiting us. No worries, you never need reservations. Are you here on business or pleasure?"

"Neither," Sabrina said. "In fact, we're in the midst of an emergency."

"From what I understand emergencies happen quite frequently to you and your family," Harry said with a knowing grin. "Can I be of any help?"

"We want to use the main portal. The one that leads to the real world."

Harry nodded. "Oh, so you slipped in the back way. Interesting. Of course you can use the portal. This way," he said, leading everyone through the hotel lobby. "The boss has been using the portal a lot lately. He's pretty busy with his camp. I explained that he could have all the refugees stay here with room to spare but he said he didn't want the riffraff to sully the sheets."

"What does *riffraff* mean?" Daphne asked.

Sabrina opened her mouth to explain but remembered the girl's reaction the last time she had tried to define a word. Instead, she decided to let someone else be the dictionary for a change.

"*Riffraff* is a mean word for people who are of a lower class," Veronica explained. "It's not a very nice thing to say."

"Harry, you said something about refugees?" Goldilocks asked.

"Yes, those terrorized by the Scarlet Hand," Harry explained. "Prince Charming has offered them sanctuary in his camp. It's gotten to be quite a large population."

"Wait a minute!" Henry cried. "This mirror belongs to Prince Charming? This is going to take us to his camp? This plan is insane! Have you forgotten that he has threatened to destroy our family? He and Dad couldn't have been bigger enemies. Charming said he would bulldoze our house."

"I can't promise he won't someday," Granny said as she wiped Uncle Jake's brow with a damp cloth. "But now he's the closest thing the Grimm family has to an ally, and Mr. Canis has learned to trust him. We'll be fine."

"Mr. Canis is there, too?" Red Riding Hood whimpered.

Granny took her hand. "He won't hurt you, child."

Harry pushed a button on a bank of elevators and the doors slid open, revealing the portal to the outside world.

"Hey, there's Charming now," Daphne said, pointing into the portal. Sabrina could see the former mayor and his diminutive assistant, Mr. Seven, in a dimly lit room, propping another full-length mirror against the opposite wall. Seven was one of the world-famous seven dwarfs, and despite his boss's frequent insults and humiliations had been at Charming's side ever since the day Sabrina and Daphne had met him. Sabrina wondered what kept him there now that the prince could no longer afford to pay his salary.

"This is foolish," Henry warned. "Charming can't be trusted."

"It's the best plan we've got," Veronica said. Granny nodded in agreement, then sent Poppa Bear through the portal with Uncle Jake on his back. Everyone else followed.

The world on the other side of the portal couldn't be more different from the opulence of the Hotel of Wonders. Sabrina found herself inside a crude log cabin with a dirt floor and a thatched roof. A few chairs were scattered around and a rough table had a scale model of Ferryport Landing resting on top. Charming and Seven, startled by the sudden appearance of visitors, nearly dropped the mirror they were holding.

"Careful now!" a face cried as it appeared inside the mirror. He had dark skin and long, untamed dreadlocks.

"Are you people touched in the head?" the prince bellowed. "I am hanging a magic mirror! Do you have any idea what would happen if I dropped this?"

"Let's try not to t'ink on it, my friend," the man in the mirror said in a thick accent that sounded as if its origins were Caribbean. "I'll have nightmares."

"You can relax, Reggie," Charming said. "You are perfectly safe."

"T'is is a good t'ing, man," Reggie said, and then disappeared.

Charming and Seven set the mirror safely against the wall. "Relda, is there more of this rabble out there or is it safe to say you've brought the entire town?"

"My son is injured, William. He was shot by one of Nottingham's arrows. He needs help," Granny Relda pleaded.

"Seven, lead the bear with Jacob to the medical tent. Tell Nurse Sprat to take good care of him," Charming said.

Mr. Seven nodded, and, along with Poppa Bear, raced out of the cabin.

"Sprat will send for us when she has treated your boy, Relda," Charming said. "In the meantime I suppose you'd like to take a look at our little community."

He led the group through the door and out into an open courtyard. Sabrina was stunned by what she saw. They were inside a huge fort with walls twenty-five feet high. The compound was wide enough to fit dozens of cabins, barracks, a mess tent, a makeshift hospital, an armory, and a small farm. Hundreds of Everafters were busy gardening, working with horses, tilling the land, and building more cabins.

Granny looked around in awe. "William, what exactly is this place?"

"Welcome to Camp Charming," the prince said proudly. "The Everafters' last stand against the Scarlet Hand."

3

ook familiar?" Daphne asked Sabrina.

An icy feeling crept up Sabrina's back as she studied the fortress. She had been here before. In their trip to the future, Sabrina and Daphne had seen a handful of Everafters build a fort to fight the Master exactly like the one she was now standing in. Seeing the fort in the present was a chilling reminder for Sabrina that parts of the future had not been changed, and events might unfold despite the girls' best efforts to prevent them.

The prince smiled as he gestured to the camp. "The Scarlet Hand is harassing Everafters, especially ones that have associated with you and your family. I've sent word out that our camp is a safe haven, and we've had a steady flow of people seeking shelter ever since."

"How did you build this so fast?" Granny Relda asked. "You and Mr. Canis fled into the forest only yesterday!"

"We work fast around here," a voice said from behind them. They spun around and found Mr. Canis. Their old friend was as skinny as ever, with a tangle of gray hair and a black patch on his left eye. He pointed toward a wizard who was levitating a load of rubble left over from the construction of a stone sewer.

Daphne raced to the elderly man and gave him a hug. He would have toppled over if not for the cane he carried at his side. Its presence bothered Sabrina. Canis had never needed one before, and it was a reminder that their friend was a very old man. Still, even weakened he looked more at ease than she had ever seen him. His trademark scowl and pensive expression were gone, replaced with an easy smile. "It's good to see you, child," he said to Daphne, then turned his attention to Sabrina's parents. "Henry and Veronica, among the world of the wakeful. I am pleased to see the spell has broken and you have been revived."

"Goldilocks woke them up," Daphne said. "With a kiss."

Puck stuck his tongue out as he if was about to be very sick.

Granny took her friend by the hand. "How are you feeling?"

Canis shook his cane. "Tired—my age is catching up with me. Rather quickly, too. It appears that I have lost some of my youthful strength now that I am free from the Wolf."

"Wow!" Veronica said. "We've missed a lot, haven't we?"

Sabrina quietly agreed. Only the day before the girls had used a magic weapon to remove the demonic spirit that had inhabited their friend for so many centuries. Now that it was gone, it could no longer torture Mr. Canis, but it appeared he no longer possessed the strength, energy, and keen senses of the monster.

"My yoga and meditation have been invaluable to me. Though it's coming slowly, I'm starting to access memories of my life before I became the Wolf," he said as he stepped close to Red Riding Hood and held out his hand in friendship. "Perhaps you would like me to show you how it works?"

Red trembled and hid behind Granny Relda.

Granny knelt down to Red and put her hand on the little girl's cheek. Red looked panicked and her eyes darted about like a cornered animal's. Granny tried to calm her. "Red, there's nothing to worry about. The Wolf is gone, *liebling*."

Red nodded but did not look convinced. It was clear she was still terrified of the old man who had killed her grandmother so many centuries ago, even though she herself had been controlled by a similar devil until the girls cured her, too. Still, all of these changes had happened so recently, Sabrina was sure it was natural to not want to be best buds with a guy who ate your granny.

"Perhaps another time," the old man said, breaking into a coughing fit. When he regained control he turned back to Granny Relda. "I'm told that Jacob has been attacked."

Granny nodded. "The Hand surrounded the house. Nottingham shot him with an arrow when he went out to confront them."

"The tension has escalated," Canis said. "Charming predicted something like this would happen."

"I'm rarely wrong," Charming said, as if it was a matter of fact and not an opinion. "Now maybe everyone will realize we need to start training an army."

"An army?" Goldilocks cried.

"So this little camp is really a military base?" Sabrina's father asked suspiciously.

Charming stood defiant. "Not yet, but it's clear that the tide is certainly turning in that direction. The Hand has taken over the town and run all the humans out. They're turning on their own now, pushing Everafters out of their homes and businesses. It won't be long before they are hunting down anyone that doesn't agree with them. We need to be prepared."

"And once you have beaten the Hand you can point your little army toward taking over the town for yourself," Henry said.

Charming sneered. "I liked you better when you were asleep."

"What does Snow White think of this?" Granny Relda said, referring to the prince's on-again, off-again girlfriend. Sabrina was curious as well. There was no way the pretty former teacher would support a war effort. Sure, she taught a self-defense class called the Bad Apples, but Sabrina had taken her class and Ms. White spent most of the time teaching her students how to avoid a fight.

"You can ask her yourself," the prince said, gesturing to an open field near the far wall of the camp. There, they could see two dozen Everafters doing pushups in the mud while a woman stood over them barking insults and spraying them with a hose.

"Snow is training to fight?" Goldilocks asked.

"No," Charming explained. "She's doing the training. She's in charge of the camp's security. Unfortunately, the only Everafters who have volunteered are the biggest collection of feeble nincompoops ever to grace a storybook. Ms. White is doing her best to turn them into fighting machines."

"Ms. White?" Daphne said.

"Trouble in paradise, Billy?" Sabrina asked.

The prince's eyes lowered and regret filled his face. "She and I are not talking . . . at the moment. Now, if you'll excuse me,

Mr. Seven and I have to check on the state of some cots. The refugees keep coming and the supplies are getting scarce."

The former mayor and his assistant left the group behind and marched across the field.

"I suppose you would like to say hello to our resident drill sergeant?" Canis said, gesturing toward Snow White and her ragtag collection of soldiers. The group rushed in her direction. As they got closer Sabrina noticed Ms. White was dressed in full army fatigues and was blasting a whistle at her trainees. The recruits quickly got to their feet and ran in place, their boots filled to the brim with the heavy mud. All the while Snow called them "worthless," "weak," and "spineless maggots."

"Snow! What in heavens are you doing?" Granny cried as she hurried toward the teacher.

"Getting these plebes into shape," Ms. White said, though she never took her eyes off her recruits. "We need to be prepared for hostilities. Have you come to volunteer? We can use all the soldiers we can get."

"Dear heavens, I think I'm a little old to go to war," Granny replied.

"That's a shame. Any other volunteers?" Snow said. "It would be nice to have one of the Grimm boys helping out. What about you, Hank? Now that you're up and about you could make yourself useful."

Henry shook his head. "We have no intention of staying in this town any longer than we have to."

"Can't say I blame you," Snow said. "This town is a disaster. Taxes are outrageous, no one is safe, homes are being searched without warrants, not to mention the disappearances. Relda, your son may have a point. I'd go with him if I were you."

Granny Relda shook her head. "I'm not leaving."

Henry scowled and stamped the ground.

"So, what's the scoop on you and the prince?" Daphne asked.

"Daphne! Don't be rude," Veronica admonished.

"No worries, Veronica. The girls have been privy to my soap opera for some time. If you must know, Billy proposed."

"Gravy!" Daphne cried.

"And I declined," Snow added.

"What? Why?" Granny asked.

"'Cause he's a jerk. He's arrogant. He's mean. He's selfish," Sabrina said.

"Sabrina, that's not nice," Veronica said, though she didn't sound convincing.

Just then, a gray goose hobbled over to the group. "New refugees are coming in now. One of them is asking for Geppetto," it honked.

"Geppetto, what do you know about this?" Snow demanded as she turned her attention back to her troops.

An elderly man covered in mud fell out of formation and ran to Snow White. He saluted her nervously. "Nothing, sir!" he shouted.

"Geppetto!" Granny cried. "You're training to be a soldier?"

Geppetto nodded. "Things have gotten very bad, Relda. It's not just harassment and stupid laws anymore. Now if you don't take an oath to the Scarlet Hand and the Master they just burn your home and business. The toy store is ashes. It's time to fight back."

The rest of the troops let out an exuberant *Hoo-ah!*

"Well, it appears you have a visitor, maggot," Snow shouted. "Let's go see who it is."

A large group followed Geppetto as he hurried through a throng of excited Everafters crowded into the courtyard. Many were hugging friends and family as they trudged through the open gates. Sabrina and Daphne squirmed their way to the front and watched the toy-maker report to King Arthur, who was making a list of people as they entered the fort.

"Sir, I was told there is someone here asking for me?"

King Arthur looked at the list. "Oh yes, the kid. Over there."

Everyone turned to find a small boy sitting on a huge traveling bag. He was no older than Daphne and was wearing a pair of red overall shorts and a button-down shirt. He had on a yellow hat that sported a quail feather. His face was angular and his nose a bit pointy, and he had a pronounced overbite. His expression was tired and agitated. He stood up and scanned the crowd until his eyes landed on Geppetto. At once his scowl became a wide, toothy smile.

"Papa?" he said. "Dearest Papa!"

"Papa?" Sabrina and Daphne repeated. The old man was trembling, as if in the midst of an illness, and tears were gushing from the corners of his eyes.

"Pinocchio?" he cried, rushing to the mysterious child. In one quick motion he scooped the boy off the ground, swung him around in his arms, and hugged him tight. "You've come back to your father."

"Pinocchio!" Henry exclaimed. "That's *the* Pinocchio?"

"It appears so," Granny Relda said, a happy tear sliding down her cheek. Geppetto was an old family friend and the Grimms knew that the toy-maker's heart was broken the day he and his son were separated.

"Gravy," Daphne said just before she bit down on her palm.

Sabrina should have been happy for Geppetto, but an odd bitterness stabbed at her heart. Instead of joy she was filled with envy. It was hard for her to see this family reunion and know that her own experience just that morning had been less than sweet. She looked to her father, hoping the scene wouldn't be lost on him, but he was busy talking to King Arthur about possible ways out of the forest. Suddenly she knew the moment she had imagined for two years would never come to pass. Her family had chosen to argue. That was their reunion.

"My little pine nut, where have you been?" Geppetto asked his son. "Why didn't you get on the boat with me? I've been a mess for so long worrying about you."

"I'll explain it all in good time, Papa," Pinocchio said. "Just let me embrace you one more time!"

"He talks funny," Puck said.

"You smell funny," Sabrina grumbled.

Puck raised an arm and sniffed his armpit. "Can't argue with you there."

"I thought Pinocchio was a puppet," Daphne said to her grandmother.

"He was," Granny Relda said. "But after he proved he could be good, the Blue Fairy granted his greatest wish—to be a real boy."

"Where has he been all this time?" Sabrina asked.

"It's none of our business," Henry said. "Arthur has given me directions to a path that will take us out of the woods. Girls, say your good-byes. We're leaving."

"But, Dad! We can't leave. Uncle Jake is hurt!" Daphne said. "Besides, that's Pinocchio. I want to get an autograph."

"Daphne, I've had enough of your attitude," Henry snapped. "Now, be a big girl and get your suitcases."

Daphne stomped off to do as she was told.

"Relda, are you sure you won't come with us?" Veronica begged.

"Veronica, you know I can't go," Granny said. "Look around you. The Everafters need us more than ever. If the family abandons Ferryport Landing, the barrier will fall and the chaos will spill out into the surrounding towns. It wouldn't be long before war spreads all over the world. It's this kind of thing that the barrier was created to prevent, so I have to stay."

"Jacob is still here," Henry said. "When he feels better he can take over the responsibility."

"Jacob is a free spirit," Granny said. "I'm surprised he's stayed here as long as he has."

Henry shook his head. "If you won't come with us then you should go back to the house. The protection spells we've put on it will prevent anyone from getting inside. A hurricane could hit that house and you'd be safe. Don't come out until this blows over and don't get involved! I don't want you to end up like Dad."

Granny Relda's face fell with disappointment, but Henry either didn't notice or chose to ignore it.

"I'll keep you informed of where we land," he continued. "C'mon, Daphne, don't dilly-dally. We've got a train to catch."

Daphne slammed Sabrina's suitcase to the ground. "Carry your own bag, traitor."

"What did I do?" Sabrina cried.

Daphne ignored her and hugged Granny and Mr. Canis, then said good-bye to Puck, Red, and Goldilocks. Then she stormed off to wait by the gate.

"So, you finally got your wish, frog face," Puck said. "You're getting out of Ferryport Landing."

"Yeah, I guess," Sabrina said, eyeing her grandmother. As much as she had wanted to leave the town, it didn't feel right to do it now. Not with a war brewing. Some of the Everafters might be hurt. Granny might need them. "But this isn't how I wanted to go."

"C'mon, Sabrina," her father said, grabbing her suitcase and leading his wife to the main gates. They stepped through as the latest Everafter refugees entered.

Sabrina turned to look back one more time as the guards closed the gates. Puck stood in the entrance, hands on hips, his wooden sword by his side. His wings popped out and flapped in the summer sun. Granny was next to him, smiling through tears. Red stood next to her, looking afraid. Goldilocks handed Granny a handkerchief and Momma Bear wrapped a furry arm around her shoulders. Mr. Canis leaned against his cane. Sabrina stared at them intensely, hoping her mind could take a photograph that she could return to from time to time. She wondered if she should say something to these people who had been part of her life for nearly a year. She knew she had been difficult—a downright pain most of the time. Her reluctance, distrust, and general nasty mood had not been easy to tolerate, and yet, they had all in their own way been by her side at her worst moments. *I should thank them,* she thought. *I should express some sort of gratitude. I should tell them that I love them.* But the doors of the fort closed before she could get out a single word. A heavy lock turned. A bar came down across the doors and she was outside. Exactly where she had always wanted to be, with her parents and sister by her side, safe and sound. And yet . . .

• • •

They had not walked long when Henry stopped to consult the crude map King Arthur had drawn for him. When Veronica asked if they were lost, he held up his hand for silence but said nothing. After more scrutiny he climbed atop a rocky cliff and peered over the horizon. Sabrina thought she'd seen most of the woods around Ferryport Landing—after all, she had been chased through them by enough monsters—but she had no idea where they were. If Ferryport Landing had anything in great supply, it was creepy forests. She hoped they weren't lost.

"He's like this in the car, too," Veronica said as she watched her husband turn the map one way and then the other.

Sabrina giggled but Daphne said nothing. She sat on a stump sulking, her head tilted downward as if the most intriguing thing she had ever seen were the ants at her feet.

"Well, that's new," Veronica said quietly, as if she had just come upon some exotic animal in the woods. "I don't think I've ever seen your sister angry."

"Stick around," Sabrina replied. "It's a regular event these days."

"You two have changed so much." Veronica sighed.

"We've been through a lot," Sabrina said. "We had to adapt."

Henry scrambled back down the cliff toward the family and tucked his map into his pocket. "OK, I know where we are. It'll take about two hours to get to the train station if we hurry. We should be able to catch the 6:17 to Grand Central."

"So, Henry, what are we going to do when we get to the city?" Veronica asked.

"I haven't figured it out yet," Henry said, urging everyone to their feet. He walked on, leading them along Arthur's trail.

"Oh, so we're just going to stumble into New York City with no money and no place to sleep? That's your plan?"

Henry shook his head. "I have some money—enough to get us a hotel for a night. Tomorrow we'll need to tackle our bank accounts."

"Tomorrow is Sunday," Veronica said. "The banks will be closed."

Henry's steps faltered for a moment but he soon continued onward. "I'll figure something out."

"Daphne and I slept in plenty of homeless shelters when we ran away from foster families," Sabrina said. "I know places that will take us."

"Oh good!" Veronica cried. "We can sleep in a homeless shelter. Our problems have been solved."

"Sarcasm is not necessary," Henry said.

Veronica laughed. "Oh yes it is! It's the only way to get you to react to what is going on around you. Henry, we can't leave. I'd love to go back to the city, but not this way—with your brother wounded and the entire town in jeopardy. On top of that we're broke and homeless."

"I would rather have us sleeping in a gutter in the Bronx before we spent a night in this forsaken town!" Henry said. "I know you don't agree with what I'm doing or how I'm doing it but I'm going to protect this family. I can't do that in this town; there's too much Everafter craziness. I don't want my family around it. And to be very, very clear, I mean I don't want anyone in my family around Everafters. Not even the ones that live in New York City!"

Veronica's face fell. "You were eavesdropping?"

"Imagine my surprise when I learned my own wife was working with Everafters in Manhattan behind my back!"

"I had to! I knew you wouldn't approve. I was trying to be helpful. Isn't that what Grimms do?"

"Don't throw that silly catchphrase at me," Henry said.

"So now that the secret's out, you must know there are at least two hundred Everafters running around New York City, so if you're trying to get away from them—"

"Not a problem. We're moving," Henry said.

"Moving!" Sabrina gasped. Moving away from the Big Apple was not part of the dream reunion she had imagined when her parents woke up. They couldn't move!

"Yes, we'll move to somewhere no Everafter would want to live!"

"Like where?"

"I don't know. Canton, maybe."

"Canton, Ohio!" Veronica groaned. "*Human beings* don't want to live in Canton, Ohio!"

"It doesn't matter where we move as long as it's boring," Henry shouted. "We'll find someplace where the mayor isn't a prince and the local police aren't magical transforming pigs!"

"Actually, the Sheriff of Nottingham is running the police department now," Sabrina corrected.

"I didn't say good-bye to Elvis," Daphne whimpered.

"So, you're laying down the law, huh? Do I get a say in any of this?" Veronica asked. "Or am I supposed to play the dutiful wife? Perhaps you'd like me to put on an apron and make you a pot roast, too?"

Henry scowled. "Veronica, that's a bit dramatic."

"I didn't say good-bye to Elvis," Daphne repeated.

Sabrina frowned. She hadn't said good-bye to the big dog, either.

Veronica continued the argument. "You're not going to drag the girls and me through this world hiding from pixies and fairy godmothers. They're out there, and most of them are not bad people."

"Pixies are not people," Henry snapped. "Don't try to tell me what I know about Everafters. I've lived side by side with them most of my life. My mother's best friend is one. I used to be in love with one."

The girls cringed, then turned to their father. He cringed back. Henry had stepped in it, and Sabrina's mother was boiling mad.

"I'm painfully aware of your previous love life, Henry Grimm. After all, I just woke up this morning from a two-year sleep to find your old girlfriend sitting over you with her big moon eyes!"

"Veronica! I can't believe you're jealous."

This time Henry put his head in his hands. Sabrina didn't know much about adult relationships, but everyone knew that accusing someone of being jealous of an old girlfriend couldn't be a good thing. Her mother looked like the top of her head might blow off like the cork on a champagne bottle.

"JEALOUS?"

Henry sputtered. "I didn't exactly mean jealous—"

"What do I have to be jealous about? I'm the best thing that ever happened to you, pal!"

Henry nodded sheepishly.

"You hit the lottery when you met me! I'm smart. I'm funny. I can throw a sixty-mile-an-hour fastball! And I'm a babe!"

"I agree." Henry's face was bright red. "I am the luckiest man in the world."

The family walked on for several yards in silence. Sabrina wondered if her parents would ever speak to one another again, but then Veronica broke the ice.

"Henry, I know why you want to leave. The loss of your father, the problems the girls have had for two years, our kidnapping. I get it! But we're still a family—a team—and we're supposed to make decisions as a team. Besides, there's something I've been meaning to tell you all, and I . . . wait, where's Daphne?"

Sabrina spun around but Daphne wasn't there. "She must have gone back to tell Elvis good-bye."

"Daphne, we don't have time for this," Henry shouted.

"Daphne!" Veronica called. There was no response.

Henry shook his head. "When did she get so stubborn?"

Sabrina shrugged. "Actually, that's what people usually say about me."

"Wait here. I'll go after her," Henry said. He took off running back the way they came. Veronica and Sabrina looked at one another, shook their heads, and then raced after him through brush and creek beds. Sabrina could hear her father shouting for her sister farther along the path, demanding that Daphne come back, but he was wasting his breath. Sabrina had been trying to manage her sister for some time and it was like pushing a car up a hill.

When Sabrina and her mother finally caught up with her father, he was standing in a clearing of trees with his hand clamped on Daphne's arm.

"This is unacceptable, young lady," Henry scolded.

"I'm not leaving," Daphne said. "They need us."

"What makes you think you can do anything to help?" Henry demanded. "You're only five years old!"

"Dad, she's seven," Sabrina said.

"Eight in two weeks, and I've fought plenty of bad guys in the last year. I am a Grimm. This is what I do!"

Just then, a dozen hulking figures stepped out from the trees, surrounding the family. They all stood nearly seven feet tall and each had bumpy, gray skin that looked like it had been peeled off an alligator. Their eyes were twice as big as a normal person's. Their ears, however, were unlike anything Sabrina had ever seen—sharp, pointy, and covered in what looked like porcupine quills. Most held spears, though a couple clung to knotty clubs with dozens of rusty spikes jutting out of them. Their leader, a brute with a chest full of gaudy medals, stepped to the front of the group. His face was a collection of scars, broken bones, and jagged teeth. Like all of his soldiers, his chest was painted with the mark of the Scarlet Hand. He surveyed the Grimms and then grinned like some twisted kid who has just decapitated all of his sister's dolls.

"I knew I recognized the foul stink that comes off humans, but I never suspected we'd meet ones who are so famous," he said.

"You want an autograph?" Sabrina grumbled. Henry shot her a look that told her to keep her mouth shut.

A second soldier stepped forward to join his boss. He was just as ugly, with a tuft of red hair on his decidedly pointy head. "They must be coming from Charming's camp," he said. "They've allied themselves with the traitor and his troublemakers."

"That means the camp must be nearby," the leader crowed. He turned back to the family and gnashed his yellow teeth. "The Master will reward us for finding the camp. To avoid any unpleasantness, perhaps you would like to tell us where it is?"

"We don't have the foggiest idea what you are talking about," Henry lied. "We're not coming from any camp. My family and I are just out for a picnic."

The hobgoblin leaped forward and stood as close to Henry as he could. Their faces were only inches apart and he blew his rank breath on him. "You lie. You're a Grimm. All of you lie."

"That's not a very nice thing to say," Henry said. "I'm hurt."

"If you don't tell me where the camp is you're going to be hurting a lot more."

Henry shook his head. "We've gotten off on the wrong foot. Let's start over. My family and I are not involved with Charming or his camp. We have refused to take a side in your little conflict and to avoid any further problems we are on our way to the train station. So, if you'll kindly step aside and let us pass, we'll get out of your hair."

"You'll go where I tell you, human," the monster snorted, then turned to his men. "Arrest them and bind their hands. If they won't take us to the fort, we'll beat the answer out of them, starting with their children."

One of the brutes clamped his hands down on Sabrina's arms. She tried to pull free but he was impossibly strong. She could see the rest of her family getting the same rough treatment.

Then there was a flash of fists and feet, loud groans, and the cracking of bones. At first Sabrina thought that some unearthly force had come to their rescue, but it soon became clear that there was nothing supernatural at work, only her mother and father—who fought like trained prizefighters.

Henry was like a tornado, whipping from one soldier to the next, planting punches with incredible accuracy. Sabrina had never seen someone so quick and yet so precise. The way her father fought reminded her of a dancer, kicking and punching to a rhythm only he could hear. Veronica was not quite so elegant. She snatched a thick limb off the forest floor and clubbed anyone who got close to her. Sabrina remembered one evening when her parents had taken her to the boardwalk at Coney Island. They passed some batting cages and Henry and Veronica decided to see who could hit the most fastballs. Veronica won by a landslide. Sabrina had felt bad for the balls that night as her mom drove one after another into the netting. The monster's ribs and heads weren't nearly as hard as baseballs, but she swung for the fences anyway. Working together, Sabrina's parents managed to take out eight of the monsters.

Sabrina looked over at her sister. "Our parents are so gravy."

Daphne scowled. "That's not how you say it."

"Girls, run for the fort," Henry shouted as he defended himself from one of the creatures who was charging him with a heavy chain in hand.

"We can help," Daphne said, stepping into the fighting stance she had learned in self-defense class.

"Listen to your father!" Veronica cried, jamming her branch into the belly of one of the beasts and knocking him to the ground.

Sabrina snatched her sister by the hand and pulled her down the path toward the fortress. She looked back, hoping her mother and father were right behind them, but they were nowhere in sight.

"We have to go back!" Daphne said. "We can't just leave them."

"You saw them. Our parents are tough," Sabrina said, doing her best to sound confident. "They'll be along soon."

They ran and ran and by the time they came to Charming's camp Sabrina's lungs were on fire, but she forced herself to shout for help. Daphne did the same. A sentry appeared in a tower and aimed a magic wand at them. "Stand back, invaders!" he shouted and a second later a blast of white-hot fire exploded at Sabrina's feet.

"Who goes there?" he demanded.

"Open the gate!" Sabrina cried. "It's Sabrina and Daphne Grimm. Monsters are chasing us."

The sentry blew a whistle and the big doors swung open.

Before the girls could take a single step inside, an infantry of armor-clad knights on horseback surrounded them. The girls were nearly trampled before Charming rushed to their side with his silver sword in hand. He snatched Sabrina by the arm. "Where are these monsters?" he shouted.

"We ran into them about half a mile back," Sabrina said. "There are at least a dozen, maybe more. They're attacking my mom and dad."

"You fools! You have probably led them to us," he cried in disgust.

"Freaky monsters were trying to kill us," Sabrina said. "Should I have just died out there so you could keep your clubhouse secret?"

"Absolutely!" the prince said.

"Well, well, well, look who's back," Puck said, hovering above the fortress wall. "I knew you'd show up again. This little crush you have on me is getting embarrassing."

Enraged, Sabrina would have slugged the fairy boy if not for the appearance of Henry and Veronica, slightly worse for wear. Sabrina's father's lip was bloody in the corner and her mother had a long scratch on her right arm. "We took care of them, Prince."

"How many were there?" he said.

"Fourteen that we saw," Henry replied. "They're hobgoblins. We managed to subdue twelve of them. If you walk along the path you'll find them."

"And the other two?"

"They ran," Veronica said, still clinging to her heavy branch. "Cowards."

Charming pulled a guard aside and ordered him to gather as many of Robin Hood's Merry Men as he could collect. "Find those hobgoblins. If they get back to the Hand they'll reveal where we are and we'll be overrun by nightfall!"

A moment later a well-armed posse of archers and swordsmen was racing into the forest in hot pursuit.

4

efore nightfall the camp received more than three dozen additional Everafter refugees. They looked tired and broken. Many spoke of burned homes and businesses, shattered lives, and destitution. Others shared warnings of brutal beatings, threats, and murder.

When they came in, Mr. Canis called them "guests" and informed them that to join the camp they had an obligation to all the others. Each person would be assigned tasks in the morning based on their occupations or talents, but until then they should try to relax and get some rest. Robin Hood and his wife, Marian, led the newcomers on a tour and to the supply tent for fresh clothes. They were all given hot meals and promised clean bunks.

Charming marched through the camp pulling people aside and letting them know about the hobgoblin attack. The story seemed to startle everyone, especially those who had just fled chaos.

"I told you this would happen. They are bringing the fight to us!" the prince said. "It's time to prepare for war."

His call for action didn't produce the reaction Sabrina suspected Charming was seeking. He was largely ignored. Many of the Everafters said they didn't want to get involved, even if they were shaken by the prince's dark predictions. At the end of the day, only six of the refugees volunteered to join Snow White's militia.

Dinner was served in the courtyard as the sun sank below the tree line. A witch conjured a hundred tables and enough folding chairs for everyone. The magic tables came complete with plates, utensils, and drinking glasses. Oil lamps were strung from trees for light. Everyone filed through a long line for their share of beans, brown bread, a potato, and an ear of corn. Sabrina and her family, along with Red, dined together at a table. Mr. Canis was invited to join but claimed he needed to get back to his meditation. Goldilocks and her bears were invited as well, but Henry's former girlfriend seemed nervous around him. She claimed she and the bears had already made dinner arrangements. Sabrina's mother didn't seem at all heartbroken by Goldilocks's rejection, but she said nothing. Geppetto and Pinocchio, however, happily accepted the invite.

"Good day, all," Pinocchio said. "My father has spoken highly of your family. He considers you some of his dearest friends. I'm quite honored to make your acquaintance."

Sabrina couldn't help staring at the boy. If the story was true, Geppetto had carved him from a solid block of wood. But what threw her off more was the way he spoke. He was so proper and mature.

"Nice to meet you, too," Granny Relda said. "Your father has missed you terribly."

"Indeed," Geppetto said, giving the boy a hug.

"So, where have you been?" Daphne asked the odd little boy.

"Daphne, that's a little rude," Veronica said. "That's Pinocchio's business."

Daphne shrugged. "Just making conversation."

"Well, it's not much of a tale," the little boy said.

"Then skip it," Puck said, filling his mouth with beans. "We've spent entirely too much time discussing things other than me."

Granny rolled her eyes. "Please, Pinocchio. Go on."

"I'm confident Papa told you about our missed connection aboard Wilhelm's vessel."

"What's a vessel?" Daphne asked.

"The layman calls it a boat," Pinocchio explained. "I have never cared for the sea. I had a very disturbing encounter with a great white shark once. I also had a bit of trouble on an island off the coast of Italy. Thus, I try to stay landlocked as much as possible."

"I wonder how hard it would be to hide a shark under someone's pillow," Puck said, squinting at Sabrina. She shook a threatening fist at him.

Pinocchio continued his tale. "So I stayed in Europe and took a few odd jobs. I was an apprentice at a newspaper and learned to work with a printing press. The paper wasn't much to speak of—mostly propaganda and smears. I was an artist's assistant for a few years. I sold kites in a market in Spain. I lived in the Taj Mahal for a month before security guards found me and tossed me out. I was a shoeshine boy on the Orient Express. I've had a number of occupations and saw a great many places. I even journeyed back to my home in Italy. Papa, I believe I found the actual forest I came from and met a great many of my relatives. It was very enlightening."

"You found the magic forest," Geppetto said, clapping his hands. "I found a log inside it and used it to carve my son. I had heard it was destroyed by a forest fire."

"Sad but true, though a few saplings survived the blaze," the boy said.

"Why all the moving?" Granny Relda asked.

"It's due to my condition," Pinocchio explained.

"Condition?" Puck asked. "Do you have some horrible virus? If so, could you give it to Sabrina?"

Pinocchio ignored him. "It appears that I am incapable of growing old. Every few years I was forced to vanish before anyone could conclude I wasn't getting older. I made the horrible blunder of sticking around for too long once in Eastern Europe and the superstitious townspeople chased me with torches and pitchforks. Do yourself a favor and stay away from Transylvania."

"It's 'cause you're an Everafter. You have to decide to get older or you'll stay the same age forever," Daphne explained.

"Alas, no," the boy replied. "I cannot get older. I believe it has to do with the wish I made to the Blue Fairy. I wished to be a real boy. Not to be a real boy that grows into a man."

"You have to be real specific with wishes," Sabrina said.

"Indeed," the boy groaned.

"The Blue Fairy lives here in town," Daphne said. "We could help you find her. She might fix the wish."

"Thank you, but no," Pinocchio said. "Like your sister said, her wish granting leaves a little to be desired. I might ask her to let me grow up and she'd probably make it so that I grew all the way to the moon. I'll seek other options."

"I'd like to know how you ended up here in the camp," Henry asked.

Pinocchio shifted uncomfortably. "I had a great deal of savings from my many occupations, and these days anyone can purchase an airplane ticket on the Internet. I landed in New York City and boarded the next train for Ferryport Landing. It was immediately clear that trouble was afoot, but I searched for my father nonetheless. I met a young man who had a pumpkin for a head. He was quite peculiar."

"Jack Pumpkinhead," Granny said. "He's from Oz. They're all a little odd."

"I told him who I was and he offered to bring me to the camp."

"And I couldn't be happier, pine nut," Geppetto said. "After dinner you will have to show everyone your marionettes."

Granny smiled. "So you are a puppet-maker as well?"

"Like father, like son, I suppose," the boy said. Geppetto beamed with pride.

They hugged again. Sabrina looked over at her own father, hoping he might be inspired by the family feeling, but he was busy studying a map of the town. It was clear he was looking for another path out of Ferryport Landing.

Just then, Nurse Sprat approached the table. She was an

overweight woman shaped like a nearly perfect circle. The family had met her at her former job as a nurse at Ferryport Landing Memorial Hospital, where she had had the unfortunate responsibility of looking after Red Riding Hood when she was mentally unhinged.

"Jacob is going to be fine," she told the group.

"Thank goodness," Granny cried.

"Normally he would be healing for a couple of months, but I found a container of magical salve in his pocket and it's doing wonders. He should be shipshape in a couple of days."

"Can we see him?" Henry asked.

"Tomorrow," she said. "He's sleeping and needs the rest."

"Thank you so much, Mrs. Sprat," Granny said.

"You're welcome, Mrs. Grimm," she said, then returned to her medical tent.

For the first time since her mother and father had awoken, there were smiles on everyone's faces. Sabrina reveled in the moment. It was just what she had wanted—just like it had been before her parents disappeared and all the craziness began.

But it was a short-lived celebration. A loud bell rang and the gates of the fort opened. Robin Hood and his men marched inside with a dozen of the hobgoblins Henry and Veronica had pummeled earlier that day. The brutes were tied together at the wrists and then linked by a single heavy chain. They grunted and complained as they were roughly shoved along. Charming appeared and ordered the men to lock all of the creatures in his cabin. He pulled Little John and Will Scarlet from the group and ordered them to have the prisoners guarded twenty-four hours a day. "We can't have them escape before we question them."

"You can forget interrogation," one of the hobgoblins barked. "You won't get anything out of us."

Snow White, who had appeared in the courtyard for dinner, still in her fatigues, cracked her knuckles loudly. "We'll just see about that."

"Relda, you seem to have a knack for getting information. Could you help?" Charming asked.

"She's not part of your war," Henry said.

Granny stood up. "I'll do what I can."

Sabrina watched her father quietly seethe.

• • •

After dinner, the girls went on a walk to give their parents some privacy. It was clear another argument was brewing and Sabrina had had enough fighting. Puck followed them. Sabrina tried to ignore him, as he was being especially annoying and had already driven her to the brink of murder several times that day.

They wandered aimlessly around the fort, taking in the strange sights, until Daphne spotted Red Riding Hood sitting behind Charming's cabin. Daphne rushed over and sat down next to her.

"Hey," she said.

"Hey." Red forced a smile on her face.

"Are you hiding back here?"

Red nodded. "I'm trying to stay out of the way. I don't want to be any trouble."

"I'm all about trouble," Puck crowed.

Sabrina leaned against the cabin and pretended to be fascinated with a dusty stone near her foot. She did not want to have a conversation with Red and was surprised by Daphne's acceptance of the demented child. Just a few days ago Red was locked up in an insane asylum for trying to kill Sabrina's family, and now, with a little magical help, she was "cured" and living with the Grimms. It was obvious that this "new" Red needed some comfort, but why should Sabrina have to give it?

"You're not trouble," Daphne said. "Granny invited you to live with us so that makes you one of us. You don't have to run off and hide."

"Your grandmother is very kind," Red said.

"My grandmother is gravy," Daphne agreed. "You'll be safe with her, and plus she's an excellent cook—"

Sabrina laughed out loud and Daphne flashed her an angry look. "Well, you shouldn't lie to her," Sabrina said defensively.

Daphne turned back to Red Riding Hood. "Like I was saying . . . Granny's a great cook and soon you will have your own room. Granny promised to build me one, too. Maybe you and I could have a secret door that leads into each other's rooms—one only we know about."

"I would like that," Red said, grinning.

Sabrina bristled. The first time the girls had slept in separate beds had been the night before. Daphne had refused to share a bedroom after Sabrina had lied and stolen from her. Apparently, her sister's desire to have her own room hadn't gone away yet. Sabrina knew what she had done was wrong, but they were sisters! Wasn't blood thicker than water, or whatever the saying was that meant you had to forgive your family's mistakes?

Prince Charming's booming voice exploded from a window directly above them.

"What's going on?" Red asked.

"I think they're questioning a hobgoblin," Sabrina said as she got up on her tiptoes to get a peek in the window. The rest of the children did the same, elbowing one another for a good view. Inside, Sabrina saw a hobgoblin sitting on a chair. His hands were still bound and he looked exhausted. Charming and Snow hovered over him while Granny sat in a chair, patiently. Mr. Canis and Mr. Seven looked on.

"Does the Master know where our camp is?" Charming barked.

The hobgoblin smiled and dipped his head. "Not yet, Prince, but soon."

Charming turned to Mr. Canis and they exchanged a worried look. Snow and Mr. Seven, who stood on the opposite side of the room, shared the same worried expression. Granny Relda, however, seemed relaxed.

"You speak of the Master as if you know him. Who is he?" Granny Relda asked.

Sabrina's heart skipped a beat. She, too, had wondered who the Master was and why he had caused so much heartache for her family.

The hobgoblin snorted a laugh. "I have not earned the honor of sharing the presence of the Master. But one day I hope to meet him in person and kneel before his feet."

"So you take orders from someone you have never met?" Snow asked.

"I do not need to meet the man when his genius is so clear. He has a glorious plan for Everafters," he barked at her.

"Not all Everafters," Ms. White corrected him. "He has no use for many of us."

"Nonsense! You have turned your back on him! You've turned your back on all of us," the hobgoblin cried earnestly. "You and Charming and the rest of your ilk mingle with the humans. Worse, you conspire with the Grimm family, the very people responsible for our imprisonment. The Master says you are traitors to our race."

"What does your Master plan to do about it?" Charming asked.

"He will free us, of course," the commander said smugly. "He will destroy the barrier that traps us here and we will march through every nation, recapturing land and treasure from the weak and pathetic human population, then ruling over them as it was always meant to be."

Charming rolled his eyes. "I've heard enough from this fool. Was he searched?"

Seven, who had been sitting directly beneath the window, stepped forward and handed Charming a filthy burlap sack. The prince emptied it onto a nearby table and studied each item: a rusty dagger covered in what looked like dried blood, a couple loaves of moldy bread, a compass, a map of the woods, and a small pocket mirror. Charming looked at the mirror with some amusement. "I had no idea hobgoblins were so vain."

The hobgoblin chuckled, sending a shiver through Sabrina. It was not a nervous laugh. It was the sound of someone who knows a secret.

Charming frowned, then turned to Granny Relda. "Mrs. Grimm, I have a favor to ask."

Daphne elbowed some more space at the window. "I can't see. What are they talking about?"

"The Master," Sabrina said.

"Oh, he gives me the shudders," the little girl said.

"The ugly one says he wants to take over the world," Puck added. "Been there. Done that."

"Did he tell who the Master is?" Daphne asked.

Puck shook his head. "Not even a hint."

"Wait a minute," Sabrina said, turning and crouching next to Red. "Haven't you seen the Master?"

Red Riding Hood shifted uncomfortably and looked away.

"Yes, you have!" Sabrina cried. "You told us that you had talked to him when you first attacked us with the Jabberwocky—"

"I don't remember," the child said.

"Sure you do," Sabrina said. "Who is he?"

"It's blurry," Red said as she clamped her hands onto her head. The subject seemed to cause her physical pain.

Sabrina was so excited she could hardly talk. "Try! If you tell us who he is then Charming can send people to capture him. Then no one else will be hurt!"

"I don't think I can," Red whimpered.

"You have to!"

Daphne stepped between her sister and Red. "Sabrina, leave her alone. She says she doesn't remember."

"She's not trying," Sabrina said.

"Her memory is messed up. Don't you remember what Mr. Canis said? Since his madness has gone he can't remember big parts of his life. It's the same with Red," Daphne said.

"Daphne, she's got to remember. Stopping the Master will end all this nonsense. The town will go back to normal and we can go back to New York City."

"What? You don't want to stay?" Puck said.

"Duh!" Sabrina said, spinning on him. "I've wanted to get out of this town since the first day I stepped into it. My mom and dad were supposed to make that happen but of course Everafters have to get in the way."

"Don't *duh* me!" Puck snapped. "Trying to figure out what you're thinking from one day to the next takes more brains than I have."

"Well, maybe you should stop. I'd hate to burn out that little peanut in your head."

"You wish you were more like me, Grimm. I'm magnificent," Puck said, puffing up his chest.

Sabrina's face twisted in anger. "Magnificently smelly. I doubt too many people would list themselves as exceptional when their greatest talent is eating with their feet!"

Daphne laughed but clamped a hand on her mouth when Puck glared at her.

Red watched, bewildered. "Are you two in love or something?"

Daphne lost it and fell to the ground, rolling and laughing beyond control. Perhaps it was Daphne's amusement, or Red's embarrassing question, but before Sabrina could stop herself she blurted out the one thing she promised herself she would never tell—the truth.

"In love? As if! How on earth we end up getting married is beyond me! How could I have held my nose long enough to get through the ceremony? Ugh!"

There was a silence unlike anything Sabrina had ever experienced. It felt as if someone had turned the volume knob on the world to the Off position. Her sister's giggling expression was now replaced with shock. Even Red seemed bewildered. Sabrina was sure she was about to hyperventilate. She closed her eyes and quietly prayed for another rip in time—one that would allow her to go back and kick herself in the rear before she opened her dumb trap. All she could do was hope that Puck was as slow as he seemed and that he wouldn't understand what she had said. But his face said otherwise.

"MARRIED?"

"It's nothing," Daphne said, trying to dispel the tension.

Puck's huge insectlike wings popped out of his back and lifted him off the ground. He rose a few feet above them and hovered there, flapping his wings furiously.

"Tell me now!" he shouted.

Sabrina tried to talk but all she could do was stammer.

Daphne stepped in to explain. "Do you remember when Cinderella's husband built the time machine that nearly ate the town? Well, we got pulled into it a couple times and saw the future and—"

"NO!" Puck cried before Daphne could finish.

The little girl nodded. "You two are married in the future!" Daphne confirmed.

Puck's wings were beating so hard and fast he was shaking

the air around him. "I'm a little boy. Little boys do not get married."

Sabrina's face was so hot she felt she had somehow taken over the work of the sun. "You grew up."

Puck's face fell. "What would make me do that?"

Daphne pointed to Sabrina.

"I would never do that!" Puck roared.

"You're already doing it," Daphne said. "Haven't you noticed you've gotten taller lately? I heard Granny tell Mr. Canis you were going through puberty."

"What's that?"

Daphne shrugged and looked to Sabrina.

"Oh, now I'm good for definitions?" she fumed. Sabrina had never dreaded explaining a word more than at that moment. "Puberty is when a child starts to become an adult. You're going to get taller and grow hair on your face and get zits."

"This puberty you speak of—it must be triggered by some kind of disease. You've given me your cooties, dogface!"

"Puck, you're not sick," Sabrina said, trying to calm him down.

Blistering flames shot out of Puck's eyes. "I am the Trickster King. I'm a villain. I am the King of Loafers, the Prince of Low Expectations! The spiritual guide for millions of complainers, criminals, and convicts! Villains do not get married. They do not get zits. You have poisoned me, Sabrina Grimm. This means war!"

"War?" Sabrina repeated.

"Yes, war! And when I'm done you'll wish the Scarlet Hand had gotten to you first!" Puck blasted into the sky like a rocket. He went so fast there was a loud boom and then he was gone.

"That went better than I expected," Daphne said.

Before Sabrina could respond, Uncle Jake staggered around the corner. His arm was bandaged in a sling that hung around his neck. He looked pale and in a great deal of pain. "Girls, I've been looking everywhere for you. I need your help."

"Uncle Jake, you should be in bed," Daphne scolded.

"I can't. I have to go," he said.

"Go where?" Sabrina asked.

"To rescue Briar Rose. And I need you to help me."

5

ncle Jake, we were just out there and we nearly got stomped to death by the Scarlet Hand's goons," Sabrina said. "If we walk through the forest we won't come back."

"We're not going to walk," he replied as he shuffled unsteadily toward the courtyard. "C'mon."

The girls left Red Riding Hood in her hiding place and followed Uncle Jake to Prince Charming's cabin. It was empty except for the two magic mirrors. Once inside, he lit one of the oil lamps. "Briar Rose didn't come in with any of the refugees. We're taking the flying carpet to find her. Daphne, you can steer it better than me even when I'm a hundred percent. Sabrina, I need your help, too. My arm feels like a dead limb. You can keep me from falling off the carpet."

"It's dangerous out there," Sabrina said.

"Which is exactly why I need to find Briar. Something's wrong. She and the fairy godmothers would have come here already, especially if the town is as bad as everyone is saying."

"Maybe they're leaving her alone," Sabrina said.

"The Scarlet Hand? Leaving my girlfriend alone? Not likely, 'Brina. Listen, I know there could be trouble so if you or your sister want to bail I'll understand. I'll find a way to manage."

"I'm in," Daphne said.

Sabrina weighed the options. On the one hand she knew that letting Daphne go by herself would win her points with her sister. Daphne would see this as a vote of confidence. On the other hand, if she didn't go, Daphne and her wounded uncle would be flying into a war zone all by themselves. If something happened to them she'd never forgive herself. It was decided. Daphne's forgiveness would have to wait—again.

"Let's do it," Sabrina said.

They crept through the Hall of Wonders and to the back door that led to the Room of Reflections. Once there they asked Mirror to retrieve the magic carpet for them, then they tiptoed back the way they came and into the fort. Guards were milling about but gave them no trouble, though they became alarmed when Uncle Jake unrolled the carpet and climbed aboard.

"Charming has ordered that no one leave the camp," a guard pleaded.

"Charming isn't the boss of us," Daphne said then turned her attention to the rug. "Up!"

The elegant Persian rug rose into the air, its tassels rippling with the evening breeze. Sabrina couldn't help admiring the intricate weaving of the carpet, and focusing on it prevented her from getting vertigo as they were suddenly propelled skyward. When the rug had cleared the high walls of the fort, Daphne instructed it to take them to Briar's coffee shop, Sacred Grounds. In their previous experiences with Aladdin's rug, they had learned that it seemed to know where everything was and the best way to get there. At Daphne's instruction, the rug jolted forward, nearly knocking Sabrina over the edge. Her uncle grabbed her hand just in time.

"You're supposed to make sure *I* don't fall off," he reminded her.

"Sorry," she said. "This thing really needs seat belts."

"It's easier if you sit down," Daphne explained over the wind. Jake and Sabrina took her advice and found she was right. The more relaxed they were the better the ride became.

Still, it was hard not to be nervous. The quarter moon did little to illuminate the forest below, so sailing above it was like drifting over a black abyss. Sabrina watched the treetops nervously. The refugees' stories of the Scarlet Hand's army had made her paranoid, and she feared what might rocket out of the darkness below. She imagined the hideous roar of a Jabberwocky as its tiny wings lifted it up to devour them in midair. If there was any comfort in the trip, it was that it became clear to Sabrina that Prince Charming's camp was hidden deep in the woods, and it would be very difficult for the enemy to find.

Uncle Jake seemed to read her mind. "You forget that sometimes under all his arrogance the prince is brilliant. I doubt that those hobgoblins could ever find the place. Still, the refugees should be getting ready just in case."

"You think they should fight back?" Daphne said.

"Absolutely. Will they win? That's another question entirely. They're completely outnumbered, and even if they did manage to raise an army it would consist of elderly witches and princesses who have spent most of their lives being waited on hand and foot. There's only a few of them that have any wits about them at all."

Sabrina knew her uncle was referring to his girlfriend, Briar Rose. She was a lovely woman and the basis for the famous story of Sleeping Beauty, but unlike a lot of the royalty Sabrina had met, Briar was a resourceful woman. Sabrina had come to think of her, Snow White, and Granny Relda as role models. She set her hand on her uncle's good shoulder. "We'll find her."

"I hope."

"We will," Daphne said, steering the rug westward. "We're Grimms. This is what we do."

"So, perhaps we should discuss our cover story for your father," Jake said.

The girls looked at one another nervously.

"You want us to lie to Dad?" Sabrina asked.

"No! Of course not," their uncle said, then thought for a moment. "Actually, yes. I want all of us to lie to your father. He's being a bit of a jerk."

"You noticed that, too?" Daphne said.

"Hank was always the high-strung one. He can be very stubborn, too, but your dad is only trying to protect you both. He's not exactly polite about it but it's the only way he knows to keep everyone alive. He gets that from your grandfather. I'm more like Mom in a lot of ways—impulsive—"

"NO! You?" Sabrina said with a grin.

Uncle Jake laughed. "Guilty as charged."

"I've never seen Dad like this, ever," Daphne said.

"She's right. Mom and Dad have always been laid-back. Ever since they woke up it's been nonstop bickering, with us and each other. If I didn't know better I would think we woke up the wrong people." Sabrina sighed.

"Not the happily ever after you were hoping for, huh?" Uncle Jake said. "Girls, I'm sorry. I think in all the excitement I've forgotten how important waking them up was to you and then to have them snapping at everyone—I wish it had been different."

"We're coming up on the farms," Daphne said as she pointed directly in front of them.

Sabrina expected to see long plains of corn and wheat, neatly planted in rows—maybe a silo here and there, the occasional cow mooing at the moon, but what they drifted over was unrecognizable. Much of the farmland was in ruins. The little houses that freckled the fields were ablaze.

"The Scarlet Hand has been here," Uncle Jake said gravely.

"But these are Everafter farms," Daphne said. "Why burn them when there are human farms not far away?"

"These fires are about sending a message to the rest of the Everafters: Anyone who doesn't join the Hand will regret it," Uncle Jake said. His jaw stiffened and it was obvious to Sabrina that he was now doubly worried about his girlfriend. She was an Everafter, and thus difficult to kill, but, as Sabrina had witnessed, it wasn't impossible—especially if the killer was an Everafter, too. Had the Hand gotten to her?

Once again, Uncle Jake seemed to be listening in on her thoughts. "Can you make this thing go faster?" he said.

Daphne nodded and spoke a few words to the carpet. It accelerated and the ground below whipped by. Uncle Jake nearly fell off the side but Sabrina did her job and kept him upright. In no time the group left the farms of Ferryport Landing and darted into the town proper.

Daphne slowed the carpet and lowered it so that they hovered only a few feet above the ground. They floated down Main Street, absorbing the shocking scene before them. Stores were gutted with fire, their contents coughed onto the street and smoldering into ash. Old King Cole's Restaurant was not much more than a shell, as was the Blue Plate Special diner. Cars lay on their backs like hunters' trophies. Bicycles were scattered about the street, bent beyond repair. The town's one and only traffic light had snapped off its wire. It lay shattered on the road.

"Get this thing to the coffee shop, now!" Uncle Jake blurted out.

The rug seemed to understand and didn't wait for Daphne's command. It zipped down the street toward the bank of the river where the little shop was located, but when they arrived all of Sabrina's worst fears were realized. Sacred Grounds was destroyed. The windows were black with soot. The roof had collapsed. All that remained was the sign that once hung over the door, and it had fallen to the ground. A red handprint covered the name.

Uncle Jake leaped off the rug before it came to a full stop. He rushed to the shop and threw the door open. A blast of still-smoldering fire exploded out and Uncle Jake fell backward. The girls rushed to his side and helped him to his feet. His face was red from the heat, and it was clear the fall had jarred his shoulder. He could barely stand.

"You can't go in there," Sabrina said.

"I have to," he cried.

"Looking for your sweetheart, Jacob?" a voice called out from behind them. The trio spun around to find Sheriff Nottingham glowering beneath a dead streetlight. The flames from the open door illuminated his face, exaggerating his already disgusting scar and causing the red handprint on his chest to cast an eerie glow.

"Where is she, Nottingham?" Jake said, his fists clenched.

"She's dead . . . or she soon will be," the sheriff said, his white teeth flashing in the flames.

Jake charged the sheriff. Before the villain could pull his weapon Jake swung widely, and his fist slammed into Nottingham's cheek. The sheriff collapsed to the ground. Bewildered, he grasped for his dagger, aiming it upward at the girls' uncle.

Jake didn't give Nottingham a chance to strike. His hands were in his coat pockets before Sabrina could clearly see what was happening. In a flash Nottingham was enclosed in a perfect green bubble. When Jake lifted his hand the bubble and its prisoner lifted as well. Nottingham kicked and fought like an angry marionette, but he was completely helpless.

"You've made a terrible mistake, Grimm," the sheriff shrieked.

"The mistake is yours, Nottingham. You think that I am good-natured like my mother, or tough but fair like my father, God rest his soul. But you and the rest of your thugs are wrong."

"Is that so? Then what are you, Jacob?" Nottingham sneered.

"A man who will kill to protect the people he loves."

Nottingham's face grew pale.

"Where is she?" Jake continued.

Nottingham shook his head.

Jake swung his arm around and the bubble followed. He whipped it into an abandoned building. Nottingham slammed into the wall and let out a pained groan. Uncle Jake swung the bubble at a building across the street, with similar results. Then he returned Nottingham to the center of the street. The sheriff's nose was covered in blood.

"The mayor and several others have surrounded her home," he groaned. "Her fairy godmothers are fighting them off, but they can't last forever."

A long ropelike stream appeared at the top of the bubble. It wrapped itself around a streetlight, where the sheriff hung like an evil Christmas ornament.

"I'm going to her, Nottingham," Uncle Jake said. "If she is harmed I'll be back for you. Think about what I've said. I'm not like the rest of my family."

Nottingham sneered and wiped his bloody nose on his sleeve.

Uncle Jake stepped onto the flying carpet. The girls joined him and Daphne commanded the rug into the air. A second later they were gone, but not out of trouble. Once they were in the air, Uncle Jake collapsed. Sweat poured down his forehead and he looked ashen.

"What's wrong?" Daphne asked, trying to steer the rug and attend to her uncle at the same time.

"It's nothing. Just remind me to punch people with my good arm," he said weakly, then passed out.

"What do we do now?" Daphne said.

"The sensible thing to do is to go back to the fort and get Uncle Jake back into his cot, but—"

"But?"

"But if Nottingham was telling the truth then Briar is in serious danger. She needs help. But we're just a couple of kids, Daphne. Can we stop an entire mob by ourselves?"

Daphne reached into various pockets in Uncle Jake's jacket and pulled out handfuls of rings, amulets, and wands. "We're a couple of kids with a whole lot of magic stuff."

"Do you know how to use any of those?" Sabrina asked.

Daphne shook her head. "How hard could it be?"

The little girl's eyes were filled with confidence, and perhaps some of her bravery rubbed off on Sabrina, or maybe she just realized her little sister could accomplish anything she put her mind to. While her father had been treating Daphne like a baby, her skills and talents had become clearer to Sabrina. Maybe it was time to trust her.

"It's your call, then."

Daphne looked stunned. "Really?"

Sabrina nodded. "I have more faith in you than anyone I know, Daphne."

Daphne smiled but it was brief. "I'm still mad at you."

"I know."

"Carpet, take us to Briar Rose's house, and step on it."

The carpet made a sudden turn and they were off. Daphne gave it instructions while Sabrina attended to her uncle. He looked pale and small in the night sky. His blond hair fluttered about his sallow face. Sneaking out to save Briar had not been a good idea, but the family, as a whole, wasn't known for its good ideas. They were all impulsive, Sabrina concluded. Odd that she would start to see how they were all connected at such a time. Why had she never noticed it before?

The carpet flew along an old country road, narrowly dodging a speeding pickup truck that was fleeing a vehicle filled with well-armed trolls hanging out of the windows. Sabrina was about to tell Daphne they needed to help the poor pickup driver but the trolls took a turn too fast and drove into a ravine.

They came up over a rise in the road, and Daphne brought the carpet to a slow crawl. Briar's house was a sturdy Victorian with a round column on each side of the door and a rose window in the center. It was painted sea green and stood out from all the other homes in the neighborhood. Sabrina had been there once with Jake and she had noticed the attention and care Briar had given the numerous rosebushes that surrounded her home. They were still quite a distance from the house but she could see those bushes had been trampled by the horde of Everafters surrounding the house. The mob was made up of goblins, witches, knights, and a near-giant—a man nearly twenty feet tall with an ax to match. He wore a flannel shirt and had a big, bushy red beard that matched the handprint on his enormous chest.

"Paul Bunyan joined the Scarlet Hand," Daphne said.

"I see him," Sabrina replied with a shiver. Giants, even small ones like Bunyan, gave her the willies.

"Look who's leading the pack," Daphne said, pointing to a woman in a gaudy dress decorated with hearts. Mayor Heart had her electronic megaphone in hand and was barking orders to the mob.

"Do you think Briar is still alive?" Daphne asked, peering at the trinkets she'd pulled out of her uncle's jacket.

"Absolutely! Look!"

A green bolt of electricity shot out of an open window on the second floor. It hit a goblin on the ground, and his fierce metal armor was transformed into a silk gown that reminded Sabrina of the kinds of dresses women wore in movies like *Gone With the Wind.* The goblin tripped over his giant hoop skirt and tumbled onto his back, unable to right himself.

Another blast came out of the window and nailed a troll, who found himself sporting a feathery headdress and high heels, like a Las Vegas showgirl. He cried indignantly and shook a mace at the house.

"At least we know her fairy godmothers are here," Daphne said. "Let's go give them some help."

Sabrina thought they should spend some time trying out the magical weapons first, but Daphne urged the carpet forward and soon they were barreling into the midst of the Scarlet Hand's army. Everyone turned their attention from their attack on Briar's home to the magic carpet. Swords slashed at them and wands launched deadly spells, each narrowly avoided as the nimble carpet banked and weaved through the crowd.

"Uh, you want to use one of those magic doohickeys?" Sabrina asked.

"I'm working on it," Daphne said as she slipped on a huge ring with a stone scorpion set inside an emerald. "Abracadabra!"

The ring popped and sparked like a fork inside a microwave but did little else. Daphne shrugged and replaced it with a second ring, this one with a small tooth embedded in amber. "Gimme some magic!"

This time there was nothing. Sabrina was starting to worry, especially when the carpet hovered too close to an angry knight in full armor whose sword nearly cut her in two. Without even thinking she kicked the knight in the helmet and slammed his visor down on his nose. He staggered, finally falling into a rosebush and crying out when the thorns held him fast. The carpet veered away from the mob to a quieter patch of air. Once there, Sabrina turned to her sister, who was working her way through the magic wands. "Any luck? That knight almost gave me a haircut."

"Hold your horses," Daphne said. The wand she held was made of little red jewels fused together like a long stick of rock candy. Daphne waved it in the air and it started to glow. "Now we're talking."

"What's it do?" Sabrina cried as Paul Bunyan's gigantic ax came crashing down only inches from the carpet.

Daphne shrugged. "Your guess is as good as mine. OK, wand, shrink everyone."

There was nothing.

Daphne frowned. "Set something on fire!"

Nothing.

"Freeze the bad guys!"

Zilch.

"Shoot everyone with electricity!"

Nada.

Daphne snarled and shook it as if perhaps its batteries were dead. "This thing is for the birds."

Suddenly, an eerie hum came from the wand and a flash of light blinded Sabrina.

"No way!" Daphne exclaimed, her eyes big with surprise.

"What?"

"OK, don't be mad. I didn't know it would do that," Daphne said.

"WHAT?"

"Take a look at your back," Daphne mumbled.

Sabrina craned her neck over her shoulder and choked out a scream. On her back was a set of huge white wings. The feathers bristled and fluttered in the wind and when she tensed up they flapped.

"Oh no! Change me back. I can't go through life with wings!"

"It's not the wings that's the problem," Daphne said. "It's the beak."

Sabrina crossed her eyes and saw that her nose and mouth had been replaced with a hard, golden beak with a hooked tip. She screamed, but what came out sounded an awful lot like a squawk. "Fix it!"

At that moment Mayor Heart's voice ripped through the air, courtesy of her electronic megaphone. "They're only children. Attack the house until backup gets here!"

"I wonder who the backup is," Daphne said, steering the rug out of the way of a flying spear.

"Who cares? I look like Big Bird," Sabrina complained. She could feel feathers sprouting along her arms and legs.

"OK! OK!" Daphne cried. She flicked the wand at Sabrina and said "change her back" but nothing happened. "OK, let's not panic."

"Not panic? Listen, I'm starting to get a craving for worms. I think it's definitely time to panic."

Daphne steered the carpet back toward the crowd, flying low and buzzing the tops of their heads. With one hand she removed her sneaker and did her best to wallop a few as they zipped by. "I realize this is inconvenient but you need to focus. We're here to rescue Briar Rose."

Sabrina scowled as her feet ripped through her shoes, revealing tough, spiky talons. She stood up and realized her entire lower body was now that of a fat, pear-shaped goose. She looked down at her hands only to find they were no longer there—they had vanished inside the feathers of her wings. It was official. She was a bird.

"Excuse me if I'm a little distracted—*honk!*" Sabrina was horrified by the sound she had just made and hoped it had been her imagination. Daphne looked just as startled.

"Did I—"

"Yeah . . . you honked," Daphne said as she smacked a few more trolls with her shoe. "Try to think of the bright side. At least Puck isn't here to see this. He'd never let you forget it."

Uncle Jake began to groan. He opened his eyes slowly and peered around. Sabrina saw his face twisted in confusion. She tried to ask him how he felt but in her excitement she let out a series of honks. Startled, Jake shoved Sabrina off the rug in midair with a "Shooo!"

"NO!" Sabrina cried as she plummeted toward the ground. In desperation she flapped her wings as hard as she could. The action seemed to slow her, and she found she could control her direction. Without thinking she sailed face first through an open window and crashed to the floor, tumbling and sliding to a stop.

When she was on her feet she turned to call for Briar only to find the two fairy godmothers standing over her, wands drawn. Buzzflower and Mallobarb were stout women with serious faces. Their threatening eyes told her everything she needed to know. Sabrina had better not move a muscle—or a feather, in this case.

"Take your filthy, traitorous bottom out of here, goose, and tell the rest of the Scarlet Hand they're going to have to send more than a bird if they want take us down," Buzzflower said, her voice fierce.

"I'm not a goose!" Sabrina cried.

"Well, you aren't a Bengal tiger," said Mallobarb.

"I'm Sabrina Grimm!" she honked. "I'm here to rescue you."

The fairy godmothers looked at one another in disbelief, then back at Sabrina.

"Really?"

"Listen, my uncle is here and my sister, too."

"Jake is here?" Buzzflower said.

"He is?" a voice said from down the hall. A moment later Briar Rose raced into the room. Even distressed, Briar was a vision. She had green eyes and skin like cocoa. She was enchanting . . . except for the baseball bat she held threateningly. "Where is he?"

Sabrina pointed out the window with her wing just as the flying carpet zipped past.

"So, what's the plan?" Buzzflower said.

"Yeah . . . a plan. We hadn't really gotten that far," Sabrina said.

"Great," Mallobarb said sarcastically. "What we need is a distraction. If we can get those lunatics outside to focus on something other than the house, we can fly Briar out of here ourselves."

"Sounds good to me," Sabrina said. "What do you have in mind?"

"I think a giant goose might confuse them for a bit," Buzzflower said.

"You want me to fly out the window and let them shoot at me?"

The fairy godmothers nodded.

"I could be killed!"

The fairy godmothers nodded again.

"No," Briar said. "She's right. This is too dangerous. Those people out there intend to kill someone. If something were to happen to Sabrina I could never live with myself."

Sabrina peered out the window. Her sister was still buzzing the crowd but seemed to have had no more success with Jake's magical possessions than before.

"OK, I'll do it, but I haven't mastered flying yet since I've only been a bird for five minutes. If I manage to stay in the air you have to act fast. Get out as soon as you can."

Briar looked nervous but agreed. "But where are we going to go even if we do escape? The town is overrun by the Scarlet Hand."

"Prince Charming and Mr. Canis have built a camp. We'll

take you there," Sabrina said, returning her attention to the window.

"Good luck," Buzzflower said.

"Here goes nothing!" Sabrina said as she leaped out the window and flapped her wings as hard as she could. She would have described the experience as awkward and unnatural but she had no time to contemplate her situation. Her appearance drew the full ferocity of the crowd and before she could react, dozens of arrows, magical blasts, and even an electronic megaphone were flying right at her. She dodged the best she could, feeling a spear clip her tail feathers. It startled her and she landed awkwardly on the head of a hobgoblin. Enraged, the creature tried to clobber her with his lumpy club but she leaped off and landed on the head of another hobgoblin. The first brute brought his club down on his colleague's head just after Sabrina leaped onto another. Not wanting to wait for another assault, she leaped off the startled head of the third hobgoblin onto a fourth, then a fifth, then she landed in the beehive hairdo of the Queen of Hearts, who screamed and slapped at Sabrina. Instinctively, Sabrina pecked at the mayor's hands and leaped into the air. She flapped wildly, and much to her surprise, rose into the air and away from the mob.

When she turned her head to look over her shoulder, she

spotted Buzzflower and Mallobarb lifting Briar Rose out of the window and into the air, a stream of magical dust floating behind them. The trio floated off to the shelter of the woods that bordered Briar's property.

Sabrina found Daphne and Uncle Jake, who had slipped back into unconsciousness. She angled her wings so that she could fly alongside them and together they rose high enough to be out of danger.

"Briar and her fairy godmothers are out of the house," Sabrina said. "Have you figured out that wand yet?"

"I think," Daphne said.

Just then, the Mayor's wretched voice filled the air. "Don't follow the traitors. We'll let the pack handle them."

"The pack? What's the pack?" Daphne asked.

Before anyone could hazard a guess, the temperature of the air rose dramatically. It was accompanied by a sticky, humid cloud that invaded all of Sabrina's pores. There was a sound like a hurricane crashing through a strip mall and then something as big as a jumbo jet flew overhead. It flew by at such an incredible speed all Sabrina could see were red wings and a long tail and then it was gone.

"Uh, what was that?" Daphne asked.

Sabrina wasn't sure, but she knew anything that big and that fast couldn't be good. Worse still, it was not alone. A second creature appeared in the sky. This one was green and covered in black spikes. It had bulbous yellow eyes that scanned the sky.

"There's another one!" Daphne cried, pointing to a third creature that had appeared in the west. This one was purple and slightly bigger, with birdlike talons and a white snout. Fire blasted out of its nostrils and lit up the sky.

"Are those dragons?" Sabrina gasped, flying out of the way of the green one's leathery wings. Her answer came in the form of a crackling voice broadcast from a megaphone far below her.

"Dragons, your target and her cohorts have fled into the woods," the mayor bellowed. "Retrieve them anyway you can. Bringing them back alive is not necessary."

The creatures turned their massive bodies in the direction of the woods and flew over it with amazing speed. They blasted several areas with fire as if to clear the trees for a better glimpse of their prey.

"We need to find Briar and the fairy godmothers before they do," Daphne said as the flying carpet dipped into the trees below. Sabrina tilted her wings and followed, surprised by how easily flight was coming to her. If she hadn't been on the edge of terror she might have actually enjoyed the sensation.

Flying beneath the canopy of trees made navigating much harder. Several branches scraped her soft belly and a few lashed across her face. Daphne seemed to be having the same problem, and the trees got denser as they flew farther into the forest. Soon Sabrina spotted Briar and her fairy godmothers, hurrying along through the bramble. The girls flew alongside of them and stopped.

"They've sent dragons after you," Sabrina said. "We need to get you out of here, now."

"Dragons!" Briar cried. "Where did they get dragons?"

"We can worry about that later," Daphne said as she lowered the rug. "Briar should climb on board with me. Buzzflower and Mallobarb will have a better chance of escaping by air."

"She's right," Buzzflower said as she took out her wand. "And they might find we're a little harder to kill, too."

Briar climbed on the rug and knelt down next to Uncle Jake. "He looks so weak."

"This camp you spoke of," Mallobarb said. "Where is it?"

"At the farthest edge of the barrier," Sabrina explained. "If we get separated and show up first I'll let Charming know you're on your way. But we don't have a lot of time to talk."

She had no idea how right she was. At that moment the purple dragon's head dipped down from above. It studied the group. A blast of hot breath scorched everyone.

"What do we do?" Sabrina whispered, wiping the sweat from her face with one wing.

"Just get out of here!" Daphne shouted and at once, everyone scattered. They hadn't moved a second too soon. The dragon opened its mouth and roasted the area with flames.

Sabrina sailed into the air, flying higher and higher. Getting above the scene seemed to make sense to her. It would allow her to survey the area and keep an eye on the monsters. When she felt she was high enough, she tilted her body a little and moved in a wide circle. She could see the entire forest. Daphne, Jake, and Briar Rose were racing in the direction of the town and the two fairy godmothers were firing magical attacks at the dragons. She had to give her sister credit: Daphne was leading them for the first time and everyone was still alive. She couldn't have done better herself.

Unfortunately, her feeling of security was short-lived. She looked down to see the red dragon rising from the ground like a missile, its deadly mouth open wide and closing in on her. She flapped furiously to the left, narrowly missing the jaws that clamped down just inches away from her. The creature's gnashing teeth sounded like a twenty-car pileup.

She flew as hard and as fast as she could but the dragon was in pursuit and gaining. If only Daphne had changed her into a faster bird! She flew to the left, then to the right, with the monster's broiling breath scorching her little goose feet. No matter where she went, it followed. Even when she sank into the trees the dragon blasted through them, pulverizing huge oaks and giant maples like a child running through grass. She knew she couldn't keep her pace for long; she was already tired and the tree limbs kept clipping her wings, making it impossible to coast on the breeze. Then one of the branches caught her across the chest, and she tumbled to the ground. The fall knocked the wind out of her. With her breath gone the best she could do was stagger to her feet and hop along the forest floor.

The red dragon landed in her path, and its head dipped down to look at her. Its milky-yellow eyes had two sets of lids, like a crocodile's, and when they focused on her she could hear the creature let out a satisfied chuckle. It reared its head back, inhaling oxygen into its mouth and nose, apparently fueling the furnace inside it. Sabrina knew there was nothing she could do to escape and she braced herself for death.

"Run, child," a voice said from above. Sabrina looked up to see Buzzflower floating above the dragon's head. She waved a wand at the creature and a bolt of blue energy exploded into the dragon's chest. The dragon screeched and fell backward.

Buzzflower turned to Sabrina. "RUN!"

Sabrina fled into the woods as fast as her legs would allow. She heard a horrible roar and turned to see flames rising up into the trees. She hoped that Buzzflower had not been the target of the fire and feared the worst when she felt the beast stomping behind her. She heard more fiery blasts and angry roars. And then it was in front of her, using its tail to knock down huge swaths of forest. It turned toward her, eyes focusing, and this time there was no chuckle. This time it was impatient.

Sabrina looked right at the creature. "Fine! You want to kill me. I'm right here. But if you were looking for a trophy for killing a Grimm you won't get it. I'm weakened by this stupid spell. If I was my normal self you would never catch me."

"You speak gibberish, child," the dragon said, his voice like a thousand volcanoes exploding at once.

Child? How did he know she was a child? She looked down, wondering if he could see her true self through her magical transformation, and realized her feathers were gone. Her wings had vanished. Even the hard yellow beak was nowhere to be found. The magic had worn off and she was herself again.

"OK . . . good," she grumbled. "Just in time to be roasted like a marshmallow."

"Not tonight, big sister," a voice said and suddenly she was hoisted upward and onto the flying carpet. Before Sabrina could hug Daphne they darted away, with the monster roaring in frustration.

"Hey, you changed back," Daphne said. "See, I told you it was temporary!"

"You did not," Sabrina said, trying to get her bearings.

"Well, I meant to," Daphne said. She turned to Briar Rose, who held Uncle Jake's head in her lap. "Briar, we need all the magic we can get. Can you dig in his pockets and see if there's anything we can use to fight these dragons?"

"Preferably something with instructions," Sabrina added.

Briar pulled out small bottles of strange liquids, weird rings, and even a smelly fur hat. She laid them all on the rug for Daphne and Sabrina to examine. "Anything?"

Daphne shook her head. "I don't recognize any of that stuff."

"Wait, there's something else here," the princess said as she pulled a small felt box from her boyfriend's jacket. She flipped it open and her face lit up like a candle.

"What is it?" Daphne asked.

"Please tell me it's the world's tiniest rocket launcher," Sabrina said.

Briar reached inside and took out a bright diamond ring. It was emerald-cut and mounted on a platinum band.

"Is that—?" Daphne gasped as she watched Briar Rose slip it on her ring finger. Though she was laughing and smiling widely, Briar's cheeks were wet with tears.

"YES!" she cried. "Yes, I will marry you, Jacob Grimm."

"You might want to wait until he's awake," Sabrina said.

"You may be right." Briar giggled, took off the ring, and put it back in its box.

Then she slipped it back into Uncle Jake's pocket.

Mallobarb joined them, flying alongside with a trail of glitter falling behind. "My wand has almost no effect on them," she said. "It's only making them angry."

"Making who angry?" Uncle Jake said blearily as he tried to sit up.

"The dragons," Daphne said. "Three of them are chasing us."

"Look what happens when you take a nap," Briar teased.

"Briar, you've been crying," Uncle Jake said, taking her hand.

"Here comes one now!" Mallobarb shouted.

Jake had Briar and Sabrina help him to his feet. He reached into his jacket and removed a small black coin. He rubbed his hand over it for a moment and it began to spin. The spinning increased until a ferocious wind surrounded them. Luckily, the spell didn't seem to affect them or Sabrina knew she would be swept right off the flying carpet. Uncle Jake clenched the coin tight and when the first of the dragons, the green one, got close enough he tossed it into its open mouth. Bolts of lightning poked out from inside its jaws, then erupted out of its fat belly. The dragon fell out of the sky, but before it hit the ground an enormous hole opened in its torso and the creature exploded.

"Gross," Daphne said. "Next time warn a person you're going to blow a dragon up in front of her. I'm going to have bad dreams until I'm a hundred years old."

"Sorry," Uncle Jake said. "Now for the other two."

"Shouldn't we just try to outrun them?" Sabrina asked.

"You can't outrun a dragon, 'Brina," her uncle said. "I've tried."

The purple dragon circled above them then dove like a kamikaze pilot. The carpet easily dodged its attack but the monster was not discouraged. It swooped back to try an attack from below. Once again, Daphne proved her skill at steering the carpet.

"Land this thing," Uncle Jake said.

"Is that a good idea?" Briar Rose said.

"No, but we won't last long in the air," he replied. "Daphne, take us down."

Daphne did as she was told, landing in a clearing surrounded by heavy trees. Once they were on the ground, Uncle Jake shooed everyone from the rug and told Mallobarb to take them all to shelter.

"Use whatever protection spell you have in your wand," he said.

Mallobarb looked surprised by Uncle Jake's commanding tone. A frown came to her face but Briar tugged on her arm. "Don't argue. Just this once—don't argue."

Mallobarb forced a phony smile onto her face and did as she was told.

Just as the group reached the safety of the trees, the purple dragon slammed into the ground right in front of Uncle Jake. He didn't even flinch. In fact, he smiled.

"You are either brave or stupid," the dragon croaked.

"Maybe a little bit of both," Uncle Jake replied.

"You know I'm about to roast your bones and you don't run?"

"No need," he said as he began digging into his pockets. "I've got the Amulet of Roona. It will turn your bad breath into a cool summer breeze."

"You lie," the dragon said.

"No. It's right here. I mean, it's in one of these pockets," he said, fumbling nervously.

Sabrina noticed the handful of rings and necklaces in Daphne's hand. "Could one of those be the Amulet of Roona?"

Daphne cringed. "Uh, Uncle Jake, what does the Amulet of Roona look like?"

"It's a black necklace with a silver crescent moon. The moon has a carving in it that looks like a puff of wind."

Daphne sorted through the items she had taken from Jake's pockets. She held up a necklace that looked exactly like the one her uncle had just described. "Uh-oh."

"Uncle Jake? You might want to go with plan B. We have the Amulet of Roona," Sabrina cried.

"Fudge," Uncle Jake said as he shoved his hand into another pocket. It was the only word he could get out before the dragon blasted him with flame. Sabrina shrieked as she watched the fire engulf her uncle.

"NO!" Briar Rose cried. She raced to his side but there was nothing she could do. Jake's body looked like a piece of charcoal—his features reduced to that of a volcanic rock.

Tears squirted out of Sabrina's eyes and sobs filled her ears. Her sister was trembling and in hysterics. Briar collapsed. Mallobarb attended to her but she was just as shaken, her face cracked and confused.

And then the fire was gone. The forest was full of smoke and cinders burned Sabrina's eyes.

"We should go," Mallobarb said.

"GO?" Briar Rose cried. "I can't go."

"Princess, he is gone. If we stay we will all join him," Mallobarb said.

Sabrina shook her head. If they wanted her to leave then they would have to carry her away. She turned back to the spot where her uncle had stood. She was prepared to fight the dragon with her bare hands, but Briar was already there, kicking and punching at its huge feet. The dragon looked down and laughed, then swatted her away like she were an insect. She slammed into a tree. There was a sickly cracking sound and then she collapsed to the ground like a rag doll.

"Briar!" Mallobarb cried and rushed to her side.

Sabrina tore her attention away from Briar and back to the dragon. He could easily do the same to her and her sister. As the smoke dissipated around her uncle she saw something that should have been impossible. The black shell that covered Jake cracked and broke. Pieces fell off and crumbled to dust on the ground. Inside the shell was Uncle Jake, unhurt and whole. In his hand was a dark-green crystal, glowing like a small star.

"My turn," Uncle Jake said. He reached into one of his pockets with his free hand and pulled out a long broadsword. In one quick motion he shoved it under the dragon's chin, easily slicing through the creature's steel-strong skin. The dragon let out a muffled cry and then, with a ground-shaking thud, fell over dead.

"Luckily, I also have an invulnerability stone," Jake said.

High above, the red dragon roared in rage.

"You want some?" He laughed as the dragon flew off, either to protect itself or warn its masters. "That's what I thought, punk!"

Buzzflower flew into the clearing. She looked frazzled. When she saw Mallobarb hovering over Briar she cried out and flew to them.

"No!" she shouted. She waved her magic wand over the fallen princess and a stream of colors and lights flooded into her. But Mallobarb held her hand and forced her to stop.

"What happened?" Uncle Jake said, rushing to the group.

"She's gone, Jacob," Mallobarb said.

Uncle Jake fell to Briar's side and cradled her broken body in his arms. He buried his face in her hair and wept. "No, no, no."

Sabrina and Daphne stood on the edge of the clearing. For the first time in days they hugged each other like sisters. They shook their heads in disbelief and their tears fell on the charred ground.

6

abrina, Daphne, their parents, and Granny Relda
stood in the huge crowd gathered around a vacant
space of the camp, now set aside as a cemetery. Mr.
Canis stood shoulder to shoulder with Robin Hood and Prince
Charming. The three men looked somber as they stared down
at the casket that Geppetto had hurried to construct. Pinocchio
had helped, and together they had carried it to the plot where
Briar Rose's body was placed. Red Riding Hood placed a
bouquet of wildflowers she had gathered along the camp's walls
in Briar's hands. She looked beautiful, as if she were once again
the sleeping princess from the storybooks.

Uncle Jake stood by the casket with Mallobarb and Buzzflower.
The godmothers sobbed, and though his face was cracked with
misery, Jake did his best to appear strong. His love affair with

Briar was well known in the town and the entire crowd seemed to be bearing his heartbreak for him.

Daphne was inconsolable. She wept and clung to her mother. Elvis sat next to her, licking the tears from her face. Sabrina found herself sobbing as well.

"Today is a dark day for us," Prince Charming said as he stepped before the casket. "We have lost one of our own and one of our most precious. Like many of us, Briar Rose came to America aboard the *New Beginning*, searching for a new life. She left a family and kingdom behind, but she brought with her two fairy godmothers, Mallobarb and Buzzflower, who have been by her side since she was a baby, nearly seven hundred years ago. Mallobarb and Buzzflower kept Briar safe from wicked witches and a few foolish suitors and an even more foolish husband."

The crowd chuckled. Sabrina knew that Charming had once been married to Briar, but he had never spoken of their relationship. She had also never heard the prince be self-deprecating before.

"Sadly, they could not have stopped a freak accident. She was killed by a dragon—"

A gasp rose in the crowd. Robin Hood shouted for everyone to remain calm.

"Where did this dragon come from?" a stooped old witch asked.

"It was sent by the Master and the Scarlet Hand," Charming said.

"They have a dragon!" Little Boy Blue cried.

"They have more than one," Charming said. "Jacob Grimm managed to kill two of them and claims to have seen a third. We have no idea how many more there might be."

"Where did they come from? I thought the Grimms had all the dragon eggs," Morgan le Fay said.

"We have what we were given to look after," Granny said. "I have no doubt there are others."

Charming raised his hand for the crowd's attention. "We can discuss that matter later, but first I would like to let some of the people who knew Briar Rose speak," Charming said. "Starting with myself. I stumbled upon Briar Rose's castle wrapped in a thorn hedge centuries ago. My youthful zeal for exploration and treasure urged me to cut through it. Little did I know the treasure I would find. She was one of the most beautiful women I had ever seen in my life. But her true beauty was hidden inside her like she was hidden in her castle. She was, above all, kind and patient. She was thoughtful and encouraging. She was smart, and funny, and wise, and I knew that I did not deserve her. I was not the husband I should have been to her and she knew it as well, but she never held a grudge. She was mature about the end of our marriage and moved on to a new life. I was not a good man when I met her, but I am all the better for knowing her. I count myself as one of the luckiest people in the world for having shared a love with her. Now, I'd like to ask Mallobarb and Buzzflower to speak."

The fairy godmothers stepped forward and lifted their sad faces to the crowd. "Briar was a brave woman. She was also strong, stubborn, and opinionated . . . but brave," Mallobarb said, holding back tears.

"She faced a dragon with no hope of victory . . . but that's the way she was," Buzzflower said. "I will miss her humor, her strong sense of right and wrong, and her companionship. Though my sister and I were assigned to raise her, I feel I learned more from her than she ever learned from me. Good-bye, my sweet rose."

Buzzflower blew a kiss to the casket and the two rejoined Jake at the front of the crowd.

Jake stepped forward. He turned to the Everafters as if preparing to speak about the woman he loved, but instead, he reached into his pocket and took out the felt box that held her engagement ring. He took it out and slipped it on Briar Rose's finger. Then he leaned over and kissed her on the lips. A tear streamed down his face and landed on her forehead, then Jake rejoined the group.

Charming stepped forward and looked over the crowd. "So death has come to our door. I've told you all that this day would come, and now that it is here I get no satisfaction from being right. Today, we all lost a friend and a member of our unique community. She was our first casualty and I know what you are thinking. *Casualty* is a word people use for death in the midst of war, and I say we are at war. Just because some of you have chosen not to fight does not mean you are not in the battle. They will find this camp and they will slaughter us all. If we stand idle we might as well start digging our own graves."

Mr. Seven appeared with a shovel on his shoulder. He handed it to Charming. "Who wants to dig their own grave?"

The crowd eyed the shovel like it was a scorpion preparing to strike.

"These are your choices. Join Sleeping Beauty or fight."

Sabrina scanned the crowd. There she saw so many familiar faces—Snow White, Friar Tuck, Puss in Boots, Morgan le Fay, Old King Cole, Frau Pfefferkuchenhaus, Rip Van Winkle, Sawhorse, the Scarecrow, the Pied Piper and his son Wendell, Lancelot, Cinderella and her husband, Tom, and Jack Pumpkinhead. There were Munchkins and Lilliputians, Yahoos and shoe elves. There were brutish creatures like the blacksmith troll and a Cyclops, but also delicate beauties like Little Bo Peep and her flock of sheep. There were also many Everafters Sabrina had never met and couldn't identify.

"Why should we trust you, Charming?" Ichabod Crane said from the middle of the crowd. "You have a history of manipulating this town for your own selfish concerns."

Charming was taken aback. "Because—"

"And weren't you a member of the Scarlet Hand yourself? How do we know this is not some trap you and your toadies are laying?" a duckling quacked.

"Let me explain," Charming said as the crowd erupted into shouts and arguments, but the noise stopped when Mr. Canis stepped forward.

"He is not lying to you, but since you need to hear it from someone else, here it is. The war is coming. If we fight many will die, but there's a chance we could beat them back. If not, we will all die anyway. None of you are safe. We can train you. We can prepare this camp. But we have to do it together. You decide. Join this battle or pick up the shovel and dig."

The crowd looked bewildered, and then Uncle Jake stepped forward. "I will fight."

Sabrina's father gasped. "Jake, no!"

"Thank you, Jacob," Charming said, then turned back to the crowd. "Is there no one else? A human has stepped forward to fight for you! A human!"

Mallobarb and Buzzflower joined him. "We will fight."

"Anyone else?" Charming said, raising the shovel over his head.

Poppa, Momma, and Baby Bear were next. They roared. Puss in Boots joined the rest. "I will fight."

The tabby was followed by Beauty and her beastly daughter, Bella, then former deputies Mr. Boarman and Mr. Swineheart. Soon Morgan le Fay had joined the group as well as the bridge troll and Rip Van Winkle. The Munchkins followed, then the Winkies, then the Gillikins. The Lilliputians were the next to join, followed by the Mouse King and a sea of his royal subjects, then several Houyhnhnms, then a huge contingent of knights, princes, princesses, and witches.

Soon, the last one left in the crowd was Ichabod Crane, who frowned and eventually stepped forward himself. "Fine, but if I see one of those Scarlet Hand thugs is missing a head, I'm deserting."

"Very well," Charming said. "We will train and we will fight. Let the Hand come because we will beat them back with our bare hands if necessary."

The crowd roared approval and shook their fists in the air.

Charming turned to his team. Mr. Seven, Robin Hood, Snow White, and Mr. Canis nodded at him and he nodded back. Then he took off his purple suit jacket and tossed it aside. He scooped up the shovel off the ground and began to dig, but Uncle Jake stopped him and took the shovel from the prince. Charming nodded respectfully and stepped aside.

Sabrina and Daphne watched Uncle Jake dig. When the hole was big enough he pounded the casket lid closed. He and Charming lowered it into the hole as rain clouds circled and eventually soaked the camp. Uncle Jake filled the hole while Charming looked on. When it was finished, Mallobarb and Buzzflower planted a single seed on top of the plot and a moment later, fed by the rainwater, a rosebush sprouted and grew.

• • •

There was little time to mourn. The next morning Camp Charming became Fort Charming, and Sabrina was surrounded by a flurry of fight training, forging, and the construction of several lookout towers. Mr. Boarman and Mr. Swineheart directed the building, and with the help of some witches and wizards the fort grew in size dramatically. Teams of volunteers fortified the lookout towers with cannons, while others built a catapult big enough to hurl a pickup truck over the walls.

Everyone else was drafted into Snow White's army and trained in hand-to-hand combat. Under her command Everafters of all shapes and sizes ran drills, rappelled down the tall fort walls, and of course, Snow's favorite, dropped at a moment's notice for muscle-straining pushups. It was very strange to see the ancient Frau Pfefferkuchenhaus crawling beneath barbed wire on her belly.

It quickly became clear that the Grimms were in the way. The girls were left to their own devices, and as they searched for some way to be useful they came across Pinocchio sitting under an oak tree. He was resting on a stack of logs, one of which he had used to carve a dozen small marionette legs with a sharp knife. His work was detailed and marvelous, and his mastery of the blade was incredible. The legs were proportioned and elegant. There were several other arms, a few torsos, and a number of heads resting at his feet.

"You're making puppets," Daphne said, picking up one of the heads and examining it.

"They are called marionettes," Pinocchio said.

"What's a marionette?" Daphne asked.

"It's a wooden figure with limbs attached to strings, and the strings are manipulated by someone," Sabrina explained.

"And that's not a puppet?" Daphne asked.

Pinocchio seemed to bristle at the little girl's confusion. "No, a puppet has someone's hand up its bum. Marionettes can walk, dance, and perform in any way its master desires."

"And now you're making them, just like your father," Sabrina said, continuing to admire his work.

Pinocchio nodded. "It's a skill I've been working on for some time. The secret is to use the right wood. If it's too hard it's impossible to carve but if it's too soft then the whole piece can fall apart in your hands. It took me forever to find the right wood, but now that I have some I carry it with me."

"Must get heavy," Sabrina said, noticing the huge bag the boy had brought with him to the camp.

"A tad," the boy said as if slightly annoyed. "My condolences for your loss."

Sabrina thanked him and struggled not to cry. Her eyes and cheeks still hurt from the funeral. "She was the best."

"I did not know her other than what I had heard from others," Pinocchio said. "She seems to have been quite an exceptional woman and an asset to the Everafter community."

Sabrina nodded, though she was unnerved by Pinocchio's manner of speaking. He was such a little boy, yet he spoke as if he were a college professor.

Before she could respond, Goldilocks appeared. "Girls, your

grandmother would like to see you in Charming's cabin. She's having some kind of meeting."

The girls said good-bye to Pinocchio and crossed the fort to Charming's cabin. When they entered they found their father and grandmother in the midst of a heated argument.

"If he does it again I'll knock him out," Henry said. "None of you have a right to sneak my children out in the middle of the night to fight dragons."

"Good heavens," Granny Relda said. "Your brother didn't sneak them out to fight dragons. I'm sure he had no idea they would run into trouble."

Henry looked as if he might scream. "We're lucky any of them came back alive."

"Henry!" Veronica cried. "Lower your voice. He might hear you."

"I'm sorry but this is not cool. If he needed to go after Briar he shouldn't turn to two children for help."

Granny stepped forward. "Henry, I'm not happy about it either, but the girls are very capable. They've encountered dragons before. Why, Sabrina killed a giant once."

"She nearly kills me every time she looks at me." Puck snickered as he strolled into the cabin. He looked as if he had been playing in a toxic waste dump; he was dirtier than Sabrina had ever seen him and was grinning from ear to ear. "What's going on here?"

Henry ignored him. "These are my children, Mom."

"Hello?" Veronica interrupted.

Henry scowled. "They are not sidekicks. Not personal flying carpet chauffeurs. They are not junior detectives or monster-fighters in training. They are little girls."

"Little girls?" the girls said at once.

Henry ignored them, too. "If anyone tries to involve them in another stupid scheme, any of you, I will personally wring your neck," Henry shouted.

Just then, Uncle Jake entered the cabin. He looked at the group but said nothing as he sat in a chair by the window. He was followed by Mr. Canis, who, much to the shock of Sabrina and Daphne, was accompanied by Little Red Riding Hood.

Granny stepped into the center of the room. "I'm glad you are all here. We need to have a family meeting."

"Since when do we have family meetings?" Sabrina said.

"Since now," Granny said.

Red turned to leave.

"Where are you going, *liebling*?" Granny asked.

"I'm not a member of your family," Red said.

"Yes, you are," Granny replied.

Red smiled and rejoined the group. "What does *liebling* mean?" she asked Sabrina.

"It's German for *sweetheart*," she said.

Red's smile was so big it looked as if her face might not contain it.

"Mr. Canis?" Granny said, gesturing to the old man.

"Thank you, Relda. We have been through a terrible tragedy, but there are other pressing matters that must be considered. First, as you all know, Red and I share some memory loss. Fueled by recent events, Red has found the courage to work with me in restoring some of those memories. I believe, with the proper meditation techniques, she may be able to lead us to the Master."

Sabrina studied the little girl. She looked like a nervous wreck, but Sabrina was proud of her. She wasn't sure she would have had the courage to trust a man that terrified her in order to help the rest of her community.

"That sounds like good news," Granny said.

"Red will let you know if she uncovers anything useful. Unfortunately, there is bad news as well. Mr. Boarman and Mr. Swineheart have uncovered some acts of sabotage around the camp."

"Sabotage!" Granny said.

"What does *sabotage* mean?" Daphne asked.

"It's when someone intentionally tries to ruin a plan or destroy something that's important."

"Are you sure, Canis?" Uncle Jake said.

Canis nodded. "The pigs have found several important parts of the main gate stolen. The roof of the medical tent was tampered with and there was some sort of effort to destroy the camp's well. Boarman and Swineheart assure me that these are not mere accidents or acts of poor workmanship. Someone in our community is intentionally trying to make things difficult."

"Any suspects?" Veronica asked.

Everyone turned their eyes to Puck, who was making disgusting faces in the mirror leaning against the wall. He looked at them and grinned. "You guys just made my day, but it isn't me."

"Do you think it might be someone from this Scarlet Hand group?" Henry asked.

Canis nodded. "I suspect we have a spy in our midst. They must have entered with the refugees. Unfortunately, we don't have any clues to their identity. Charming, the pigs, and I are the only ones who know about the sabotage and we ask that you keep it to yourselves. Knowledge of a spy in the community could hurt the morale of everyone and start a panic." Canis paused and looked to Granny. "Lastly, I come to you with a request."

"What kind of request?" Henry said suspiciously.

Granny interrupted. "I'll take it from here, old friend. Henry, Jacob, Veronica, Sabrina, Daphne, Puck, Mr. Canis, and Red—you are my family. Whether you are of my blood or invited to my family, you are a Grimm."

Elvis whined.

"And of course, you as well, Elvis," Granny said, scratching the big dog behind the ears. "And being Grimms, we have certain responsibilities. Our role in this community has been to document what we see, investigate any unusual crimes, and act as peacekeepers when possible."

"What's this got to do with anything?" Uncle Jake said.

"As you know, the Everafters are building an army. They plan on confronting the Master and the Scarlet Hand, despite my pleas for them to reconsider. It appears that peace is not a possibility."

Mr. Canis nodded in agreement.

"So, Mr. Canis and Prince Charming have asked us to join their efforts."

Sabrina looked over at her father. She could already tell he was angry, but he stayed silent.

"Join their efforts?" Veronica asked. "They want us to join their army?"

"No," Mr. Canis said. "As much as we need recruits, you're human, and far too fragile."

"Then how can we help?" Daphne asked.

"By opening up some of the rooms in the Hall of Wonders to Charming's army," Granny explained.

Henry nearly exploded. "You want to open up the Hall of Wonders to Prince Charming—our family's bitterest enemy?"

"The prince is not the man you remember," Mr. Canis said.

"Am I really hearing you say this? You and Charming—best buddies!" Henry scoffed.

"I would not count him as a friend, but he has earned my respect and my trust. He is not being deceitful when he says the Scarlet Hand is on the march. They won't be stopped until this town is ash and I won't sit idly by. I may not have the senses of the Wolf any longer, but I still smell war in the air. We come to your family because we are outnumbered. The Hand counts amongst its number the most ferocious of us, the most powerful, and the most bloodthirsty. If you won't help us we have little chance of defending Ferryport Landing, let alone saving our lives."

"They only require a few items from select rooms," Granny said.

"Give it to them," Uncle Jake said.

"Now, Jacob, don't you want to know what they want?" Granny asked.

"No. Give it to them," he said. "Whatever they want."

"We've taken the liberty of making a list," Mr. Canis said in the awkward silence. The old man pulled out a sheet of paper. Sabrina's father snatched it.

"Thirty trained unicorns!"

"We have unicorns?" Daphne asked, amazed. "No one told me we had unicorns. You do know that I'm seven years old, right? Unicorns are everything to me."

Henry ignored her. "Two dozen Pegasus horses, the shoes of swiftness, Excalibur, the Wicked Witch's flying broom, and Aladdin's flying carpet."

"Plus as many fairy godmother wands as you can spare," Mr. Canis said. "As well as the horn of the North Wind."

"Absolutely not!" Henry said. "The only reason this town doesn't destroy itself is because this stuff is not in the hands of Everafters. Who's to say that once we turn this over to Charming he won't use it to kill us all?"

"I'm to say," Mr. Canis said, tapping his cane on the floor angrily. "Do you believe I would allow harm to come to your family?"

Henry shook his head feebly.

"This request is an enormous departure from our family's traditional role," Granny Relda said. "So I present it to you for a vote. I believe Jacob has cast his vote, so I turn to Daphne."

Daphne held her hand out to her grandmother. Granny seemed to understand what she wanted and reached into her handbag. She removed a small velvet bag with the words "The North Wind" embroidered on it and handed it to the little girl. Daphne opened it and took out a small silver kazoo. Though it looked like a toy, Sabrina knew its destructive nature. The Big Bad Wolf had used it to huff and puff his way into mayhem. Sabrina herself had accidentally destroyed a bank with one simple note. She wished that the army hadn't asked for it—it was the most powerful magical item she had ever come across and if it fell into the wrong hands it could be a catastrophe. Daphne, however, readily handed it to Canis, who tucked it into his suit jacket and thanked the little girl. "You have my vote," she said.

Granny turned to Red. "And you?"

Red seemed overwhelmed. A happy tear appeared in the corner of her eye and then streaked down her face. She nodded, another vote for the cause.

"Puck?"

The fairy boy flashed Sabrina a nasty look, then shrugged. "Whatever. Why should I care? Do what you want."

Granny frowned at his bad attitude but moved along. "Which brings us to Veronica."

Veronica looked at Henry then back at the rest of the group. "I say empty the whole hall out. The Master kidnapped Henry and me. He's responsible for my daughters living in an orphanage. He stole two years of my life. Open every door, Relda."

Henry scowled. When the old woman turned to him he was furious. "You know my vote. Dad would say we were crazy for even talking about this. Releasing magic into this town is why he's dead."

Uncle Jake stared out the window.

"But it doesn't matter what my vote is," Henry said. "The majority has already spoken."

"Hank, your concerns are noted," Canis said. "But your involvement in our training would help to ensure your fears never come true. You have considerable talents. You were, after all, trained by Basil Grimm. You could—"

"This is not my war, Canis," Henry snapped.

Granny nodded. "Sabrina?"

Sabrina wanted to say no. She had seen the kind of havoc magic could produce. She had gotten so caught up in the powers of enchanted objects that she now had what amounted to an addiction to it. What if the same thing happened to one of the soldiers, or worse, the entire regiment? But there was a flicker of hope in Daphne's eyes that Sabrina believed meant that the little girl's forgiveness might be attainable if she voted in favor of the proposal. And if she was to say no, would she be betraying her uncle or would saying yes be betraying her father?

"Sabrina, what do you say?" Granny asked again.

"Open the doors," Sabrina said.

Daphne looked at Sabrina as if she had never seen her before in her life. It wasn't total forgiveness, but it wasn't the glare she'd been sporting for days.

Henry, however, scowled and stormed out of the cabin.

Granny frowned but did not chase after him. "Then it's decided, Mr. Canis. Tell Charming he can have what's on the list. I hope it helps."

"I pray so as well," Canis said.

"OK, let's get to work."

• • •

"Did you say 'army'?" Mirror asked as he studied the list.

Granny nodded. A team of thirty or so soldiers along with Veronica, Sabrina, and Daphne stood behind her. The soldiers were a mixed lot—mostly Arthurian knights and Merry Men. Morgan le Fay was there, as was Puss in Boots and the Scarecrow. There were a few fairies that Sabrina had never met, each more obnoxious than the last, and a rather smelly banshee. All of the visitors were completely bewildered when they stepped through the back door in the Hotel of Wonders into the Hall of Wonders. Even Charming, whose own magic mirror was nothing short of incredible, was struck speechless.

"I had no idea," Mr. Seven said as he marveled at the enormous hall.

"Yes, you never really get used to this place," Snow said, though she had spent many evenings in the hall training the girls in martial arts.

"The Wicked Queen described this mirror as a botched first attempt," Charming said, referring to the woman who created all the magic mirrors and their guardians.

"A *botched first attempt*?" Mirror cried.

Charming ignored Mirror. "I was expecting something much less grand." He marched around the Hall of Wonders directing the recruits as they set up tents and unrolled sleeping bags. "We'll be able to train them right here. We could store the entire infantry in here, as well as the weapons."

"Relda, am I missing something?" Mirror asked.

Granny handed Mirror her massive key ring. "My family and I have agreed to aid Prince Charming's army with supplies and training. The list will tell you what they need."

Mirror looked incredulous. "I'm not a young mirror, Relda, but my memory is fine. No Grimm has ever gotten directly involved in the Everafter community in this manner. I must protest."

"Tut-tut," Charming said, stepping up to Mirror. The prince towered over Mirror. "No one cares about your opinion. You are a servant. Hurry along and get those doors opened."

"Mr. Charming!" Daphne cried.

"He's not a servant. He's our friend," Sabrina said.

"Child, this 'friend' of yours is not even real. He's nothing more than a security system designed to look after this hall and to obey your every command. He only has a personality to make dealing with him pleasant. His stubbornness, however, is obviously a malfunction, one we should have his manufacturer take a look at right away. He's wasting valuable time. My troops need to train."

"Billy Charming, you're forgetting your manners," Snow White said as she stepped between the two men. "Mirror is a big part of this family and he is well respected. I know firsthand that he's a sweetheart." She turned to face Mirror. "Now, I can explain more in detail what our plans are but for now let's just say we're outnumbered and don't have the magical firepower to put up a good fight against the Master and the Scarlet Hand. You can help us balance the scales."

Mirror looked down at the keys he had been handed, then at the list. He shrugged and shuffled off to do as he was told.

"Don't be mean to him," Daphne snapped at the prince.

Charming rolled his eyes.

Veronica stepped forward. "What can we do?"

Snow smiled. "You and your family are the key to our success. We need you to train us in how to use this stuff."

"We'd be happy to help," Veronica said. "But I don't want the girls involved in anything dangerous."

The family spent the entire day instructing the Everafters in the proper use of magical gizmos. Sabrina did her best to help without actually touching anything, and so she eventually found herself instructing people on how to direct the flying carpet. Its magic had never fed her addiction, so she helped several people learn to steer, fly straight, and build speed. It was nice to be treated like a hero by the soldiers, but helping them felt like she was betraying her father. Henry had not accompanied them to the hall. Instead, he was sitting in the courtyard of the fort grumbling. Sabrina thought of all the times she had sulked rather than helped, and for the first time she could clearly see how annoying she could be.

Daphne quickly became the go-to expert on many of the items. Sabrina knew her sister had a knack when it came to wands and rings, but she was surprised to see the respect the Everafters had for her. Sabrina couldn't help but watch her with a mix of pride and regret for treating her like a child. It was clear Daphne was growing up.

Granny Relda trained a number of Merry Men in the art of flicking a fairy wand to turn on its magic. It didn't come naturally to the burly men, who were used to clubbing villains and shooting arrows. A wand took a bit of delicacy, so there was a lot of shouting and frustration. Little John was so furious he punched a nearby marble wall and broke his hand. Veronica assisted as Nurse Sprat set the broken bones and Uncle Jake lent her more of the magical healing salve. After treating Little John, the two women were kept very busy with other minor training injuries.

Uncle Jake, who had quite a bit of experience with magical creatures, saddled the unicorns and did his best to calm the nervous beasts. They were stubborn animals and their single pointy horn made them particularly dangerous. Elvis was frantic when they were around and hid behind Veronica whenever one was loose. Despite the obvious pain he was in from heartache and his wounded shoulder, Jake never took a break.

Sadly, at the day's end, Sabrina worried that the army was a lost cause. Most of the soldiers were hopelessly inept and a few were showing signs of an unhealthy addiction to magic. Worse, there were just too many Everafters to teach and it was clear that time and practice were the only ways to master the new weapons. Snow told Sabrina that there were nearly three hundred more soldiers back at the fort waiting for their training the next day.

"Sabrina, could you show me how to fly this?" Snow White asked, pointing at the carpet.

"It's really simple," Sabrina said. "You just tell it what to do and it does it."

"If it's so simple why does it look so awkward?"

"That's me, I think," Sabrina said. "I can't seem to get it to work as well as Daphne. Even Uncle Jake says she's the best. She's busy teaching the Merry Men how to use a genie's ring but she shouldn't be too long if you want to wait for her."

"I think I'll stick with you," Snow said, stepping onto the rug. "So, how do we get it into the air?"

Sabrina joined her. "Well, you just tell it to go up." Suddenly, the rug rocketed into the air and came to a screeching halt with Ms. White's head just a few inches from the Hall's ceiling. Sabrina cringed. "Sorry—like I said, I'm not the best driver."

"Perhaps it's easier if we sit?" Snow said, easing herself down. Sabrina did the same. "So if I want it to go down the hall?"

"Just say the word."

"OK, rug, let's move," Ms. White said. The rug shook and dipped a little but sailed forward. It reminded Sabrina of the time she and her family had flown to Mexico on a family vacation. The plane had flown through some clouds and bounced around in midair. The pilot had called it turbulence. Sabrina had almost lost her lunch.

"I'm sorry you and your family can't seem to get out of town," Snow said. "I know how much you would like to leave."

Sabrina nodded. "It's causing a lot of fighting between my mom and dad."

"I've noticed."

"My parents are a little obnoxious, huh?"

Snow laughed.

"They weren't always cranky."

"I know. I met them as a couple before you were born. One look and you could see how much they adored one another. I've only seen one other couple who looked at each other the way they did."

"Oh, who?"

"Charming and me," she said wistfully. "What if I want to fly in a circle?"

"You can explain it to the rug. If you're just cruising along it tries to follow your directions but when things get crazy, like if you're being attacked, it sort of has a mind of its own. I guess you could say it wants to save its own butt just as much you want to save yours."

Snow explained a route she wanted to take and the rug followed her every command.

"So if you two were so happy why aren't you getting married? You said he proposed, right?"

Snow nodded. "It's complicated."

"I've got time," Sabrina said. "I'm sure I have to train Ichabod Crane next and he sweats a lot when he's nervous. He's so funky it makes my eyes water."

"Well, it all started about six hundred years ago," Ms. White said with a laugh. "You see, there was a time when I was—well, pretty naive."

"Huh?"

"In a nutshell, I was dumb. In my defense, they didn't exactly educate women back in my time. There used to be a joke back then—the reason they were called the 'Dark Ages' is because the women couldn't figure out how to light the candles. Jokes weren't really that funny back then, either." Snow laughed at her bad joke. "Anyway, I lived on my family's lands. I coasted on my looks, didn't worry about my brain, and assumed that eventually I'd find some handsome prince to come and take care of me.

And then there was the whole situation with the apple and my mother. I don't know if I had an epiphany while I was sleeping, but when I woke up I was mad. Not only had I let myself get into a bad situation, my own mother had had a hand in it! And then there's this guy who the mystical world decides is the man I'm supposed to marry. Who's to tell me whom I'm supposed to love? But even that's not what really, truly bothered me. It was the realization that I couldn't take care of myself. While I was riding off into the sunset on the back of Billy's horse I made a decision. I would never allow myself to be a victim again."

"So you learned kung fu and started the Bad Apples self-defense school to teach other women how to fight back. And now you're training an army. What does that have to do with Billy's proposal?"

"Nothing, really," Ms. White said. "The problem is I broke my own promise. I let myself be victimized again."

"How?"

"Bluebeard."

Sabrina shuddered. It had only been a few days since her run-in with Bluebeard. The infamous murderer had a twisted attraction to Ms. White. He had abducted her during a chaotic riot. Luckily, Prince Charming appeared in the nick of time to save her.

"When he grabbed me and pulled me into that alley I literally forgot all my training. I was helpless," Ms. White said, ashamed.

"You shouldn't give yourself a hard time about it," Sabrina said. "He gave everyone the heebie-jeebies."

"I'm not everyone, Sabrina. I'm Snow White, this town's resident fighter. I pride myself on my smarts and my right hook, but they both failed me. So I am right back where I was six hundred years ago with a handsome prince saving my butt. At Briar's funeral all I could think about was whether I was fooling myself. I mean, this soft-spoken, demure woman stood up to a dragon. She died with her fists in the air, like a hero. Could I do the same?"

"You're one of the bravest people I know," Sabrina said as she showed Snow how to make the carpet do a loop-the-loop without falling off of it.

"I'm not so sure, Sabrina, and until I know, I can't get married, even though I love Billy. I won't marry someone who has to take care of me. I'm going to take care of myself. I have to prove to myself that I can, again."

• • •

All in all, the three heads of the army—Mr. Canis, Prince Charming, and Robin Hood—seemed happy with the day's progress. At the end of the very long day the troops marched back through the portal to their well-earned cots. Mr. Canis told the family that the mysterious saboteur had struck several times that day and had yet to be identified. Luckily, he said, the destruction had been repaired before anyone could be hurt. Canis thanked the family for what they had done that day and excused himself, saying that he and Red had work of their own to do.

Unfortunately, preparations for the war started another war entirely—this one about the family's sleeping arrangements. With fears that the fort might be attacked at any moment, Henry was insistent that the family spend the night elsewhere. His first suggestion was to sleep in Granny's house, until the old woman reminded him that it didn't have water or power and was probably still surrounded by noisy lunatics. Daphne suggested they check into a room in the Hotel of Wonders, but everyone suspected that Prince Charming would never allow it. Instead, after much shouting and throwing up hands, it was decided that everyone would camp out inside the Hall of Wonders. Mirror seemed put out by his sudden overnight guests, but plodded down the hall to a room that held camping supplies. Uncle Jake drifted back to the fort without a word. Sabrina guessed he was going to visit Briar's grave. She wondered if she shouldn't go with him but Granny told her that Jake probably wanted to be alone.

Sabrina nestled into her sleeping bag and watched her sister do the same. Elvis lay between them, his big head resting on Daphne's belly.

"Daphne?"

The little girl opened a single eye.

"Are you OK?" she said. "I mean, about Briar and—"

"I'm fine," the girl said quickly.

"It's just, I mean, you probably feel very sad and you can talk to me if you want," Sabrina said.

Daphne rolled over so her back faced Sabrina.

Sabrina sighed and stared up at the vaulted ceiling of the Hall of Wonders. She was tired but too restless to sleep. She thought about Briar Rose, who had always been so kind. Snow White had been right about Briar; despite her soft-spoken personality, she had been a fighter. Sabrina liked to think of herself in the same way, though she had to admit most of her battles had been selfish in nature. *Can I be a hero, too?* she wondered.

As she lay there in the dark she heard someone rustle in a sleeping bag. Sabrina turned and watched her mother stand up, slip on a pair of flip-flops, and pull a sweatshirt over her head. Sabrina's father was sleeping deeply and it was clear to Sabrina that her mother was trying not to wake him up. She tiptoed down the hallway toward the Room of Reflections. Curiosity piqued, Sabrina shook her sister awake.

"Iiiiiiidddooooooghwannnnagiiiiiiiitupppffff," the little girl grumbled.

"Wake up," Sabrina said.

"Didn't I tell you I'm mad at you?" Daphne muttered.

"Mom just snuck out of here. Let's follow her," Sabrina said.

"Maybe she's just getting a drink of water," the little girl complained.

"I am the queen of the sneaks and I know sneaking when I see it. She was sneaking," Sabrina said, pulling the little girl out of her sleeping bag. "C'mon!"

Daphne grumbled but followed Sabrina down the hall to the Room of Reflections. They passed without disturbance into the Hotel of Wonders and then through the portal that led to the fort. Outside, the night had grown chilly and damp.

"It's cold," Daphne complained. "Let's go back."

"Sssh! There she is," Sabrina said, pointing toward their mother. Veronica rushed toward the medical tent and disappeared inside.

"Why is she going into the medical tent?" Sabrina wondered aloud.

"Maybe she's got a bellyache," Daphne said, nearly asleep on her feet.

Sabrina grabbed her sister's hand and dragged her to the back of the tent. There they got on their hands and knees and tucked their heads underneath a loose section of the canvas. Lying very still, they watched Nurse Sprat take their mother's blood pressure.

"Thanks for meeting me so late," Veronica said.

"Not a problem," the nurse replied. "But I do think this is something you want to discuss with Henry."

"I can't. Not until I'm sure."

Sabrina looked over to her sister. Daphne was mouthing the words, "What are they talking about?"

Sabrina shrugged and turned her attention back to her mother.

"I'd go to a human doctor but we're kind of trapped here," Veronica said. "And this particular problem might be a little difficult to explain."

The nurse nodded. "Have you been feeling funny since you and your husband woke up?"

"No," Veronica said, "which is what worries me. I should be tired. I should feel nauseous. But I feel better than fine. I'm worried that the spell might have done something terrible."

"Well, I have to admit it's the most unusual case I've ever heard. I mean, I don't think anyone who's ever been placed under a sleeping spell happened to be pregnant at the time."

"Pregnant!" the girls cried, then clapped their hands over their mouths. But it was too late. Nurse Sprat and Veronica were already standing over them, hands on hips, with looks of disapproval on their faces.

7

eronica snatched the girls by the pajamas and pulled them into the tent.

"You're going to have a baby?" Sabrina cried.

"I'm going to be a big sister, finally!" Daphne crowed.

"Girls, let's not get ahead of ourselves. This is very early. All kinds of things could happen," Veronica said.

"She's right, girls," Nurse Sprat said. "The miracle of life is the most unpredictable magic there is, so we don't want you to get your hopes up just yet."

"You knew you were having a baby before you and Dad were kidnapped?" Sabrina asked.

Veronica nodded. "I invited your father to meet me after work so I could tell him the good news. We met at the carousel in Central Park. Last thing I remember, my friend Oz was rushing down the hill toward us, and then we woke up in Ferryport Landing."

"Oz! If I could get my hands on him," Daphne said, stepping into her warrior stance. "He's not your friend at all."

"But you've been asleep for almost two years. Do you think something's wrong with the baby?" Sabrina asked her mother.

"We don't know," Nurse Sprat said. "I don't have a lot of experience with sleeping spells, but I know that being put under one is not the ideal way to grow a baby. All we can hope is that the baby slept as well. Most of the victims of these spells report that they didn't age a day while they slept. Briar Rose, God rest her soul, was asleep for a hundred years and she didn't age a day. But she was an Everafter, of course."

Veronica nodded. "Girls, this has to be our secret, OK? If something is wrong I don't want your father to know. He's already blaming all the world's problems on Everafters. If he found out we lost our child because of one he might do something rash."

"Like fight a dozen hobgoblins at once," Sabrina said.

"Exactly," Veronica said with a sigh. "He's dead set on escaping this town. I don't need him dragging us through the woods again."

"I won't say a word," Sabrina said.

"You can trust us," Daphne added, pretending to lock her lips with an imaginary key she then tossed behind her shoulder.

"So, Mrs. Sprat," Veronica said, turning back to the nurse. "How can we find out if my baby is OK?"

"Well, unfortunately I don't have all the fancy machines like the hospital, but I did manage to grab some essential supplies before the Hand burned it down. I have a simple test that will tell us for sure. All I need is a blood sample."

Sabrina's mother rolled up her sleeve as Nurse Sprat prepared a needle. She wiped Veronica's arm with an alcohol-soaked cotton ball and pierced the vein at the crease of her arm. The crimson blood slowly filled the vial. When the nurse had what she needed, she removed the needle and applied a bandage to the wound.

"I'll have some news in three days," the nurse said, removing the vial of blood from the plunger and carefully labeling it with Veronica's name. "In the meantime, take it easy. Get some rest and stay off your feet. And let me know if you get a craving for pickles and ice cream."

Sabrina followed her mother and sister out of the medical tent. She felt like she had a million happy questions to ask but also knew that her mother was nervous and didn't want to discuss the baby. Daphne was so happy she was skipping across the courtyard, but her silence told Sabrina she must have come to the same conclusion.

"Girls, come here," Veronica said, pulling Sabrina and Daphne close to her. The three Grimm women hugged tightly.

"Mom, look," Daphne said. Sabrina turned to see where her sister was pointing. There, lying next to the fresh grave of Briar Rose, was Uncle Jake. He was sleeping with one of the roses resting on his chest.

Veronica frowned. "He really loved her."

Sabrina nodded. "The way you and Dad love each other."

Just then, Red Riding Hood came rushing out of Mr. Canis's cabin with the old man hobbling behind her. The little girl looked terrified and was sobbing uncontrollably.

"What's wrong?" Veronica said, swooping the girl into her arms.

"We've had a breakthrough," Mr. Canis said.

"He's everywhere," Red cried. "He can see us wherever we are."

"Who are you talking about?" Daphne asked.

"The Master. I remembered him!"

"You know who he is?" Sabrina asked hopefully.

"No! Just his eyes! I saw his eyes. They were everywhere I went, watching me."

Red buried her face into Veronica's shirt and sobbed.

At that moment there was a terrible explosion. Sabrina turned to find the newly built water tower on fire and in the process of toppling over. It slammed into the ground and cracked open like a cantaloupe, spilling hundreds of gallons of water into the courtyard. Everyone was swept away by the flood and dragged nearly to the other end of the fort before they regained control of themselves. Sabrina scampered to her feet and was about to help her family and friends do the same when she saw a figure dart away from the water tower. It was too dark to identify him, but she saw where he went.

"I'll be right back," Daphne said, racing after the saboteur.

"Daphne, no!" Veronica cried, but the little girl ignored her.

"I'll get her," Sabrina said, rushing into the shadows after her sister. The fort was not well lit, especially after the explosion, and for much of the chase Sabrina was running in total darkness. She listened for Daphne's footsteps, racing around a corner at the far end of the wall, and then backtracked beside the medical tent and along the obstacle course. Sabrina lost her in the maze of equipment, but when she heard Daphne shouting she turned toward the noise and ran. She found her sister standing before the high fort wall with her hands on her hips.

"Where is he?" Sabrina asked.

Daphne shrugged. "He either went over the wall," which Sabrina could see was over fifteen feet high, "or through that hole."

Sabrina spotted a small opening at the base of the wall. A portion of the timber had broken. No one could have crawled through it—at least, no one human. It was too small for even a child. Sabrina scowled. Whether the villain had flown out or shrunk himself, it didn't matter. He was gone.

• • •

Charming appeared to supervise the cleanup of the water tower and the mess it had left behind. A small handful of Everafters came out of the tents to investigate, and Charming told them there had been a small accident and there was nothing to worry about. They seemed to believe his story and drifted back to their sleeping bags.

"What did you see, child?" Charming asked.

"He was small and fast," Daphne said. "I couldn't see him clearly in the darkness."

Charming frowned and walked away.

Veronica led the girls back into the Hall of Wonders where the rest of their family was still asleep. No one inside the mirror had heard the explosion. Veronica helped her daughters back into their sleeping bags and after a quick lecture about the dangers of running after bad guys in the dark, she kissed them both on the forehead and wished the girls a good night.

Wrapped in her sleeping bag, Sabrina dreamed of naked babies flying in and out of clouds. Their rosy cheeks beamed like tiny suns and the sky was filled with giggles that transformed into tiny hearts and flowers. Sabrina had never cared much for babies before—they were smelly and always covered in food. But the idea of having another little brother or sister was exciting. It was a wonder she could sleep at all. Unfortunately, her lovely dreams were interrupted by a loud huffing sound and the sudden sensation of something moist and slippery rubbing against her cheek. Without opening her eyes she made an educated guess about who was bothering her.

"Elvis, I'm sleeping. Go get Daphne to feed you," Sabrina grumbled and pulled her sleeping bag up over her head. For a moment she was sure the big dog was going to let her drift back to sleep but with a sudden jerk her pillow was yanked out from under her head and her skull rattled against the cold marble floor. Pain rocketed from her temples around her head. Angry and aching, Sabrina sat up spewing threats of trips to the dog pound when she realized that the culprit behind her pillow's theft was not the Great Dane but an enormous white stallion hovering ten feet off the ground. Two powerful wings kept it aloft. Sabrina recognized it as one of the Pegasi the family had lent Charming's army. Behind it hovered a dozen more that looked like identical copies, aside from the fact that the one chewing on her pillow also had a rider. Sabrina snarled. Puck was sitting on its back looking as if he was about to open his biggest Christmas present.

"What's the big idea?" Sabrina demanded.

"I declared war on you, remember?" Puck said.

Sabrina rolled her eyes. "Is this another one of your stupid pranks?"

Puck sniffed. "You have contaminated me with your puberty virus and you called my villainy into question."

"First of all, puberty isn't a virus," Sabrina said as she fought a tug of war with the Pegasus for her now rather damp pillow. "Secondly, I'm sorry if I gave the itty-bitty baby the boo-boo face. Do you want me to give you a hug?"

Puck curled his lip in anger.

"Oh, now the baby is cranky. Perhaps we should put him down for a nap?"

"We'll see who's laughing soon enough," Puck said. "You see these flying horses?"

"Duh!"

"These horses have a very special diet," Puck said. "For the last two days they have eaten nothing but chili dogs and prune juice."

Sabrina heard a rumble coming from Puck's horse. It was so

loud it drowned out the sound of its beating wings. Sabrina couldn't tell if the churn or the sound of the churn was worse for the Pegasus but it whined a bit and its eyes bulged nervously.

Puck continued. "Now, chili dogs and prune juice are a hard combination on a person's belly. It can keep a human being on the toilet for a week. Imagine what would happen if I fed chili dogs and prune juice to an eight-hundred-and-fifty-pound flying horse. Oh, wait a minute! You don't have to imagine it. I *did* feed chili dogs and prune juice to an eight-hundred-and-fifty-pound flying horse. In fact, I fed all of them the same thing!"

Puck's Pegasus let out a tremendous fart and then whined uncomfortably.

The horror of Puck's plan began to sink in and Sabrina started to panic. As she looked up at the fleet of horses she wondered what she could do to save herself. She decided a threat might be her best approach. "You'll regret this, fairy boy," Sabrina said. It sounded hollow and pathetic even to her.

Sabrina heard a splat on the floor several yards away. She knew if she looked at it she'd be sorry, so she averted her eyes, but there was no protection from the smell. It invaded Sabrina's nose like an unwanted house guest. She feared it might never go away.

A second splat followed and Sabrina scampered to her feet.

Her only strategy, she realized, was to stay mobile. She leaped out of the way just before a third horrible brown bomb crashed near her foot. Sadly, she found herself directly below another Pegasus suffering a similar gastrointestinal crisis. She rolled out of the way and collided with her sister.

"What's the big idea?" Daphne groaned. A second later she was pinching her nose. "Geez, Sabrina. You should really lay off the beef stew in the mess tent tonight."

"That's not me!" she cried. "We're under attack. Get up if you want to save yourself."

Daphne gaped for a second, unsure of what was happening, but when her sleeping bag suffered a direct hit she cringed and dove to safety. In her efforts to escape the next attack she knocked Sabrina down and the two flailed like a couple of desperate fish in the bottom of a boat.

"There's no escape," Puck shouted to the girls. "And just so you know, I'm not taking any hostages." He laughed so hard it echoed off the ceiling of the Hall of Wonders.

Another bomb fell with a splat.

"Is it on me?" Daphne cried, flipping her head back and forth. She calmed down when Sabrina assured her she had not caught any shrapnel.

The commotion finally roused Granny Relda. "Puck! You cut

this nonsense out at once," she demanded, her shouts waking Henry and Veronica.

"Forget it, old lady. I'm done doing what I'm told. The Trickster King has returned," he shouted, steering his horse so that it flew uncomfortably close to Granny Relda. A splat landed mere inches from her feet and she gasped in horror. She turned to Sabrina and gave her an impatient look.

"What did you say to him?" she asked.

Sabrina was shocked. "Why is it always me!"

"Because you're the only one that can get under his skin," Granny said. "You've obviously hurt his feelings. He's very sensitive."

"Sensitive? This kid hasn't brushed his teeth since the Civil War and suddenly he cares about someone's opinion?" Sabrina asked.

"Not someone's opinion," Daphne said. "Yours."

"Why does he care so much what Sabrina thinks?" Henry asked suspiciously.

Sabrina could feel her cheeks blush and she looked to the floor.

"You've got your first boyfriend!" Veronica exclaimed, clapping her hands happily.

"Ugh!" Henry complained. "I'm so not ready for this. Couldn't you have at least picked a boy who doesn't smell like a broken sump pump?"

"I didn't pick anyone, Dad. I don't like him!" she cried.

Daphne grinned. "Whatever."

"Sabrina, apologize to him before this gets out of hand," Granny begged.

"Mom, this is already out of hand," Henry said, holding his sleeping bag over himself and his wife. Henry turned to Puck and shook a commanding finger at him. "Now you listen to me, boy. This is unacceptable behavior. You get off that Pegasus and come down here and start acting your age!"

"Honey, he's over four thousand years old," Veronica said, cowering under the sleeping bag.

"Well, then this is even more immature," Henry said.

Puck sailed over Sabrina's head. "Hey, ugly. I want to thank you. You actually did me a favor."

"Oh yeah?" Sabrina said suspiciously.

"I've gotten too comfortable living in the old lady's house, eating the old lady's food, acting like a human. I am the Trickster King. The Crown Prince of Snips and Snails and Puppy-Dog Tails, the ruler of Gremlins, Rascals, and Miscreants, the guiding light of every instigator, agitator, and knave from here to Wonderland. I shouldn't be living with a bunch of heroes like you and your family. I should be causing the chaos you are trying to prevent. I am, after all, a villain of the first rate."

"Fine, go be a villain. But don't you think this is all a little overdramatic? Flying horses? Poop bombs?"

"Actually, I think it's just dramatic enough," Puck said. "Charge!"

There was little the Grimm clan could do. They ran about the Hall of Wonders like escapees from a mental hospital, shrieking and racing around in circles. Eventually Mirror appeared, and despite his desperate cries and a very rich bribe, the boy and his chili dog–eating horses would not relent. Puck chased Sabrina until she tumbled over her own feet and fell. Helpless, she lay on the floor as the Pegasi drifted directly above her.

"Would saying I'm sorry make a difference?" Sabrina asked.

"Not in the least," Puck crowed.

Like a lot of people who have experienced horrible, nightmarish events, Sabrina's brain blocked what happened next from her memory. She wouldn't remember being carried out to the fort where dozens of soldiers, all safely far away, tossed bucket after bucket of soapy water on her until she was clean. She wouldn't remember how her family wrapped her in towels and carried her to a cot where an elf sprayed her with several cans of air freshener. She wouldn't remember how her mother sang to her and fed her soup or that she slept for nearly twenty-three hours after the ordeal. It was good that she didn't remember, but those who witnessed it would be haunted by it for the rest of their lives. Daphne said she would never look at ponies—or chili dogs, for that matter—the same way again.

• • •

Unfortunately, that was not the end of Puck's pranks. By the time Sabrina had recovered, she found snakes in her sleeping bag, stinky cheese sewn into her socks, and the word "fat head" spray-painted on her jacket. Granny promised to have a talk with the boy but Sabrina didn't have a lot of hope that his pranks would end. The old woman's efforts to discipline Puck in the past had been slightly less than successful.

Sabrina had missed a day of training, and in that time the troops had become near experts on many of the magical items, including mounting the unicorns and riding the flying carpet. Mr. Boarman and Mr. Swineheart had been busy, too, designing and building a new water tower and various upgrades to the fort, including a trench around the perimeter, a new medical clinic, and two massive catapults, each loaded with boulders as big as a family car. But the two little pigs in disguise were most proud of the high-pressure water cannons they had attached to the watchtowers. Mr. Boarman said they were the best weapons for fending off dragons if any happened to attack the fort.

The biggest change, however, wasn't in the soldiers or the fort but in the mood of its inhabitants. Gone were the frightened Everafter refugees resisting confrontation. They were replaced by an eager team of fighters determined to be the best they could be. It seemed to Sabrina that they were all itching for a fight with the Master's Scarlet Hand army. With each hour they became more of a real army, and the fort became an imposing structure. She should have been happy and proud of the community, but everything seemed eerily familiar to the camp she had visited in Ferryport Landing's dark future. There were things that were different; for example, Snow White was still alive and Granny Relda hadn't taken over the military planning. Sabrina hoped the differences would be enough to change the town's destiny.

The family sat down in the mess tent for a breakfast of oatmeal and wild berries, along with bread, eggs, and juice. Sabrina took her seat and glanced at the people around her. Her mother and father were there, as was Granny Relda. Uncle Jake sat on the other side of the table, picking at his food. Mr. Canis and Red sat together, though the little girl still looked haunted by her memories. Puck was nowhere in sight, which meant he couldn't ruin her breakfast with some disgusting noise or smell. She smiled and ate a big spoonful of oatmeal, only to feel something pop inside her mouth. She didn't think much of it until she noticed her mother staring at her in surprise.

"What?"

"Sabrina! What are you eating?"

Sabrina looked back down at her food but there was nothing unusual in the bowl. But when she looked at her hand she noticed it had turned a murky shade of green.

"Granny, is this one of your recipes?" Sabrina asked.

The old woman shook her head. "Oh, *liebling*, I think Puck has pulled another prank."

Sabrina ran into Charming's cabin and peeked into one of the two mirrors hanging on the wall. Then she shrieked. Her face, hands, feet, and even her ears were swampy green.

Reggie's face appeared. "Girl, you look like you were attacked by a mob of broccoli."

Behind her she heard Harry. "Let me see," he said from inside his mirror.

Sabrina turned. "Kids," Harry said as he shook his head disapprovingly. "They jump on the latest fad no matter how ridiculous they look."

"This isn't a fashion statement," Sabrina cried as she stomped back to the mess tent. She found Puck sitting in her seat, finishing her breakfast. He smirked when she entered.

"Puck! What did you do to me?" she asked.

"Don't get all freaked out. It'll wear off by the time you start college," Puck said, stealing a handful of eggs from Red Riding Hood's plate.

"Looks like he slipped you a water toadie egg," Uncle Jake said. "Relax. It's not harmful and I have a remedy somewhere, but—"

"But what?"

"Well, the remedy has side effects," Uncle Jake explained.

"What kind of side effects?"

"You'll grow a tail," he answered.

"Gravy," Daphne said. "Can I take it?"

Before Sabrina could strangle Puck, Prince Charming stormed into the mess tent demanding that someone do something about Goldilocks.

"She's running around here moving things."

The blond beauty followed close behind. "Things are very out of balance in this fort. You can't have the catapult near the water tower. Water has a calming effect on people. You should put the catapult somewhere that people have their blood up—like the fire pit."

"See, she talks nonsense!"

"It's feng shui! It's thousands of years old," Goldilocks said.

"And I would presume painfully annoying for every year!" Charming shouted. "This is a military complex. It's not supposed to flow harmoniously."

"You asked me for my help," the blond woman said stubbornly.

"This is not what I had in mind, Goldilocks. I need fighters, especially ones with unique abilities. You can command an animal army, but instead you're moving the ammunition and the horses so they are one with the universe. Woman, we're launching an attack tonight!"

"Launching an attack!" Henry cried as he leaped from his seat. "What are you talking about?"

Charming looked Sabrina up and down. "You are a strange child," he said, then turned his attention back to Henry. "The Merry Men only managed to track down one of the hobgoblins you let get away. That one has most assuredly returned to the Hand to report where we are located. We'll be under attack any day now. I have no intention of sitting and waiting for it to happen. We're going to strike first and let them know we mean business. It may be our only opportunity to surprise them."

When Charming strolled off Goldilocks sighed. "I'm just trying to be useful."

"You have other talents," Henry reminded her.

She walked away, frowning.

When they were finished with breakfast, Uncle Jake retrieved the toadie egg antidote and gave it to Sabrina. It was a little glass vial with a cork stopper. Inside was a strange yellow liquid. She stared at the bottle uncertainly.

"A tail, huh?"

Uncle Jake nodded. "A really long one."

Sabrina shook her head. "No way. I am not going to have a monkey tail."

"It will disappear after a day or two, but without this antidote you're going to be green for a very long time."

Sabrina sighed. She wouldn't be able to hide green skin. She'd look like a blond-haired crocodile. She could at least hide a tail. She took the top off the bottle and drank the liquid. It tasted like soda pop and cabbage.

"How long before it takes effect?" Sabrina asked.

"Your skin is changing back to normal now. The tail, who knows? It could happen any minute or it could take a couple days."

Henry shook his head in disgust. "Magic," he muttered.

"There's always a side effect."

Sabrina knew if she sat and worried about when the tail might appear she would go crazy, so she plunged into training to keep herself occupied. It was a busy day as everyone prepared for the battle ahead. Each minute that ticked by caused tension to grow amongst the soldiers. Their eyes changed from those of eager students to those of an animal who knows the zookeeper is unlocking its cage. They were loud and full of bravado. Raucous versions of ancient Irish war songs filled the fortress. Whether their bravery was real or manufactured had yet to be seen.

But beside the hunger for confrontation, many of the Everafters were going through a rather different phenomenon that surprised everyone who witnessed it—the Everafters couldn't help but be honest with one another. Maybe with so much on the line, people were giving their lives a second look. But the floodgates of truth swung open and Everafters rushed about confessing their undying love for one another. Ms. White and Morgan le Fay were nearly mobbed.

Still, there were some that were panicked. Snow gathered them together and gave them a pep talk. Sabrina watched her speak and how the recruits reacted to her. Perhaps it was Ms. White's many years as a teacher, or perhaps she was just a natural leader, but she had a command over the crowd that amazed Sabrina.

It was hard for Sabrina to believe this was the same woman who expressed so much self-doubt just days before. Snow told the troops that the battle would be dangerous, but it was well planned. She told them that people might be injured, but everyone was well trained. She told them that it was understood that fighting back was a tremendous risk, but that their names would be synonymous with the word *hero* and they would be celebrated wherever Everafters lived, either in Ferryport Landing or beyond. Sabrina watched their nervous faces harden and their frightened eyes transform into fire. When Snow walked away the group was demanding to be launched at the Scarlet Hand. They couldn't wait to fight.

"She's impressive," a voice said behind Sabrina. Prince Charming stood behind her watching his former girlfriend.

"You should tell her that yourself," Sabrina said.

Charming shook his head. "I don't want to encourage it. She could get hurt. I want to keep her safe."

"That's not what she needs from you," Sabrina said.

"Bah! You're just a child," Charming snapped. After a long moment he spoke again. "Did she say something to you?"

Sabrina nodded. "Yes, but I don't think she'd appreciate it if I repeated it to you. Let's just say that treating her like a china doll is not going to work."

Mr. Seven approached.

"Are they assembled?" the prince asked the little man.

Seven nodded. "Some are waiting in the Hall of Wonders and the rest of the soldiers are moving there now."

"Very good, my friend," Charming said, patting Mr. Seven on the back. "I think tonight a few of us are going to become legends. You included. But know this, if you get killed out there I'm going to fire you."

"I don't work for you anymore," Seven said through a smile.

"Details, details. If you ever plan on working for me again, then you better stay alive. Understand?"

Seven nodded and reached out his hand. The two men shook respectfully, then Mr. Seven raced away.

"Have you noticed that despite everything we did to change the future a lot of it is happening anyway?" she asked the prince.

Charming nodded. "And a lot sooner."

"Maybe we can't avoid it."

Charming shook his head. "I was in the future longer than you, child. I know what happens and when it happens. That gives us an advantage. Don't worry. Tomorrow is not set in stone."

• • •

The troops gathered beneath the vaulted ceiling of the Hall of Wonders. Charming entered and joined Snow White, Robin

Hood, and Mr. Canis at the front of the crowd. He called for everyone's attention and the Everafters grew still.

"There has been a lot of talk about fighting against the Scarlet Hand. Now it is time to tell you how you're going to win."

Sabrina and her family watched from the back of the crowd. Mirror had joined them and seemed quite interested in the plan. It was explained in complicated detail but when Charming was finished Sabrina understood that the assault would be on the Ferryport Landing Marina. It sat on the very edge of town only half a block from Sleeping Beauty's former coffee shop. Charming claimed that he had spies living outside of Ferryport Landing, and according to their reports the Scarlet Hand was receiving shipments of supplies and magical weapons from Everafters sympathetic to the Master's plans. If the troops could destroy the dock, there would be no place for the supply ships to land, thus cutting off a valuable source of aid to the evil army.

To accomplish this, Charming claimed the army needed a four-pronged attack. The first assault would be commanded by a new volunteer—Goldilocks. Sabrina was shocked to hear the woman had joined the effort and looked to her father. He seemed distressed but said nothing. Since Goldilocks had the unique ability to speak with animals, she would direct a literal air force of non-English–speaking birds who would draw the fire of the Hand's guards. While the enemy was focusing on the birds, Robin Hood would launch a second assault with his trained archers, raining arrows down on any Scarlet Hand soldiers guarding the marina. After the first wave of arrows was launched, Mr. Seven would lead a team of Lilliputians and other small Everafters down to the docks, where they would attach explosives to the marina right under the nose of the Hand.

"Then we drop the hammer," Prince Charming explained. "King Arthur's knights will storm the docks and run off the guards. Anyone foolish enough to stick around will face Camelot's swords and shields."

"And what do I do?" Snow said. She was visibly angry. "If you think you're going to prevent me from fighting so you can keep me safe you better think again."

"Relax, Ms. White," Charming said. "You've got the best job of the whole attack. You get to push the plunger on the explosives."

Snow raised her eyebrows. "I get to blow everything up?"

Charming nodded.

"Oh." Snow smiled. "I'm a big fan of this plan."

"What about you, Canis?" Puss in Boots asked the old man. "What's your part in this plan?"

"My assistant and I will be fighting our own battle tonight," the old man replied. From behind him stepped Red Riding Hood. He placed his wrinkled hand on her shoulder. "Red has made tremendous progress. We have hopes that together we can reveal the identity of the Master."

Prince Charming gestured into the crowd. "And now, Friar Tuck has offered to lead us in a prayer."

A bald, overweight man with a veiny nose stepped forward. He had kind eyes and a childlike face. "Let us join hands and lower our heads."

Sabrina felt Daphne slip her hand into her own, and Mr. Boarman's hand took the other. Geppetto held hands with the Scarecrow. Rip Van Winkle held hands with Jack Pumpkinhead. Beauty held hands with Frau Pfefferkuchenhaus. Though they all held their own beliefs and traditions, many entirely unique from all the others, they stood silently hoping for the safety of themselves and others, for the success of their fight, and for the enlightenment of their enemies. Sabrina lowered her head and did the same. She hadn't been to church since her parents' abduction and wondered if anyone would still listen to her in heaven, but she closed her eyes and whispered her hopes anyway.

• • •

That night, the troops put on whatever armor they possessed, picked up their shields and weapons, and filed through the massive gates of the fort. Sabrina and her family stood by, waving to everyone and wishing them the best of luck. So many familiar faces passed by with no guarantee they would ever return. Pinocchio watched as his father marched to war. Geppetto's uniform was too big and he was having a difficult time with his bow and quiver, but he continued onward.

"Watch my boy, Relda," he said.

Granny nodded. "Just until you get back, Geppetto."

"Farewell, Papa!" Pinocchio said.

Uncle Jake, dressed in his long jacket, trailed behind. When Granny spotted him with the other soldiers she cried and begged him not to go.

"I have to, Mom," Uncle Jake said.

"This is not your fight, Jake," Henry said, joining the argument.

Uncle Jake turned and pointed at Briar's grave. "It is now."

A moment later he and the troops were gone. Together, the family pushed the heavy doors closed and locked them the way the guards had shown them. Sabrina could still hear heavy boots marching and fading away.

"They're not ready," Sabrina whispered to her grandmother.

The old woman nodded sadly. "No one is ever ready for war."

The waiting was excruciating. Sabrina couldn't sit still and walked about the fort aimlessly. She stopped by the new clinic and waved to Nurse Sprat, who was busy eating a pulled-pork sandwich. Nurse Sprat was a nervous eater, and considering her already rotund shape, Sabrina was sure a legendary binge was going to take place that night.

Hours passed, and the family huddled together in the mess tent. They said nothing to one another but their worried eyes spoke loud and clear. Even Elvis was fidgety as he chomped at a fly that kept resting on his nose.

After some time, Pinocchio approached, and his smiling face seemed to dissolve some of the tension. He carried a burlap sack slung over his back and seemed excited by its contents. Sabrina wondered how he could be so positive with his father off to war.

"I come bearing gifts," the little boy said, setting his sack on a table and untying the string that held it tight. "They're not much but I hope you enjoy them."

He took out a marionette and handed it to Sabrina. She peered at it closely and smiled when she realized it looked just like her. The figure had blond hair and blue eyes and even had her little dimple on its right cheek. She marveled at its intricacies all the way down to the dingy sneakers and her favorite blue shirt. The limbs clanked in her hands as the strings went this way and that.

"What are these for?" Daphne said, when Pinocchio handed her one that looked just like her.

"You have all been such wonderful friends to my dear father," the boy said. "I wanted to find some small token of thanks. I do say they manage to capture some of your qualities."

Granny Relda smiled as she looked down at her marionette, which wore a bright pink dress with a matching bonnet—complete with a sunflower painted in its center. "I love it," she replied.

Pinocchio was elated and smiled his big toothy grin. He reached into his sack and removed marionettes for Henry and Veronica. Puck's featured his filthy green hoodie.

There was even one for Elvis.

"It's nearly as good looking as I am," Puck said, admiring his gift.

"Pinocchio, these are truly remarkable," Granny said.

"You must have worked so hard," Veronica added.

"One can be quite industrious when one has the right inspiration," the boy said.

"I don't know what to say," Henry said. He moved the strings and his marionette did a funny little dance.

"If I knew we were giving presents I would have gotten you something," Sabrina said, slightly embarrassed.

"Well, there is something you could do to return the favor," the boy said.

"Name it," Daphne said.

"I was hoping Sabrina might instruct me in the methods of the flying magic carpet. I find it most curious but did not want to get in the way of the soldiers. Now that they are gone I would be grateful for a lesson."

Sabrina nodded and looked at her marionette. "For you, anything. You chose not to paint this thing green so you've got a friend forever." She flashed Puck an angry look. The Trickster King laughed at her and manipulated his marionette so it bent down and stuck its rump at her.

• • •

"Look at all these doors!" Pinocchio cried as he and Sabrina soared through the Hall of Wonders aboard Aladdin's carpet. "How many do you think there are?"

"I'm not sure," Sabrina said. "My grandmother said there were hundreds but she wasn't sure herself."

"What do you suppose is in all of them?"

Sabrina shrugged. "For the most part . . . trouble."

"It must be fascinating to have the keys at your leisure," the boy said. "I have to admit I'm quite envious of the freedoms and responsibilities your family has granted you. I have found myself held back at nearly every turn. It can be quite perplexing."

Sabrina laughed. "You've got one big vocabulary there."

Pinocchio blushed. "I've picked up a few words here and there."

Sabrina could see she had embarrassed the boy and she apologized. It was clear that he wanted to speak further, but he was so odd he made her uncomfortable. She decided to focus on the lesson and try to avoid any conversation. The boy was a good pupil. He took to the carpet very well and within minutes he had reached a comfort and control that surpassed Sabrina's. It wasn't long before she realized there was nothing more she could teach him. He seemed to have sensed it, too, and he returned to his angry rant.

"Being so young in appearance has been nothing short of frustrating," the boy said. "You must be able to understand. Adults presume that since you look like a child you have the interests of a child, or worse, need to be protected like one. Father forbade me from learning to operate this carpet. It was only after much begging that he agreed to let me take a ride with you."

"Well, adults are good at making rules, but I guess it's usually to keep kids safe," Sabrina said.

Pinocchio scowled. "Well, I am not exactly a child. I'm nearly two hundred and fifty years old. At least my mind is! I have the interests of a full-grown man. I have a passion for art and music, culture, and politics. Besides this stupid, childish form I am an adult in every way!"

The rug seemed to sense his anger and it dipped and flipped, crashing to the ground and sending the children skidding across the floor. Aside from a bump on the head, Sabrina was uninjured. Pinocchio seemed fine as well.

"The carpet likes its driver to be calm," Sabrina explained.

Pinocchio blushed again. "I apologize."

Sabrina shrugged. "I get plenty mad sometimes. Don't worry about it."

She crossed the hall to fetch the rug, which had slid against one of the many doors. This one was not unlike the one on the front of Granny's house: It was red with a stone set into the wood. The stone had a hand carved into it. On the floor below was a woven mat with the word "Welcome." Once she had the rug in her hand she looked at the brass plaque on the door to find out what was inside, but unlike all the other doors in the hall, there was nothing inscribed on it.

"That's odd," Sabrina said.

"What's odd?" Pinocchio said.

"There's nothing to tell you what's in this room," Sabrina said as she studied the door. "And there's no hole for a key."

Pinocchio didn't seem interested. "Perhaps we should get back to the fort. Is it too much to ask that we walk?"

Sabrina rubbed the bump on her head gingerly. "Sure."

• • •

One step into the real world and Sabrina's throat was filled with smoke. Pained cries of the wounded came from every direction. Dozens of Everafters were being carried into the fort on stretchers. The soldiers had returned.

"What happened?" she asked, but the soldiers were either too busy or too exhausted to explain. They rushed past her, jostling her amongst their ranks like a pinball.

"Close the gates!" Charming shouted when everyone was inside. The guards quickly slammed the immense doors and braced them tightly with a bar as big as a tree. The prince commanded everyone to take a position around the fort wall in case the Hand had followed them from the battle.

"What happened, William?" Granny Relda asked as soon as she could reach him.

Charming scowled. "They knew we were coming. They were ready and they beat us badly. I have no idea how many are wounded or dead."

"That can't be!" Daphne cried. "How could they know?"

"It can be and it is," Uncle Jake said, his face full of disgust. "Nottingham and his thugs were on us the second we arrived. They seemed to understand our whole strategy and countered it at every move. If I didn't know better I would think Nottingham had been part of the planning."

"Do you think the guy who's causing all the trouble inside the fort could be a spy, too?" Sabrina asked.

"Hush, child!" Charming snapped.

Nurse Sprat raced to the group. "I can't handle all of these people," she said. "There's only one of me."

"I'll help," Granny said. "I worked for the Red Cross during the war. I can dress a wound as well as anyone."

"You can count on all of us," Veronica added.

The rest of the day Sabrina and her family ran for medicine, helped bathe patients, and did whatever they could to make the suffering Everafters comfortable. There were twenty critically wounded people and dozens more in need of stitches or a splint for a broken bone. Robin Hood's close friend Will Scarlet had been hurt badly. Little Boy Blue had two broken ribs. Sadly, a few of the Everafters died while poor Nurse Sprat tried to save them, including Frau Pfefferkuchenhaus. The gingerbread witch had taken a blow to the head and had fallen into the river, and she was too far gone for Nurse Sprat's skills.

The nurse wept, cursing the Master and his Scarlet Hand. "I'm not a trained doctor," she cried. "I can only do so much." No one blamed her. They were grateful for what she could do and at the end of the day she managed to save the lives of sixteen people.

Exhausted, Sabrina and her family stumbled back to the Hall of Wonders. There they found a hundred and fifty or so soldiers, all of whom looked beaten and afraid. Charming, Ms. White, Mr. Seven, and Mr. Canis looked over them like shepherds watching a flock.

Mirror met the family when they arrived. "I hear that things did not go well."

Uncle Jake nodded. "It's true."

"Charming has asked that we all meet. He says he has a new plan," Mirror replied.

"New plan!" Henry exclaimed. "The last plan nearly got everyone killed."

"Relda, perhaps you can talk some sense into him," Mirror said. "The prince can't send these people into battle again. They're not soldiers. Does he think that a collection of princesses, talking animals, and elderly witches can beat back the Master?"

"Shut up, Mirror," Uncle Jake said.

The little man was dumbfounded. "Jacob, I—"

"We are in the middle of a war, Mirror. If you come in here talking about how it's hopeless, you are going to crush them. They know it went badly. Leave it at that," Jake said, then stormed off into the crowd. Mirror shook his head but didn't say any more.

Standing in the front of the crowd, Charming raised his hand until he had everyone's attention. "Tomorrow we march on the sheriff's office."

A gasp went through the crowd.

"This is madness," Puss in Boots declared.

The Scarecrow joined in. "My calculations tell me we have a ten percent chance of surviving another confrontation with the Hand."

"That's suicide," Ichabod Crane shouted, nursing a wounded arm. "You saw what they did to us. We're no match for them!"

Charming ignored their protests.

"The sheriff's office is a central planning base for the Hand. If we can destroy the office we take a valuable asset from the enemy. My hope is that we can capture Nottingham as well. To accomplish this I believe we need a four-pronged attack."

"You and your four-pronged attacks!" Morgan le Fay cried bitterly.

Charming continued. "The first attack comes from the Pied Piper, who will use his abilities to command rats and squirrels to infest the office, driving Nottingham and whoever else might be inside out into the open. We assume the offices will be filled with card soldiers. My spies have informed me the Jack of Spades and the Three of Diamonds were seen going into the office this morning. Once they are in the street, the second attack comes from the sky. Buzzflower and Mallobarb will lead a squadron of flying wizards and sorceresses over the crowd, zapping as many as they can with their magic wands. The third attack will commence with Goldilocks and the three bears, along with an army of intelligent animals, going after Nottingham. And finally in our fourth prong, Mr. Seven will deliver the final blow by leading our knights, archers, and swordsmen into the fray."

"Charming, listen to reason," Beauty begged. The poor woman was nearly in tears and her little dog was yapping in panic. "Are you determined to get us all killed?"

The prince's jaw stiffened but he didn't get to respond. Snow White stepped forward, and there was fire in her eyes.

"Charming has told you the truth!" she said. "You have two choices. Fight or die under the heel of the Master. That's it. There are no other alternatives. Now, I know you wish someone else could do it for you, but that's not going to happen either. So it's time to grow up. You people have received your orders. If I hear another one of you crybabies questioning them, I'm going to make you wish you had died at the marina!"

The crowd grew quiet.

"The fort is not safe tonight," Snow continued. "All of you will camp in the Hall of Wonders. Get some sleep. We march at dawn."

 enry shook his head in disbelief. "I think everyone has lost their minds."

He turned and found Granny Relda crying into her hands and shaking uncontrollably. Sabrina and Daphne raced to her side and hugged her tightly.

"Those poor people," she said. "I can't give them any hope. Billy won't change his mind and he shouldn't. We all have to fight, tooth and nail, or we are all doomed."

"It's going to be OK, Mom," Henry said, resting his hand on her shoulder.

"No, it's not!" she cried angrily. "Look about you. Of all the craziness this town has been through, have you ever seen Ferryport Landing like this? It has never been this bad. But you want to run off, back to your New York City. You would leave if you could—just when they need us the most."

Henry said nothing. He looked around at his family and walked away by himself.

"Veronica, I'm sorry," the old woman said. "I'm very tired."

"He'll be OK," Veronica said.

Sabrina wasn't so sure. When he didn't come back for an hour, she went looking for him. She searched through the Hall of Wonders and didn't find him anywhere. He wasn't at the camp or the Hotel, either. Sabrina suspected he might have gone back to Granny's house for a little privacy. There was no way she could walk all the way back to the house's portal, so she looked for Mirror, who could take her in the trolley. She found him inside the Room of Reflections, pulling a shard of a mirror from one that was shattered. When he saw Sabrina he slipped it into his pocket and snatched a broom.

"Good, I could use a hand," he said as he pointed to a mop and a bucket on the far side of the room. The bucket was filled with steaming, soapy water. Sabrina took the mop and ran it over the floor that Mirror had swept. "People have been tracking mud and leaves in here all day. You'd think some of them grew up in a barn."

"I think some of them did," Sabrina said, recalling the talking goat who had nearly killed her while steering the flying carpet earlier.

Mirror chuckled. "Don't miss that spot over there," he said. "I like to keep this place sparkling. One of these days *Architectural Digest* is going to want to take pictures. I plan on being ready."

"I guess you're not used to so many people in here," Sabrina said.

Mirror shook his head. "Not that I mind visitors. The hall can actually get quite lonesome at times, but this has been unprecedented—all these wannabe soldiers running around leaving their filthy fingerprints on everything. And I thought Puck was a mess."

"So you just clean when we aren't around?" Sabrina asked. She had never once wondered about her friend's personal life.

"Oh no, I keep myself busy with my little projects," he said. "So, why aren't you with your family?"

"I'm looking for my dad," Sabrina said. "He's pretty uspet."

"I took him back to the house. Give me a second and I'll take you."

They swept and mopped until the room was sparkling, then stepped into the hall and boarded the trolley. Mirror took the driver's seat while Sabrina stood nearby, holding a strap hanging from the roof. In no time they were zipping down the hall.

"In all the fuss I haven't had a chance to say how sorry I am about Briar. I know she was important to you and your family. It was a terrible tragedy," Mirror said.

Sabrina nodded and tried not to cry.

"Not to mention the return of your parents. It must be particularly hard on you to hear them bickering."

"You're reading my mind," Sabrina said.

"If I said your sister's attitude was bothering you, too, would I qualify as a full-fledged psychic?"

Sabrina smiled. "You've been paying attention."

"I see everything that goes on around here," Mirror said.

"I'm sorry that Uncle Jake snapped at you," she said. "He's very . . ."

"He's upset, Sabrina, and he has a right to be. Just like you do."

And then it dawned on Sabrina. She was angry. It wasn't fair to have suffered for so long only to have her parents wake up to chaos. She had done what she was supposed to do: She grew up. Took the responsibility of looking after her sister. Even learned to appreciate her family's legacy and responsibility. She had done all this in the hope that there would be something at the end that made all her struggling worth it. But that's not what happened. She felt cheated.

"Starfish, do you believe in happy endings?" Mirror asked.

"You mean like in fairy tales?"

Mirror nodded. "Quite a number of them have happy endings. Even the story they wrote about me is a happy ending for Snow and the prince. Do you believe in them?"

"In real life?"

"Snow and William might argue their story *is* real life. What I'm asking you is, do you believe one might happen to you?"

"I used to," Sabrina said. "I thought when my parents woke up, we'd all move back to the city. Granny and Uncle Jake would come for visits. Things would go back to normal. That's my happy ending."

"And you've given up on it?" Mirror asked.

Sabrina shrugged.

Mirror sighed. "I believe everyone deserves a happily ever after. But I think that happy endings don't just happen by accident— you can't wait for one. You have to make them happen."

"I'm not sure what you mean," she said.

"I'm saying you are responsible for your own happiness," Mirror said as he brought the trolley to a stop at the end of the hall. "If you want to be happy you have to work to make it happen. You can't just wish for it and you can't put it in the hands of other people. I know you thought when Henry and Veronica woke up they'd give it to you, but that's not how it works, Starfish."

"So what should I do?"

Mirror shrugged. "I can't possibly know, Sabrina. Only you know how to end your story. It took me a long time to realize it myself. I'd hate to see you grow bitter waiting. If you want a happy ending you have to go out and take it."

Sabrina nodded. Mirror always made her feel better. She felt like she could tell him anything and he'd understand. In many ways he was her best friend.

"So I suppose you'd like me to wait while you talk to your dad?" Mirror asked.

Sabrina smiled. "You're the best."

She hugged the little man and climbed down from the trolley.

"Hurry up, the meter is running," he said. Then he took the shard of mirror from his pocket and used it to check his thinning hair.

A moment later she was standing in the spare bedroom of Granny Relda's house. The power was still out so the house was dark. The windows had been shut tight for several days and the air was stuffy. From the shouting and explosions outside, it was clear that the Scarlet Hand was still surrounding the house and doing its best to find a way inside. But the protective spells were still working.

Sabrina called out for her father and heard him reply. She

followed his voice to her bedroom—rather, his bedroom. He was lying on the bed staring up at the model airplanes he had constructed when he was Sabrina's age. A photo album rested on his chest. He turned his head when she entered and smiled.

"Need a friend?" Sabrina asked.

"I didn't think I had any friends left."

"I know that feeling," Sabrina said. She noticed the collection of marionettes Pinocchio had made of her family resting on the nightstand.

"I didn't want anything to happen to them," her father said. "He worked so hard."

Sabrina sat on the bed next to her father. He turned to her.

"I don't want you or your sister to train the soldiers anymore," he said. "No wands, rugs, rings, or unicorns. I don't want to see you helping anyone. I don't want you running off to fight. I don't want you to get more involved in this than you already are, understand?"

"Yes."

"Good."

"But, Dad, it's a lousy idea," Sabrina added.

Henry looked shocked. Sabrina realized that waking up to see that his daughters were older must have been troubling, but dealing with their independent personalities also couldn't be

easy. He rubbed his face in his hands, something he did when he was trying to wrap his head around a problem. Instead of answering Sabrina, he sat up and flipped through the photo album. Inside were yellowing photographs of the Grimm family from long before Sabrina was born. Her father stopped at a picture of himself and Jacob, dressed in long wizard robes and pointy hats decorated with tinfoil stars and moons. Each boy had a magic wand in his hand and was pointing it playfully at the camera. They couldn't have been more than seven and nine.

"I was around Daphne's age when my father opened the Hall of Wonders and its contents to your uncle and me. Back then, there weren't any locks on the doors except for the ones with very dangerous weapons or creatures. Jake and I ran wild in there. It was like a giant playground, and we didn't have to share the slide with other kids. I was learning to conjure fireballs and handling dragon eggs before I hit the third grade. Dad thought it was good for us to know how to use magic."

There was a picture of the two boys sitting atop a griffin. Despite its dangerous claws and vicious beak Jake and Henry looked like they were riding a pony on a carousel. Their father, Basil, stood by proudly.

Henry continued. "We didn't take magic seriously. Jake and I saw it as a little game. There didn't seem to be any consequences. Well, there are consequences, Sabrina, and they can be deadly."

Sabrina knew the story of Basil Grimm's death well. When her father and uncle had almost been men, Uncle Jake had found a way to temporarily shut off the magical barrier that surrounded the town. Once it was down, Henry's girlfriend, Goldilocks, would be free. Unfortunately, the spell also shut down a special prison intended for several very dangerous Everafters, including Red Riding Hood and a creature known as the Jabberwocky. The monster was a hulking, lizardlike creature with hundreds of teeth. Once it was free it killed her grandfather and changed his sons forever. Both boys left town and went their separate ways. The tragedy also ended her father's relationship with Goldilocks.

"Dad, that was an accident," Sabrina said.

"We're supposed to learn from accidents, Sabrina. We're not supposed to go around repeating them over and over again. That's why I don't want you and your sister fooling around with that stuff. It's why I need to get us out of this town as fast as I can."

"So what you want us learn from your mistakes is to avoid trouble? Even if you can help you should run the other way?"

"Yes!" he said, then paused. "No. I don't know. I'm confused. You know, someone doesn't come and give you all the answers the day you have a kid."

"Would Grandpa Basil run?"

Henry was quiet. He flipped through the photo album and stopped on a picture of his father. He was standing in the front yard of the house with an ax in his hand.

"Dad, Daphne and I take magic very seriously. I learned the hard way. I can't go near most of the stuff, but Daphne—sure, she gets excited when she gets to use it, but it's not a game to her. She respects it, Dad. And she's really good with it. She's better than Uncle Jake. Every once in awhile something's going to happen that we couldn't have predicted, but that's not magic. That's life. If we don't teach the Everafters how to fight they will not win this war. And we need them to win it, Dad. If we want a happy ending we have to show them how to win it."

Henry stared at his daughter for a long moment. "When did you get so smart?"

Sabrina shrugged. "I think I inherited it from you. Plus, I've got a good friend who gives amazing advice."

Henry pulled Sabrina up off the bed and hugged her.

"OK, new rules," he said. "I'll get used to the fact that my daughters are tougher and smarter than I am—"

"And older than you think they are," Sabrina interrupted. "You're driving Daphne nuts when you call her a baby. She's very sensitive about it."

"OK, I'll do all those things if you promise to still love me, no matter how obnoxious I am. Agreed?"

"Agreed. Oh, and stop arguing with Mom. It's getting boring."

Henry laughed. "Don't sugarcoat it, Sabrina. Tell me how you really feel."

"I'm sure I inherited that from Mom," she said.

"Do you have your keys with you?"

Sabrina pulled the huge key ring from her pocket. "Yeah, why?"

"I think there are a few other items this army could use."

She followed her father back into the Hall of Wonders and then from room to room, collecting a variety of magical objects. Sabrina had seen some of them, including the wicked witch's golden helmet that could summon an army of flying monkeys, but there were more she had never seen. One of them was a small metal object he explained was a magnifying projector. Henry said it had been brought from Oz and could make small Everafters bigger. He said that someone named H.M. Wogglebug was an example, but Sabrina didn't know who he was talking about. They also snatched a small vial labeled "The Powder of Life." Henry said it was responsible for bringing the Sawhorse and Jack Pumpkinhead to life and that it might be used to construct more members for the army. It was exciting to hear her father explain things. She had once thought of him as lovable but dull—a normal dad—but now he was thrilling.

• • •

Even though her mind had been calmed by her conversations with Mirror and her father, Sabrina slept uneasily. For one, there was a tingling sensation at the base of her spine that she was certain indicated a long monkey tail was coming soon. Also, she was sure that Puck would launch another attack and she feared how the boy would top flying-horse cacabombs. Sometime during the night she sensed someone standing over her and she leaped to her feet, kicking and punching, positive Puck was about to unleash something disgusting. Unfortunately, it wasn't Puck. It was Uncle Jake.

"You really like your sleep," her uncle said, nursing a red mark on his right cheek.

"I'm sorry!" she cried.

"Wake your sister. We have a mystery to solve."

After much vigorous shaking, the little girl was on her feet and the sisters followed their uncle into the fort. It was a flurry of activity. Everyone was rushing about with buckets of water, doing their best to put out the raging fire that was turning the camp's garden into ash.

"The saboteur has struck again," Uncle Jake said.

"Fudge," Daphne complained. "This guy is starting to get on my nerves."

"He freed the chickens in the henhouse, too, but that's not what we should be concerned about. Look!"

Uncle Jake pointed to the ground. There she saw the broken pieces of hundreds of arrows. Sabrina knew at once these belonged to the Merry Men. They had been working on them for days and were to play a major part in the next day's attacks.

"Did you see anything?" Sabrina asked her uncle. She knew he had spent another night next to Briar's grave.

He shook his head. "I must have dozed off. The fire was raging when I woke up. Whoever is doing this has gotten away with it three times. It's time to put the Grimm detective skills to work."

Daphne clapped her hands. "Yay!"

"I'll search the garden," Uncle Jake said. "Daphne, you take the henhouse, and Sabrina, you search the armory. If you find any clues, whistle."

The trio separated. Sabrina rushed to the armory and found the large metal lock on the door intact. How could the saboteur get the arrows out of the armory without opening the door? Perhaps he had a key. She thought about who had keys:

Charming, Seven, Robin Hood, Ms. White, and maybe a few others. None of them struck her as someone who would betray the camp. Charming hadn't always been trustworthy, but this was his camp. He was too proud of himself to sabotage it.

She circled the building to look for another way in and found a window on the far side that was slightly open. This must have been how the villain had gotten inside and removed the arrows. She was just tall enough to pull herself onto the window's ledge and force the window open. She clambered into the dark, dry room. Inside she smelled welded metal. There wasn't much light and the moon, hidden behind clouds, was not helping. She wondered if she should climb out and get a match, but decided against it when she got a strong whiff of gunpowder. The last thing she wanted to do was blow herself sky-high—it would be hard to solve a mystery on the moon. Since she couldn't see, the whole investigation seemed pointless, so she decided to climb out. The sun would be up soon and so she would have to wait.

As she made her way back to the windowsill, she stepped on something that rolled. She lost her footing and tumbled onto her backside. She quietly cursed the pain as she searched in the dark for what had caused her accident. Her fingers touched something small and sleek that felt like wood. She shoved it into her pocket. Whatever it was, it might make someone else fall.

She got back to her feet, crawled out the window, and rushed to find her sister and uncle. Both had returned to where she had left them, and they had been equally unsuccessful.

"I couldn't see a thing in the chicken house," Daphne said.

"I had the same problem," Sabrina said.

"There was nothing in the garden," Uncle Jake said. "I'll have to wait until they put the fire out to search the rest of it."

"Well, that was a bust," Daphne said.

"You want to come in to the hall and sleep with the rest of us?" Sabrina asked, seeing the dark rings around her uncle's eyes.

"Yeah, you're going to get the flu sleeping out here," Daphne scolded.

Uncle Jake shook his head. "No, I need to be near her."

He turned and walked back to Briar's grave.

• • •

It was morning faster than she expected. Henry and Daphne went to work training as many soldiers as they could in the use of the new weapons, but it did little to raise the army's morale. Also discouraging was the cold rain and fog that had drifted into camp. It was a miserable day and it reflected in the faces of the already reluctant army.

As they marched through the gates to fight their next battle, Sabrina wondered if she would see any of them alive again.

The first battle had been disastrous and, according to some, an ambush. Now as they went off to battle again, the lingering feelings of humiliation, fright, and exhaustion weighed on their shoulders more than their heavy packs of supplies. Uncle Jake was the only one among them that looked prepared and focused.

Aside from a handful of elderly guards deemed too feeble to fight and a small group of Everafter children, which included Red and Pinocchio, the Grimms were left alone in the camp. Everyone did what they could to occupy themselves until the soldiers returned.

Granny spent most of the day studying a three-dimensional map of the town that Mr. Seven had constructed. She fretted over Charming's plan and studied all possibilities. When she had a strategic idea or a good route for a retreat, she told one of the Everafter birds that had stayed behind and it flew off to deliver her message to the troops.

Henry and Veronica had a long talk as they walked about the fort. When they came back they were hand in hand and the bitterness between them had vanished. They looked the way Sabrina had always remembered them.

Daphne, Puck, and Elvis played a game in which they tossed an old pie tin through the air to see who could catch it in their teeth first—the big dog or Puck. Pinocchio was invited to join them but he refused, claiming he was not interested in baby games. Instead he wandered from one adult to the next, eager to start a conversation about art or science or chess. Sabrina felt a pang of sympathy for him. She knew what it was like to be treated like a child. Pinocchio was only a child in form, but few seemed to notice.

The day slowly ticked by, and by evening everyone was nearly dying for news. They sat together in the mess tent picking through beef stew and cornbread.

Red Riding Hood and Mr. Canis entered. It was clear from Red's puffy face and tear-soaked cheeks that she had had another startling revelation.

"I remember something about the Master. His face is so strong. His eyes are so tiny and black, but there's another face."

"What do you mean?" Sabrina said, her curiosity piqued.

"That's all she's remembered," Mr. Canis said. "I think we're going to stop for the evening. The toll on the child is too much."

Granny took the little girl in her arms and hugged her. "You are so brave."

"I'm trying." Red sighed.

Just then, a guard rushed into the tent. "The soldiers! They're back!"

Everyone rushed into the courtyard just as the massive fort doors swung open. A stream of soldiers stomped in, cheering, singing, and carrying Prince Charming on their shoulders.

"We destroyed the marina," Snow White said as she approached the Grimms. "We took them completely by surprise. The Hand won't be getting any help by boat anymore." She was suddenly lifted onto the shoulders of a troll and paraded through the fort like her former fiancé.

"The marina!?" Henry exclaimed. "I heard your plan. You were going to attack the sheriff's office!"

"That's what the prince told us all but he had a completely different plan in mind," Rip Van Winkle crowed. "The man is a genius."

Goldilocks pushed through the crowd with the help of her bears. She found Charming and called for his attention.

"Well?" he said.

Goldilocks nodded. "Your suspicions were correct. The Scarlet Hand was waiting at the sheriff's office in full force."

"William, we're confused," Granny Relda said.

"Well, Mrs. Grimm, we have good news and bad news. The good news is we just cut off a very important supply line for the

Master. The bad news is that we have a traitor within our ranks. Someone in this fort fed our battle plans to the Scarlet Hand. I knew there was no way anyone could have been ready for our last attack. To prove my suspicions I conceived a bogus mission and switched to my real plan at the last minute."

"I was at Nottingham's office. The entire Scarlet Hand army was there waiting for us," Goldilocks said. "If we had gone we probably wouldn't have come back."

"So you went to the marina to finish the original plan!" Daphne cried. "Gravy!"

"They never saw us coming," Charming said, puffing out his chest proudly. "Now all we have to do is figure out who our spy is."

Snow stepped forward. "Worry about it tomorrow. These people need to celebrate."

Charming grinned and turned to his soldiers. "We gave it to the Master, didn't we?"

The crowd roared.

"Have a little fun, people. You deserve it!" he cried.

Tables were conjured, candles were lit, and wine flowed into every cup. There was dancing and singing, and soldiers told battle stories with details that grew more exaggerated with each telling. Sabrina spotted Morgan le Fay and Mr. Seven dancing beside a supply tent. He was standing on a chair so the two were cheek to cheek. The distraught, broken army that had marched out of the fort that morning was now confident and proud. Still, Charming's concern over the saboteur was weighing heavily on Sabrina.

"I wonder what the saboteur has planned for us tonight," she said.

Granny shook her head. "It's a terrible shame that someone would turn on their own people."

"It could be anyone," Daphne said.

"And there are so many Everafters in the camp. I don't know most of them," Henry added.

Everyone took a moment to look at the huge crowd of Everafters drinking, eating, and dancing.

"Did anyone find any clues?" Sabrina asked.

Henry shook his head. "I searched the armory this morning and found just as much as you did. Nothing."

Sabrina nodded, then remembered the little wooden object she had found in the dark room. She reached into her pocket. "All I found was this thing. It nearly killed me."

She took it from her pocket and set it on the table. All eyes turned to it and everyone grew quiet. Sabrina was so surprised she could barely speak.

"It's a little leg," Granny said.

"A little wooden leg," Daphne said, picking it up and examining it. "It looks like one of Pinocchio's marionette legs."

"How did it end up in the armory?" Veronica asked.

The group grew quiet.

"It can't be him," Granny said.

"Mom, what other explanation can there be?" Henry said.

"Wait! Are you telling me that Pinocchio is the spy?" Sabrina asked.

Granny's face fell. "Poor Geppetto. He'll be heartbroken."

"What do we do?" Veronica said. "Should we confront him?"

"Follow me," Mr. Canis said as he hobbled toward Pinocchio's tent. Once there, he used his cane to lift the tent's flap. Inside were nearly a hundred finished marionettes, along with several thick reams of wood and a carving knife. On one wall of the tent was a bloodred handprint.

"Anybody have any doubts now?" Henry said. He dug through a pile of marionettes until he found one with a missing leg. It fit perfectly with the one Sabrina had found in the armory. He tossed it angrily onto the pile.

"Where is he?" Canis asked.

"It appears the party is over," a voice said. Everyone turned to find Pinocchio standing behind them. He stood calmly, as if he was not ashamed of his crimes.

"Why?" Sabrina cried.

"He's going to grant me a wish."

"Who?" Henry demanded.

"The Master. He's going to make me a man," the boy said.

Sabrina rushed to Pinocchio and shook him by his shirt collar roughly. "Explain yourself."

"The Master came to me. He offered me my heart's desire—to grow into a man. I can't expect you to understand. Do you have any idea what it's like to be seen and spoken to as a child every day?"

"Uh, yeah?" Daphne snapped.

"Try it for hundreds of years! Forced to play with other children, never allowed to grow or mature because I am trapped in this body. I wanted life from the Blue Fairy, but look how she cursed me. The Master has promised to give me what I most desire."

"And if people die in the process?" Granny cried.

"You see him as your enemy," Pinocchio said. "But he can be your friend. He can give you anything you want. You could wish everyone back to life. That princess that died, Briar Rose, he could raise her from the dead. All you have to do is ask."

Uncle Jake glared. "We need to put him somewhere he can't get into any trouble."

"I can help with that," Puck said as he drew his wooden sword.

Just then, a horrible sound filled the air. Sabrina knew it well and the look on her sister's face confirmed it.

"A dragon!" they cried.

Others recognized the sound as well and the celebration turned to chaos. People ran like nervous rabbits, screaming and crying. Everafters fell to the ground and were trampled by others. In the madness, Pinocchio pulled free from Puck and darted into the crowd, disappearing from sight.

Puck was eager to go after him but Granny stopped him. "Let him go. We'll catch him later. For now, we have to get everyone to safety."

"Get to your posts," Robin Hood shouted as he charged through the courtyard.

Charming climbed on top of a table and commanded everyone's attention. "Remember your training. We can fight this thing!"

But when a violet-colored dragon with the face of a cat appeared on the horizon, Sabrina could see the prince's confidence melt away. The creature circled the fort like an overgrown vulture preparing to feast on the body of a dead coyote. Sabrina could taste the fear in the back of her throat, but struggled to remain calm. She turned her attention to Geppetto, who stood in the courtyard aiming his bow and arrow toward the sky.

"You can fire arrows at it all day," Sabrina told him. "They're not going to help."

"I have to do something. They have to be stopped," the old man said.

"They? How many are there?"

"Three just swooped over the fort," the old man said as he pointed north. "They came from that direction. One blasted the west wall. I sent guards to put out the fire but the water tower valve is broken. There's no way to get any water out of it."

Sabrina's father and Granny Relda raced across the courtyard with Elvis close behind. The big dog was barking hysterically. "I just spotted another seven flying in from the south," Puck shouted.

"Everyone through the portal, now!" Henry shouted. Guards rushed toward Charming's cabin, where the magical escape hatch was kept.

"But we should fight," Puck argued.

"I thought you weren't a hero!" Sabrina said.

"Who says villains can't kill dragons?" he teased. "Besides, it will look great on my résumé!"

Mr. Canis shook his head. "Not this time. You have to get to safety."

"C'mon, girls," Veronica said as she grabbed Sabrina and Daphne by the hands. Before they could take a step, a white dragon with orange stripes across its belly crashed to the ground in front of them, blocking their path. A dozen knights raced to the beast and attacked it with their swords.

"OK, we need a new plan," Daphne said.

Granny Relda rose to her full height. "Veronica, seems to me you were pretty good with mechanical things."

"I fixed some leaky sinks and the TV antenna once," Veronica said.

"You're the best we've got. Get over to the water tower and see if you can't get the valves working."

She raced off to do as she was told.

"Henry, get up on the east tower and turn that water cannon on," she said. "As soon as Veronica has the water working, try to knock one of those dragons out of the air."

Puck took his sword out of his belt. "I'll go kill one," he said.

"I have another job for you. How would you like to throw some rocks at it?" the old woman asked.

Puck scrunched up his face. "I hardly think rocks will do much."

Granny pointed behind her. There sat one of Swineheart and Boarman's catapults. It was a monstrous machine with a giant boulder loaded into its arm. Several more boulders as big as cars sat nearby.

Puck rubbed his hands together eagerly. "Looks right up my alley, old lady."

"Take Sabrina and Daphne with you," she said.

Canis stepped forward. "Relda, perhaps it's time to bring the Wolf back. I have the jar in my jacket and—"

"Absolutely not. I believe we can manage without that monster. Besides, I'm going to need you and Red to get me through this camp once it's safe."

Canis didn't look convinced, but said nothing.

Everyone raced to do their jobs, though Sabrina suspected she and Daphne were just being kept busy. Once they reached the catapult, though, she changed her mind. The device was incredibly intricate. Despite its crude appearance it had dozens of knobs and buttons and a complex series of weights and counterweights. Daphne wasn't strong enough to move all the levers, so Sabrina did the heavy lifting while Puck aimed the catapult and Daphne pushed buttons and pulled ropes.

A black dragon with white tusks swooped over the fortress. Sabrina's brain was screaming for someone to push the button that would release the boulder but Puck insisted they wait. A moment later the dragon was gone.

"Why didn't you fire?" Daphne cried.

"We have to wait until we're lined up perfectly. Don't worry. We'll get another chance."

"That's what I'm afraid of," Sabrina said. "It's coming right for us!"

The creature made a beeline for the catapult. Once it was close enough it reared its head back and prepared to blast them with its fiery breath. Then Puck gave the order and Daphne slammed her hand down on a red button. The giant spring inside the machine screeched as it extended and with incredible force the arm of the catapult whipped upward, hurling the monstrous rock with it. The boulder rocketed into the sky.

"Eat that, ugly!" Puck cried just as the boulder slammed into the dragon's face. It bellowed in agony and magma poured out of the sides of its mouth and down its face. The dragon fell out of the sky and slammed into the courtyard. Its eyes glazed white and its heaving chest grew still.

"Gravy!" Daphne cried.

"That's one!" Puck crowed, celebrating with a ridiculous whooping victory dance.

"Nine to go, bubblehead," Sabrina said. She started turning

the levers to lower the catapult's arm. "We need to reload the catapult. You think you can pull that off?"

Puck placed his hands on his hips and spun around on his heels. When he stopped a bizarre transformation began. His body swelled up to an enormous size. His nose grew so large that it hung well past his feet, and his ears turned gray and inflated to the size of kites. Two huge white tusks sprang out from under his nose and his skin turned wrinkled and tough. In no time at all he was an elephant. He lumbered over to the nearest boulder, put his head against it and pushed. The huge stone rolled slowly forward but it rolled nonetheless. It was clearly an effort for Puck, but he pushed onward until the rock was firmly in the catapult's arm.

The girls went to work twisting the knobs and weights once more in preparation for another dragon's assault. While they worked, Sabrina watched her father in the east tower. The cannon he maneuvered was attached to a huge pipe that fed into the water tower, but with the valve busted it was completely dry. As a brown dragon flew by it sent flames at the exterior wall of the camp. Helpless, Henry could not put them out. When the dragon doubled back and buzzed the top of the watchtower, he had to crouch low to avoid one of its black talons.

"How's it going, Mom?" Sabrina shouted.

Veronica had climbed up on a ladder near the tower and was trying to pull something out of a knob that opened the valves. "Pinocchio shoved something in here. If I could only get it out . . ."

"Could you hurry?" Henry shouted from across the camp.

"Keep your pants on, pal," she cried.

The brown dragon turned high in the sky and flew like an arrow at her father's watchtower. Fire was blasting out of its mouth. Henry was helpless.

"Puck, we have to get the brown one now!"

Puck spun himself back to his regular shape and then turned the catapult in the proper direction. He looked through a sight to line up his shot.

"Puck, you can't miss," Sabrina said fiercely.

"I won't miss," Puck said, but he couldn't hide his agitation. "Fire!"

Daphne slammed on the red button and again a rock was flung into the sky. Unfortunately, it rocketed past the monster and flew into the forest.

"Oops," Puck said.

Sabrina looked up and saw the dragon preparing his blast. Her father stood, helpless, on the tower. There was nothing she could do.

"I got it!" Veronica cried and suddenly water was blasting out of the cannon and straight into the mouth of the dragon. It gurgled and gasped as it fell to the ground. Once there it flipped over on its back and died.

"That was the coolest thing I've ever seen," Puck said as he ran for the other watchtower. "You guys handle the rock thrower. I'm going to have fun with the world's biggest squirt gun!"

"Hey! How are we supposed to load this thing?" Sabrina cried, but the fairy boy was already climbing the ladder.

Daphne looked over at the massive rock. "That's going to take more elbow grease than the two of us have."

"You help Dad," Sabrina said. "I'll try to keep ol' stinkface focused. I wouldn't put it past him to fire that thing at us."

The girls raced off in opposite directions. Soon Sabrina reached the platform where Puck was busy spraying water all over the forest and ignoring the circling monsters.

"You really have an attention problem," Sabrina said, pointing to a jade-colored dragon zooming toward them. She wrenched the handle of the cannon away from Puck and turned it toward the flying nightmare. The device was attached to a pivot in the floor and swung in a three-hundred-and-sixty-degree circle. It also had a metal pin at the end of the cannon that acted as a sight and allowed her to aim. She pushed the firing button lightly, just to see how much water would come out, and was surprised to see a torrent wash down over the forest. As the dragon got closer she braced herself and fired. The water shot out of the cannon and hit the dragon right in the jaw. It was a lucky shot but an effective one and the creature reared back in panic.

"Hey! I called this tower. Go kill dragons somewhere else," Puck shouted as he shoved her out of the way. A white dragon appeared on his left and barreled down on the fort, sending a river of flame that left a scorched trail across the entire complex and ignited the eastern wall.

"You're not supposed to let it burn the place to the ground! If you can't do this step aside," Sabrina said.

Puck growled. "Leave me alone. I know what I'm doing."

Puck fired the cannon but without a head-on approach, the water was of little use. The white dragon was unfazed and continued circling the fort.

"Give me the cannon, Puck," Sabrina said, pushing Puck out of the way. Studying the skies for another flying menace, she quickly spotted the white dragon approaching fast. She trained the weapon on the beast and waited patiently, seeing the fire licking the insides of its jaws. She had to let it get close to make her attack effective. In fact, she realized, she had to let it get so close it would put her into a do-or-die situation. To get the best shot and put out the fire inside the dragon, it needed to be nearly on top of her. She grasped the handle of the cannon tightly and forced herself to stay put. *Closer. Closer.* She could feel the heat of the creature approaching. Her ears were full of its roars and the sound of its wings. *Let it get closer.* It was nearly at the fence; any second now it would be right on top of her. She fired right into the dragon's open jaws. It fell out of the sky but crashed inside the fort and leveled the mess tent. When it hit the ground it skidded across the yard, slamming into another dead dragon.

"I'm catching up, ugly," Sabrina said.

"Lucky shot!" Puck complained as he snatched the cannon away from Sabrina. He spun the cannon toward another approaching dragon and fired. He missed the mark and tried again.

"What's the matter, booger brain? Do you need a bigger target?" Sabrina cried, pulling the cannon away from Puck.

He yanked it back. "Who can concentrate with your breath in my face? I'm probably not hitting anything because you have infected me with your puberty virus."

"Puck, puberty isn't a virus. You go through it when you grow up."

"Well, why would I want to grow up?" he shouted. "I'm perfectly happy to stay this age forever but you come along and now all of a sudden I'm getting taller and my voice is changing."

"Don't look at me. I didn't ask you to grow up," Sabrina said, scanning the sky for more dragons. She could see three high in the sky, circling the fort. "You started this war against me, but aging is your own fault. You wouldn't grow a day older if you didn't want to."

Just then, three arrows thudded into the side of the platform. Sabrina studied the forest to find their source and nearly fell over in shock when she spotted the massive army approaching the fort. There must have been two thousand Everafters charging in their direction. Sheriff Nottingham and the Queen of Hearts were leading the throng. Even from her great height Sabrina could see the bright-red handprints on their chests.

"The Scarlet Hand is here!" Sabrina shouted down to the soldiers inside the fort. The news caused even more panic than before and many in Charming's army fled into cabins and tents, presumably to hide. She snatched the cannon back from Puck and turned it on the approaching army. She pushed the Fire button hard and unleashed an avalanche of water on them. The liquid crashed into the center of their ranks and knocked nearly a hundred goblin soldiers flat. She continued her assault, hosing down as many of the thugs as she could. She couldn't be sure but she thought she might have waterlogged nearly five hundred soldiers until something terrible and unexpected happened. The stream of water turned into a trickle.

She turned to the water tower and saw her mother peering into a glass window on its side.

"It's run dry!" she shouted.

Without the water cannon there was little they could do against the overwhelming Hand army or the five remaining dragons hovering overhead.

"Why aren't you firing?" Puck cried.

"We're out of water!" Sabrina explained.

"That can't be right. You must be doing it wrong," he said, pulling the cannon out of her hands once more. He pushed the Fire button over and over with no results. "You broke it!"

Puck swung the cannon around in anger. The nozzle spun and hit Sabrina in the chest. The force was so powerful she was knocked right off the platform and fell backward off the tower. She saw sky above her and felt the wind in her hair. How ironic, she thought, as she fell to her certain death, that at that moment she would have given anything to be a giant goose again.

9

ir rushed past Sabrina's ears and suddenly she felt her back tingling again. A moment later she was hanging upside down, inches from the ground. She looked up to find her savior, only to find that her hero wasn't a person but a long, furry tail sticking out of the back of her pants. It was wrapped around a beam in the tower and kept her swinging there like a monkey.

Puck floated down to her, his wings flapping softly enough to allow him to hover.

"I bet you think this is hilarious. Look what you did to me with your stupid pranks. I have a tail!" she raged.

Puck's face was trembling. "I'm sorry."

"What?" Sabrina said blankly.

"I almost killed you. I'm sorry, Sabrina," he said, rubbing his

eyes on his filthy hoodie. He lifted her off the tower and set her on the ground.

"Since when do you care?" Sabrina said, still stunned by the boy's apology.

Prince Charming and Snow White rushed to join them while doing their best to direct the troops. Charming looked around his fort bitterly. "We . . . we have to retreat."

"Retreat? To where, Billy?" Snow asked. "We're on the very edge of the town. We can't retreat any farther than we already have."

"Through the mirror," Charming shouted. "Get everyone through my magic mirror."

Snow White shouted to her troops to retreat. Her words brought Mr. Canis, Red Riding Hood, and Daphne to the growing group that soon included Elvis, Granny Relda, Henry, and Veronica.

"You heard the prince. Everyone into the mirror," Henry said.

"But what about big and ugly?" Daphne said, pointing to the dragon that still blocked their path into the cabin. The crowd of knights still surrounded it, but their assault seemed more of an annoyance to the beast than an attack. It hissed at them and swatted back with its long spiky tail.

"There's no way we're getting past that," Granny Relda said.

Puck's wings appeared and soon he was hovering a few feet off the ground. "Does saving the day always have to fall on me?"

"I thought you weren't the hero type," Sabrina said.

"I'm not," Puck groaned. "But the whole lot of you are constantly in jeopardy."

"Which you tend to be the cause of," Sabrina said.

"Beside the point!" Puck said.

"Puck, I forbid this," Granny said.

Puck ignored her command. "Old lady, if I die I'd like you to do one small thing for me. I want you to build a one-hundred-acre museum dedicated to my memory. Bronze my clothing and possessions. Have at least three hundred marble statues erected of me in my most dashing poses. One of these statues should stand at least one hundred feet tall and greet ships as they float down the Hudson River. One of the fourteen wings of the museum should have an amusement park with the world's fastest roller coaster inside. None of these rides should be equipped with safety devices. You can license some of the space to fast-food restaurants and ice-cream parlors but nothing should be healthy or nutritious. The gift shop should sell stuffed Puck dolls packed with broken glass and asbestos. There's a more detailed list in my room."

"Puck, no!" Sabrina cried. "You don't have to do this!"

Puck rolled his eyes. "It appears I have to do a lot of things to keep you safe, ugly." He flashed a quick smile.

Sabrina blushed and felt like everyone was suddenly watching. "What are you going to do against that monster?"

Puck took his little wooden sword from his waist. "I have this, Grimm. I'll be fine."

"You're going to get yourself killed!" Daphne said angrily.

"Don't disrespect the sword, marshmallow!" he said.

He darted toward the dragon and was soon jabbing at its ears with his weapon. The creature roared and he stuck it in the eye. It turned its massive body and exhaled a tiny blast of fire but Puck easily flew out of its path.

"Come and get me," Puck taunted, and rocketed into the air. The angry dragon did just that, soaring upward after its tiny, annoying prey.

With the path clear the family rushed into the cabin. Once inside, they helped the elderly Everafters through the mirror and then the very young and the smaller animals. One by one the frightened people stepped through to safety. Geppetto broke away to approach the Grimms.

"Have you seen my boy?" Geppetto said.

"I think I saw him heading into the magic mirror," Granny lied. "You should go look for him in the Hall of Wonders."

Geppetto thanked her and disappeared through the reflection. Granny sighed. "I couldn't tell him the truth."

"What is this t'ing that I hear outside?" Reggie said from his mirror. His dreadlocks shook nervously.

"Dragons have attacked the fort," Sabrina explained.

"Dragons! You have to get me out of here, missy."

Prince Charming rushed into the cabin with Snow at his side. "Ms. White! I won't hear another word of this. Get through the portal, now."

Snow stomped her foot. "Mr. Charming, as you may be aware, I am not seven years old. I can take care of myself."

Charming threw up his hands in frustration. "Fine. This is a direct order from your commanding officer. Sergeant, you are to get through that portal at once. Prepare the Hall of Wonders for the refugees."

"You won't be housing them in your hotel?" Veronica asked.

"My hotel?! These mongrels would destroy the place. The sheets are five-hundred thread count," he said.

Reggie looked bewildered and nervous. "Hey, my friend. The Princess Beauty lent me to you with the belief that you could keep me out of trouble. I'm fragile, you know."

"Can I take a magic mirror into a magic mirror?" the prince asked.

Reggie shrugged.

Harry appeared in his mirror. He scratched his head. "The instructions that came with me say that to do so might tear a hole in the dimensional fabric of the universe. We could all implode into a million tiny pieces."

"Has it ever been tried before?" Charming said impatiently.

"No, sir," Harry said.

Charming took Reggie off the wall and shoved the mirror into Henry's hands. "Hank, take Reggie inside when you go."

Sabrina's father tried to argue, but Charming had already bolted out of the cabin and back into the fray.

Sabrina could hear the popping and snapping of burning timber. From the irritated sensation in her nose and eyes it was clear the fort was burning. A steady stream of refugees flooded into the cabin and through the portal. Sabrina's father and mother did their best to hurry them through as a bottleneck of panicked Everafters clogged the door to the cabin. One after another disappeared through the reflection until the only people left behind were King Arthur's knights, a few brave princes, and most of the Merry Men.

"Where's Jake?" Henry cried.

Ms. White stepped forward. "I saw him at Briar's grave. He refuses to leave."

Henry looked at his mother. Granny Relda was near tears. Then he dashed out of the cabin. Before anyone could stop her, Sabrina raced after him.

Amid firebombs exploding everywhere, they zigzagged across the courtyard. One explosion was so close it knocked Sabrina off her feet and rattled her brain. She staggered upright and resumed the chase. She found her father standing with her uncle over the grave.

"You have to come, Jake," Henry said.

"I won't leave her," Uncle Jake cried.

"You have to. Do you want to join her?"

"Maybe I do, Hank. Maybe it's time to stop running. That's what we're all good at, anyway. We all run away. The girls do it. You did it. I did it. Maybe it's time to stay put."

"Jake, this isn't what she would want," Henry said.

"What would you know about what she would want?" Jake asked. "You didn't love her. You didn't hold her in your arms and feel like you just got your happily ever after. You don't know anything about her."

"I knew her," Sabrina shouted over the noise. "She would not want you to stay here and die. She was a fighter. She would want you to fight, too."

Uncle Jake looked at Sabrina. His face was thin and tired.

Tears escaped his eyes. "I can't go. I can't run away anymore."

"We're not running anymore, Jake," Henry said. "I'm here. Mom's here. The girls are here! We're all here. We're not going to run. We're going to fight, but right now we have to go."

Uncle Jake looked down at the grave. He leaned down and snatched a rosebud from the magical bush that grew there and put it into one of his many pockets, right over his heart.

The three of them raced back to Charming's cabin, counting the lucky stars that kept them alive during all the chaos. They arrived just in time to see Mr. Canis and Red Riding Hood stepping into Charming's mirror. Henry picked up Reggie and hoisted him onto his back and together the rest of the family stepped through. It was clear that the universe wasn't in jeopardy when they reached the other side.

"Are we tru, man?" Reggie said as he looked around the lobby of the Hotel of Wonders. "Hey, nice digs."

"Thanks!" Harry said. He was busy placing fresh Hawaiian leis around everyone's necks as they milled around the massive lobby. "Have you seen the boss?"

As if on cue, Charming tumbled through the portal. He was followed by a dozen fully armored knights. Many fell to the floor with a clang and begged for help righting themselves.

"Get into the Hall of Wonders, now!" Charming shouted as he pointed to the elevator door that acted as its portal.

"Why? What's the matter, William? We're safe in here, aren't we?" Granny asked.

"Not at all," Charming shouted, nudging Granny toward the portal.

They heard a massive crash. Sabrina turned to the portal and saw Sheriff Nottingham with a heavy sledgehammer in hand. He swung it as hard as he could, and it slammed into the reflective surface on the other side.

"He's trying to break this mirror," Charming said.

"Uh-oh!" Daphne said.

"Didn't you say that when a mirror is broken everything inside it is cut to ribbons?" Sabrina asked.

"You have a good memory, kid," the prince said. "By the way, your tail is showing."

Sabrina blushed and shoved her long tail into the back of her pants.

"Boss, what can I do?" Harry asked.

"There's a box in room nineteen. It's in the bureau and very important. Can you fetch it for me?"

"In a jiffy." Harry took off for the elevators. Meanwhile,

Charming was literally shoving people through the portal into the hall.

"This is a little rude, pal," Daphne said as he pushed her toward the magical doorway.

"Pardon me if I try to save your life."

Soon, Sabrina found herself sprawled out on the floor of the Room of Reflections, where the rest of her family was waiting. Elvis flew through and skidded across the floor, then turned and barked angrily at the portal. Henry grabbed him by the collar and ushered everyone out of the portal's path so that others could enter as well. As they moved Ms. White came through, nearly falling to her knees.

"He shoved me!" she cried, angrily.

"Who else is left?" Robin Hood asked. He had a terrible burn on his right arm. His wife was by his side, looking distraught.

Sabrina poked her head into the portal and saw Charming, standing alone by the elevators. "What are you waiting for?"

"It's none of your concern," the prince said. "Go help the others get settled."

She saw Nottingham charge through the other portal with his serpentine dagger in hand. He was met with a haymaker punch from the prince that sent the villain sprawling backward the way he came. A massive Cyclops took his place at the mirror, pounding on the reflection with a concrete hammer. His blow caused a tiny crack in the reflection.

"It's happening!" she cried to the prince.

Charming scowled and ran toward Sabrina. She ducked inside as he took a flying leap, knocking her to the floor. Without offering to help he scampered to his feet and turned back to the magical hole.

"Harry!" he shouted as he wrung his hands. "C'mon, Harry!"

It was then that Harry appeared. Charming slipped his hand through the portal and took from Harry a small black box just large enough to hold a ring or perhaps a small necklace. "Here you go, boss."

"Hurry, Harry," Daphne said. "You need to step through now."

Harry flashed a melancholy smile. "I'm sorry, little one. But I'm afraid that's not part of my design. I can't leave my mirror."

"But if you don't you'll die!" Sabrina cried as a ripple of cracks rolled across the glass, distorting Harry's face.

"It was fun, boss," Harry said to the prince.

Charming nodded. "Indeed it was."

A fiery-red handprint appeared at the center of the cracked mirror. It was identical to the one Sabrina had seen the Wicked Queen create when she had threatened to "fix" Mirror not long ago. It burned bright and then the reflection shattered. A million tiny pieces spilled to the floor. The Hotel of Wonders was gone forever; its guardian, the ever-smiling Harry, went with it.

Charming stared at the broken shards for a moment as he stuffed the black box into his suit jacket. His jaw was clenched, hard and cold.

"I'm sorry," Sabrina said to him. "I know Harry was a friend."

Charming shook his head. "Harry was not real. I can't mourn him."

"But—"

Charming walked away. Moments later she could hear him barking orders to his soldiers out in the hall as if nothing at all had happened.

"What about Puck?" Sabrina asked, but no one answered.

The crowd was on the verge of a panic. Many were wrapped in bandages Nurse Sprat had hurriedly applied. But there were too many injuries, even with Granny and Veronica's combined help. Worse still, it was clear their numbers had dwindled again. More than a few had perished in the dragon attack.

Charming stepped forward. He raised his hand for attention and the crowd turned to him.

"Today we suffered," he shouted. "But such is the nature of

war. Battles are won. Battles are lost. But for the sake of those who fell we fight on. I know that as you look around you a feeling of discouragement wells up in your throats. But you need to spit that feeling out on the floor. Stomp on it with your feet. Smash it into dust. It has no place here. You will fight again and I will lead you and we will show the Master and his Hand how discouragement feels."

The crowd did not look convinced. "We've heard enough of your pep talks, Charming," Mr. Boarman cried. "People died today and a lot of pretty words aren't going to make us feel better about it."

"This was foolish," Little Bo Peep said. "We cannot beat the Scarlet Hand."

Charming tried to speak but he was booed into silence. It was then that Mr. Seven stepped forward.

"We are already beating them!" the little man shouted over the crowd. A grin came to his face. "You want to know why those dragons were sent after us? The Master is furious that we beat his army at the marina. He rages because we cut off his supply line and we did it all while a spy told him our every move."

"A spy!" Rapunzel cried.

"Yes, we were all under surveillance by a member of the Scarlet Hand and we still managed to fool the Master. He sent dragons after us because we are a threat and he knows it. You see, people . . . we scared him. Listen to what I'm saying. We scared the Master. Even though we're outnumbered, we struck a fear so powerful he sent his most vicious weapons to wipe us out. And they couldn't get the job done. He took some of our friends but we took out four dragons, not to mention the two Jake Grimm killed earlier. Plus, I'm told Sabrina Grimm wiped out five hundred of his soldiers all by herself. That is astounding, people. We did what the Hand thought was impossible."

The crowd roared. Many danced and sang; others hugged and kissed one another. Sabrina was stunned. Even her sister stood with her mouth open in surprise.

"Perhaps Mr. Seven is the charming one," Granny Relda said.

"So, friends, are you going to quit now when we have the Master on the run?" Mr. Seven shouted.

The crowd shouted and shook swords, wands, and fists in the air. They snatched Seven off the ground and marched him around on their shoulders.

As they watched the celebration, Charming approached the Grimms.

"I'm told Geppetto's boy was responsible for the sabotage."

"Unfortunately, yes," Granny replied. "Worse yet, he escaped. The last we saw of him was right before the attack. I fear he may have been killed by the dragons."

Charming looked around at the huge impromptu celebration. "Or he's hiding in this crowd. I'll spread the word to the others. We'll catch him eventually."

Henry stepped forward. "You've got a bigger problem than that, Prince. Bringing the troops inside the Hall of Wonders might have saved their lives, but I'm afraid we're all stuck in here unless you're planning on rushing through one of those other mirrors we saw in the Room of Reflections."

"I wouldn't recommend it. There's no telling where they might lead or who might be on the other side," Granny Relda added.

"Not at all," the prince replied. "I was thinking we'd march right out your front door."

Henry shook his head. "If you can fight your way out you're free to try. Last time we checked the house was surrounded by the Hand."

"I'd be surprised if there were any of them still outside," Snow White interrupted. "I think the Master threw everything he had at us today."

Nurse Sprat appeared. "Excuse me, I don't mean to interrupt, but I was hoping I could borrow Veronica and the girls."

"Of course," Veronica said, then turned to Henry. "We'll be right back. Nurse Sprat needs some help with the wounded. Will you save me a dance?"

Henry kissed Veronica. "I'll save them all for you."

Veronica and the girls followed the nurse into the crowd and far from the ears of the rest of their family.

"I'm so excited," Daphne said.

"I am, too," Veronica said, then looked down at her belly. "Please be OK."

Once they were safely out of earshot, Sprat turned to the group and took Veronica's hands in her own. Her expression was serious and troubled. "I have to tell you something—"

"It's the baby," Veronica said, finishing the nurse's sentence. Her voice trembled as she slid into a seat.

"You are not pregnant," Nurse Sprat replied, leaning down to take Veronica's hands. "Anymore."

A tear rolled down Veronica's cheek and she looked to Sabrina and then Daphne. "I'm sorry, girls."

The girls hugged her tightly, as if squeezing her might prevent the tears from escaping.

"Oh, Veronica, you didn't lose the baby," the nurse said. "This is so confusing. That's why I brought in some help."

Morgan le Fay approached. "Sorry I'm late. I've had to turn

down a dozen marriage proposals in the last fifteen minutes. I got here as quickly as I could."

Nurse Sprat nodded. "Did you bring your magic?"

"Everywhere I go," the witch said, waving her hands in the air. A blue mist materialized and swirled around Veronica's belly.

"Mrs. Sprat, what is this all about?" Veronica said, startled.

"Just a moment," the nurse replied. She watched the vapor as it changed colors from blue to red. Then it vanished into the breeze.

"Just as you suspected," Morgan le Fay said. "Something magical happened."

"Can someone let us in on this big secret?" Sabrina snapped. She was tired and impatient.

"Veronica, I have a theory, but it's not good news if I'm right," Nurse Sprat said.

"Just tell me," Sabrina's mom said, grabbing the armrest of the chair as if to brace herself.

"You were pregnant. The baby was healthy but when you and your husband were placed under the spell the baby was not affected. It continued to grow at a normal pace."

"I'm not sure what you're telling me," Veronica said.

"Veronica, I found something unusual in your blood sample, a peculiar compound I'd never seen before, but it was clear it was magical. So I called in Ms. Le Fay for consultation. She's got centuries of experience with herbs and roots."

"What we found is called Donnoga Root," Morgan said. "It was used back in the old country by women who were expecting difficult births—you know, human-giant infants, things like that. The Frog Prince and his wife used it when they had their daughter—as did Beauty and the Beast and Mrs. Arachnid and the Spider. It helps the impossible birth occur."

"And this Nooganar Root was in my bloodstream?"

"Donnoga Root," Nurse Sprat said. "And yes. I found a large sample of it in your blood."

Daphne stepped forward. "My mom wasn't having an impossible birth. She was having a normal baby."

"A normal baby for sure," Sprat explained, "but not a normal birth. Someone used this on your mother when she was asleep. See, when the baby was born your mother would have had to do certain things she couldn't do if she was unconscious. Whoever gave you the root gave it to you while you were unconscious and we think—"

"They took my baby!" Veronica cried. Her voice shook with panic.

"Is that possible?" Daphne asked.

"Who would do this?" Sabrina said, but all of a sudden

she knew. She had seen a crib in Red Riding Hood's insane asylum. She had heard a child crying in the halls and seen a baby in Red's hands. The little lunatic had called him her baby brother. The former Wizard of Oz had said her parents were giving birth to a new future. That little boy she had seen with Red. He was her brother and the Master had him! There had been hints and clues all along and she had never stopped to notice. Why had the Master taken the baby and where was he now? There was only one person that knew. "Where's Red Riding Hood?"

"With Mr. Canis, I think," Veronica said.

Sabrina ran back the way they had come and into the crowd of cheering Everafters. "Let me by!" she shouted. "I need to get past!"

Finally she spotted Mr. Canis and Red Riding Hood within the crowd. The little girl had a smile on her face and was enjoying the festivities. Sabrina ran to her and snatched her cloak in her hands.

"Where is the baby?" she demanded.

"What baby?" Red said feebly.

"Don't play dumb with me. I know you had him," Sabrina said. She had never been so angry and afraid in her whole life.

"I don't remember any baby," Red shouted.

"Sabrina, leave her be," Mr. Canis demanded, but she ignored him.

"He's somewhere in that head of yours," Sabrina said. "You have to remember!"

Red pulled away. "I'm trying!"

"You're not!"

"Sabrina, that's enough," Canis shouted.

Sabrina reeled on him. "You make her remember! Right now. She and the Master stole my baby brother. She knows where he is."

"What are you talking about?" Mr. Canis said as Veronica and Daphne raced to join them.

"Sabrina, this is not the way," Veronica said.

"She knows where he is," Sabrina repeated.

"I'm sorry. I'm so sorry. I wasn't myself," Red said through streaming tears. Then there was a moment of clarity in her eyes as if something were rising to the surface.

"You remember something?" Sabrina said.

"A crib in a room filled with holes on the walls," Red said. "Little holes that let him see the whole world. Little holes that let him see you wherever you are. He keeps the baby there and watches."

"What does he look like, Red? Who is he?"

Red Riding Hood looked into Sabrina's eyes. Sabrina could see the struggle on the child's face. There was something important but Red could not get at it. She looked away.

Veronica rushed to Sabrina and scooped her into her arms. They held each other and cried. Daphne joined them. There was nothing else to do.

10

s. White's assumption proved to be correct: When they took the trolley back to the house, they saw that the mob that had once surrounded it was gone. All that remained were hundreds of broken arrows on the lawn and an abandoned cannon. The house had not been harmed, though the front yard was a disaster.

Prince Charming took advantage of Mr. Seven's heroic speech and newfound popularity and promoted him to general of Charming's army. The little man marched the soldiers through the Hall of Wonders, which took the better part of a day. When they arrived at the portal they continued down the stairs and out the front door. The family watched strangers and friends file past. They wished them well and hoped to see them all again.

Buzzflower and Mallobarb smiled at Sabrina as they left. They thanked her and the family for their kindness after Sleeping Beauty's death.

"Where are you headed?"

"Well, we're told the plan is to take Town Hall but I can't be sure that's where we are truly headed," Buzzflower said.

"Sergeant White says all we need to know is how to fight, not where it's going to happen," Mallobarb added.

Uncle Jake rushed to their side. "Ready, ladies?"

"You can't go. It's too dangerous," Granny cried.

"We'll look after him," Mallobarb said. "He didn't make much of an impression on us at first but he's grown on us."

Uncle Jake grinned.

"This isn't your war," Mr. Canis said as Uncle Jake marched ahead.

"Yes it is," Henry said. "He's a Grimm. This is what we do."

"We might never see him again," Veronica said, fighting back tears.

"We'll see him again," Daphne said. "He's Uncle Jake. He's gravy."

Goldilocks and the three bears were the next ones to file out the door.

"Goldi, are you sure about this?" Granny asked. "There's plenty of room here and the fighting is going to get worse."

Goldilocks shook her head. "I'm done avoiding my responsibilities, Relda. I'm back in Ferryport Landing. It's time to plant some roots and see what sprouts."

Veronica stepped forward. "Goldi, if you're doing this to avoid me and my family . . . you can't risk your life and limb because you might feel uncomfortable here!"

Goldilocks smiled. "You're an amazing woman, Veronica. I'm not sure you mean what you just said but you said it nonetheless. I doubt I would have done the same."

Soon all of the soldiers were gone and the family was alone. They stood in the front yard surveying their little house and silently thanking their good luck. Somehow they had survived a fleet of fire-breathing dragons, an angry mob, and an army of bloodthirsty villains. They were enjoying the peace and quiet when something massive fell out of the sky and landed in the front yard. The impact was so powerful everyone lost their footing and fell to the ground. When Sabrina got back to her feet, she realized that there was a white dragon with orange stripes on its belly lying dead in the front yard. Puck was standing atop it with his little wooden sword in hand.

"Don't disrespect the sword, Grimm," Puck said.

• • •

The first order of business was getting the water and electricity turned back on. Puck reattached the severed electricity line on the pole by flying up and carefully reconnecting the cables. Unfortunately, he held the wires a bit too long and for the rest of the day his hair stood straight up on end. Veronica worked her own brand of magic on the water pipes.

With utilities back in working order, they went about opening windows and taking out the rotting garbage that had been sitting in the hot house for five days.

Granny made a huge meal consisting of what appeared to be fried oysters in peanut butter and jelly sauce. Sabrina could barely handle the smell and sat at the table picking at the horrible culinary nightmare. Her father noticed and nudged her under the table.

"I ate her cooking for eighteen years," he whispered. "You get used to it."

"Oh yeah, when?"

"I think it happened around the seventeenth year," Henry said.

The entire table was listening to the conversation and burst into laughter. Only Granny Relda was offended at first, but she quickly joined in and eventually laughed the hardest of all.

The rest of meal was filled with jokes and stories. For what seemed like the first time since Sabrina's parents had woken, they weren't fighting. Sabrina looked about the table at her family: Mom, Dad, Granny Relda, Daphne, Puck, Mr. Canis, and Red Riding Hood, and realized this was what she had been hoping for all this time. This moment had been the one she imagined over and over when she would peek into the spare room and see her slumbering parents. If only the whole family had been there—namely Jake and her baby brother. Where was the baby? Was he safe? She looked over to her mother and from her worried expression could see she was wondering the same thing. Somehow they had to find him.

"So, Henry," Puck said as he kicked off his shoes and propped his smelly feet on the kitchen table. "I was wondering what you can tell me about puberty."

Henry turned pale and stammered.

Sabrina wanted to crawl under the table and die.

• • •

That night, as Sabrina was dressing for bed, Daphne entered the bedroom. She was carrying a pillow that she tossed on the bed.

"Are you back?" Sabrina asked.

"Not by choice," the little girl said. "Granny kicked me out of her room. Just as well—she snores."

"Well, that's the pot calling the kettle black," she muttered. "I missed you."

"I know. Think about that the next time you want to lie and steal from me," her sister said as she crossed the room and opened a drawer in the desk that sat in the corner. From inside she removed a hairbrush.

"I will," Sabrina replied sincerely as her sister crawled up behind her and brushed her hair. "You know, I'm very proud to be your sister."

"Gravy."

Sabrina smiled. "Gravy."

"We have to find him," Daphne said. "We have to stay in Ferryport Landing until he's back with us."

"I know," Sabrina said.

"No grumbling about it, either," the little girl added.

"No promises."

"Hey, where are our marionettes?" Daphne said, glancing at the dresser. "Mine was next to yours and they're both gone."

"Dad threw them out," Sabrina said. "I saw him toss them into the trash bin in the kitchen. After what Pinocchio did I don't think he wanted them around."

"Good," Daphne said. "They were creepy anyway."

"Super creepy. Nothing like a puppet to give you the willies," Sabrina said as she crawled into bed. As she lay there she felt her sister slip her hand into her own, and soon they were both asleep.

Sometime during the night Sabrina woke up. She looked at the clock on the nightstand and saw it was almost three in the morning. She was thirsty, so she padded down the hallway to the bathroom. She flipped on the light and poured some water into a glass. After drinking it she turned to go back to bed—then she spotted the marionette Pinocchio had made of herself sitting in the middle of the hallway. She nearly screamed, but quickly figured that Puck was pulling another prank. Only he would dig through the trash to have some fun at her expense.

"That's hilarious, Puck," she called. "I thought the war was over." She scooped the marionette off the floor and stuffed it into the bathroom trash can. Then she went back to bed.

She hadn't been under the covers longer than ten minutes when she heard someone shuffling across her bedroom floor. She sat up and flipped on the light. There, on her dressing room table, was the marionette.

"Aargh!" she cried, which woke Daphne.

"What's with the light?" Daphne grumbled.

"Puck's having a little fun at three o'clock in the morning," she said. "C'mon."

Sabrina snatched the puppet and walked down the hall with her sister behind her. Together, they pounded on Puck's door until he answered. He wore a pair of footie pajamas with happy cowboys on them. He looked half-asleep and annoyed. "Whatever you're selling I'm not interested."

"What's the big idea?" Daphne said.

"I don't know what you're talking about," Puck said.

Sabrina shook the marionette at Puck. "You keep trying to spook me with this. It's very immature."

"Why would I play with a bunch of girly puppets? Boys don't play with dolls."

"Don't you sleep with a stuffed unicorn?" Daphne said.

Puck stuck his tongue out and slammed the door in her face.

"Stop goofing off, freak boy," Sabrina shouted.

Puck's bedroom door opened again. "You can send your apology to me in writing." Then he slammed the door in their faces once more.

Sabrina tossed the puppet into the hall trash, and together she and Daphne headed back to their room. They complained about having to live with the king of stupid pranks for a while and then drifted off to sleep.

It didn't last. Sabrina wasn't sure what time it was when Daphne shook her awake, but it was still dark outside. She could hear crickets chirping outside her window. The little girl had her hand clamped over Sabrina's mouth and her finger over her own mouth, signaling to Sabrina that they had to be quiet. Then she pointed at the dresser across the room.

Sabrina turned and nearly screamed. The marionette was back, along with the others Pinocchio had made, but they weren't sitting on the dressing table. They were walking around the room under their own power. A few of them had opened the dresser drawers and were rooting through the girls' still-packed suitcases. Another searched in their closet, and others scurried around under their bed.

"Did you know they could do that?" Daphne mouthed the words.

Sabrina shook her head.

"What are they looking for?"

Sabrina shrugged. She turned back and saw her own marionette rummaging through the desk. "I found them," it squeaked, holding up Sabrina's enormous set of keys. The weight of the ring made the creature fall backward onto the floor, but it quickly righted itself.

"Let's go. The boss is waiting," the Granny Relda marionette commanded, and all the others followed her out into the hallway.

"What are they doing?" Daphne whispered.

"I don't know, but I think we better find out," Sabrina said, pulling her sister out of bed. Together they crept into the hallway just in time to watch the marionettes unlock the room that held the magic mirror and hurry inside.

Just then, the bathroom door opened and the girls saw their mother and father inside.

"Did you see that?" Veronica asked.

"You mean the walking, talking marionettes?" Sabrina asked.

"Yeah, we saw them," Daphne said.

"We'll get Mr. Canis and your grandmother," Henry said. "You wake up the fairy."

The girls pounded on Puck's door for what seemed like forever. Finally he opened the door. His stuffed unicorn was under his arm. "You two are really pushing your luck," Puck said. "What could be so important that you have to wake me up not once but twice?"

"The marionettes are alive and stealing the keys to the Hall of Wonders," Sabrina said.

"OK, that counts," he said, tossing his unicorn inside his room and pushing past them and into the spare room.

"We should wait for the others," Sabrina said.

"For a bunch of puppets?" Puck scoffed. "We can take care of this. C'mon!"

The spare room was empty, so Sabrina assumed the creatures had already stepped into the mirror's reflection. She led Puck and Daphne through the mirror. On the other side they found their marionettes as well as a hundred more—all the puppets Pinocchio had carved. The Granny Relda marionette was busy passing out keys from Sabrina's key ring to each of its cohorts.

"If we're quiet we can sneak up on them," Puck said, louder than he should have. His voice echoed off walls and bounced around like a ball. And then all of the marionettes turned their heads toward them. With their strings dangling behind them, they raced down the hallway, unlocking doors as they went.

"What is this all about?" Daphne asked her sister.

Sabrina didn't have a clue but she was feeling the first inkling of panic. Most of the doors near the portal were filled with useful weapons the family used frequently, but farther down, in the direction the marionettes were heading, there were terrible things—things that should not be freed.

"We have to stop this," Sabrina cried, but it was too late. Just as she said the words a door opened and out stomped a huge blue ox. It was as big as a Winnebago and had horns on either side of its head. It stomped its front leg angrily and lowered its head toward the girls.

"It's Paul Bunyan's ox," Sabrina said. She had read the plaque for its room many times and then looked up the story. She'd seen Paul Bunyan. He was huge, and Babe was even bigger.

"That's the coolest thing I've ever seen," Puck said.

"How cool is it going to be when it kills us?" Sabrina said.

"Considerably less cool," Puck replied. The three children turned to run. They heard a bellow and felt the floor beneath them roll and rock. Babe the Blue Ox was about to stomp them to death. They ran back through the portal and leaped to one side as the creature crashed into the real world. The mirror seemed to increase in size to allow the monstrous animal through. Unfortunately, Granny's house didn't have the same magical ability and the animal caused an incredible amount of damage. It knocked through the wall that looked out on the lawn and ripped off part of the roof with one of its huge horns. The confined space seemed to make it panic and it whipped its huge head around, causing even more destruction. When it stomped its feet the floor beneath it collapsed. The ox fell with it into the living room. The children stood on a thin ledge of what had once been the bedroom floor, looking down into the gaping pit. Sabrina saw her family standing by the front door, looking up at them.

"It appears we have a problem, Relda," Mr. Canis said.

"Open the front door," Granny said, and the old man did as he was told. The front door morphed like the mirror to allow the ox though and it stomped out onto the front lawn. Unfortunately, that was not the end of the chaos. A giant three-headed dog tumbled out of the mirror and immediately fell through the hole in the floor.

Puck flew over to where Sabrina was standing. "There's something you don't see every day."

The dog was followed by a wave of bizarre beasties, monsters, and nefarious-looking people. Snakes with heads on both ends of their bodies slithered out and into the hole. People that looked like zombies, vampires, and werewolves from horror movies did the same. There was a seven-foot albino man with stringy muscles and pink eyes. There were pirates, wizards, witches, and unearthly creatures that looked like they were from other planets. They came in wave after wave after wave as if being pushed forward by an even bigger crowd behind them. Creatures made from ice and fire, a man surrounded by his own tornado, and a headless knight sitting atop a black horse. All the children could do was watch the macabre parade as it went by. Each creature fell into the pit then stumbled outside to freedom.

When the last of the creatures had come through and a few

peaceful seconds had passed, the children carefully edged toward the magic mirror.

"Kids, just stay where you are," Henry said. "I'll get a ladder and help you down."

"We have to check on Mirror," Daphne said.

"It's not safe," Veronica said.

"He's our friend, Mom," Sabrina said. "He's part of our family. We'll be careful."

The children headed into the reflection. Once inside the Hall of Wonders, Sabrina realized that every door was flung open wide. The marionettes were nowhere to be seen and neither was Mirror.

"Mirror!" Sabrina shouted, but the little man did not respond.

"We can't go room to room looking for him. It would take forever," Daphne said.

"If he's alive he's probably at the other end of the hall. The trolley isn't here," Sabrina said.

Puck's wings expanded and flapped briskly. He grabbed the girls by the back of their pajamas and hoisted them into the air. Then he flew down the hallway so fast the open doors along the way slammed shut. In no time at all he came to rest outside the closed door to the Room of Reflections.

Sabrina pushed the heavy door open and looked inside, but he wasn't there. The room was empty except for the mirrors hanging on the wall.

"Maybe one of the monsters ate him," Daphne whimpered.

"That would be awesome," Puck said.

Sabrina flashed him an angry look.

"*Awesome* in a terrible, heartbreakingly tragic kind of way," Puck continued.

In a panic, Sabrina spun back around, determined to search every room until they found their friend. As she dashed out of the Room of Reflections she heard something clicking. It sounded like an army of little wooden feet. She stopped in her tracks.

"Do you hear that?" she asked the others.

Both Puck and Daphne nodded.

She turned back toward the Room of Reflections, trying to follow the sound. It was clearly coming from inside the room, which was empty except for the mirrors.

"Where is that coming from?" Daphne said, looking about.

Puck walked around the circular room, listening closely at each mirror. "It's not coming from these."

Sabrina agreed. "It seems to be coming from the door." She studied the open door closely, then wondered if something might be behind it. She pulled it shut, closing them into the room, and that's when she saw it. A passageway!

"What's this?" Daphne asked.

Sabrina shrugged and stepped through the secret door. There she saw Pinocchio, surrounded by his evil marionettes, standing in front of a wall that contained thousands of shards of broken mirrors. They looked like tiny holes in space. None of them had a reflection, but rather, they acted like windows into places all over town and beyond. A quick glance showed her Nottingham's office, Mayor Heart's bedroom, Jack the Giant Killer's empty apartment, even the Wizard of Oz's workroom at Macy's in Manhattan. Sabrina recalled seeing huge full-length mirrors in each of those rooms, and it was clear that this room allowed a person to peer into them. There were faces in some of the broken pieces—the Frog Prince, the Beast, Mayor Heart, and Nottingham himself. They were all waiting, as if expecting some important instructions.

"Have the doors been opened in the Grimm home, Master?" Mayor Heart said from one of the shards.

"You're the Master?" Daphne shouted. Pinocchio turned and Daphne kicked him in the shin. The little boy howled and fell over. His marionettes leaped to his defense, jumping on Daphne's back and punching her. It took all of Sabrina and Puck's effort to free her from the tiny villains.

"You sick, twisted monster," Sabrina seethed at Pinocchio. "Do you know the nightmare you have inflicted on my family? You're a horrible, evil worm."

"I'm not the Master!" Pinocchio shouted.

"Why should we believe you?" Puck said.

"Because I am the Master," a voice said behind them. Sabrina spun around. Mirror was standing in the corner holding a little boy in his arms. A horrible mixture of terror, betrayal, shock, and disgust filled Sabrina's head, sending a wave of mixed signals to every part of her body. One moment she wanted to run—to put as much distance between her and Mirror as possible. The next moment she wanted to snatch him by the collar and shake him in anger until he explained himself.

"No," Daphne whispered.

"You? You're the Master? You're the leader of the Scarlet Hand?" Sabrina said.

Mirror nodded his head slightly. "Yes."

"But you—" Daphne said, trembling.

"But I was your friend? Is that what you were going to say?"

"Yes! I trusted you. We all trusted you!" Sabrina cried.

"Then I'm afraid you've made a terrible mistake," Mirror said.

Sabrina ran at Mirror, but a bolt of lightning stopped her in her tracks. She had witnessed Mirror's magic before, but never had it been intentionally directed at her. She studied the boy in Mirror's hands. He was small, maybe a year and a half old, wearing footie pajamas. He had curly red hair the color of Granny Relda's. He had Sabrina's father's face and her mother's beautiful eyes. "That's my brother. You took him," Sabrina said.

Mirror nodded. "It was unavoidable. Now, if you don't mind, I'd like to get my day started. Pinocchio, I believe I have a wish to fulfill."

"Thank you, Master," the boy said, bowing respectfully.

Mirror scooped the baby boy out of the crib again and turned to the children. "I'll be needing your help."

Sabrina shook her head but another blast of lightning told her Mirror wasn't asking—it was an order.

Mirror walked them down the hall until they reached an oak door Sabrina knew at once. It was the room that she had seen with Pinocchio a few days before—the room that had no name and no keyhole.

"One of you has to unlock this door," Mirror said.

"Uh, I don't have a key for this room, and there's no keyhole anyway," Sabrina said.

"You don't need either. You are the key," Mirror said.

"I think Charming is right about you," Daphne said. "You are defective."

"When your family acquired me, this room was created to house your most important possession. Even before there were locks on the doors, there was concern that access to this room could fall into the wrong hands. Thus, this room was given a special lock—one that can only be opened by a Grimm," Mirror explained.

"We won't open it," Sabrina said.

Mirror roughly snatched Sabrina's hand and forced it onto the stone in the center of the door. Her hand fit perfectly into the carved relief and a warm sensation came over her. She heard a chime and then watched the stone sink into the door, triggering a series of internal locks and tumblers, as well as bursts of steam that hissed out of the cracks around the door. The door swung open. Mirror's eyes welled with happy tears and he barged inside, pulling the children behind him. Unlike the other rooms that had wild, fantastical items or impossible creatures inside, this room was completely empty except for a thin wooden stand. On it sat an old book.

Mirror set the baby on the floor and rushed to the stand. He caressed the book's cover lovingly. "The Book of Everafter. After eons of wishing and praying, the power is finally mine."

"Are we supposed to be worried about an old book?" Puck asked.

"You ignorant little rodent! This isn't just an old book. This is the Book of Everafter."

"Sorry, I haven't read it. I'm waiting for the movie," Puck said.

Mirror scowled. "The Book of Everafter is a collection of every fairy tale, folk story, and tall tale ever told. Inside this book are the complete works of the Brothers Grimm, Andersen, Baum, Lang, Chaucer, Shakespeare, Perrault, and a thousand others you've never heard of. Every version of the stories of Snow White, Red Riding Hood, Prince Charming, Dorothy, Alice, Puss in Boots, and every other tale can be found in this book. No one knows where it came from or who wrote all these stories down, but there was magic in his pen. This book is the source of our immortality, our magic weapons, everything—this is what gives us our power. It also allows an Everafter a second chance at a happy ending." He turned to Pinocchio. "Boy, this book will give you the opportunity to right the wrong the Blue Fairy cursed you with so long ago."

"What do I need to do, Master?" the boy asked.

"Open the book and find the story written about you. Find the moment in the story that you would like to change and place your hand on that page. You will be drawn into the story, allowing you to relive it and, if the legend is true, revise it."

"You're saying he can go in and change his own story?" Sabrina said. "That's impossible."

Mirror shook his head in disappointment. "With everything you've seen in this town, I would have thought you would have more of an open mind about the impossible. What this book does, in essence, is turn you into a fictional character that you can then revise. Once you have made your changes you can leave the book and return to the real world. In Pinocchio's case he can step in as a boy and step out a full-grown man if he can manage to change his story to his liking."

Pinocchio rubbed his hands together eagerly. "Let's get started."

The odd little boy opened the book, but instead of opening to a certain page, the book flipped through every page, back and forth, as if it were trapped in a relentless wind. He tried to stop the furious pages but failed.

"I will never be able to find my story if it keeps acting like this," Pinocchio whined.

"An unforeseen wrinkle," Mirror said. "Unfortunately, you're going to have to do it the hard way. Put your hand on a page and it will pull you in. Once there you'll have to move from story to story until you find your own. I've heard there are doors if you can find them."

Pinocchio looked uncertain.

"What if I can't find the door?"

Mirror shrugged. "Perhaps you feel you'd have better luck on your own?"

Pinocchio frowned and turned back to the book. He slipped his hand into the whirling pages, and in a flash he was gone. His marionettes chased after him, plunging into the pages of the book and vanishing.

"What does this have to do with our baby brother?" Sabrina asked.

"He's going to provide me with my happy ending, Starfish."

"Don't call me that," Sabrina yelled.

Mirror frowned and looked genuinely hurt. "Very well, Sabrina. I know you're angry, but I hope you won't judge me too harshly. I'm only after what everyone on this planet wants—happiness. I'm not expecting you to understand but try to imagine what my life must be like. I was put into this world—born, you might say—by a cold, uncaring woman who treated me like property.

"For generations I have waited hand and foot on others. I can't say that your current family is not kind, Sabrina, but my owners have not always been so sweet. I have been in the company of mad men, lunatics, or people who simply ignored me. As good as you have been to me, you are only a temporary creature on this planet. You will die someday, and who will own me then? A tyrant? A monster? Who knows? Well, I won't do it any longer. I'm going to have my freedom. I'm going to walk out of this dreaded mirror. I'm going to get my happy ending and your brother is the key. He will lend me his body. I will become a human boy and grow into a human man."

"Why?" Sabrina asked. "You have plenty of followers in your Scarlet Hand. Why not take one of them?"

"Because they're Everafters," Mirror said. "If I took one of their bodies I'd still be a prisoner in Ferryport Landing. Why would I trade one prison for another? If I take the body of a human I can walk out of this town with the magical weapons stored inside this hall. It will be easy work for me to conquer this world. It will be very nice to have others serving me."

"But you don't have to do this. You just said that this book would let you change your story," Daphne said. "Why not go in and make sure you have freedom? Why steal our brother's life?"

"Sadly, in all the stories collected in this book, the story of my glorious birth has never been documented. There is no story for me to step into and alter. Thus, I have had to come up with another solution. I believe there is someone who can help me in these pages."

Mirror scooped up the baby boy from the floor and then stepped toward the book.

"You can't go in there," Sabrina said. "You can't leave the Hall of Wonders."

"I'm not leaving the Hall of Wonders," Mirror said with a sly grin. "The book will be here the whole time."

Mirror placed his hand on one of the pages and he and the child vanished.

"We have to go after them," Sabrina said.

"We're not going in there," Puck said.

"Yeah, I think this is one of those times we should wait for an adult's help," Daphne said.

"We can't wait," Sabrina said, stepping up to the book. "They're at the other end of the hall without a trolley. What if Mirror gets lucky and lands in the story he wants? He could be stealing our baby brother's body as we speak. We've got to stop him now."

Daphne reached out a hand and Sabrina took it. They both turned to Puck.

"Are you coming?" Daphne asked.

Puck scowled and took the little girl's hand. "Every time I try to get out of the hero business you two pull me back in!"

Sabrina put her hand on one of the book's pages. There was

an odd sensation, like being flushed down a toilet, and then everything went black.

• • •

When the lights came on, Sabrina looked around. She was lying on the floor of a wooden farmhouse. Her sister was sitting on a bed, wearing a little yellow dress, and Puck was nowhere to be found.

"Where are we?" Daphne said, helping her sister to her feet.

"Inside the book, I guess," Sabrina replied. "Where's Puck?"

Daphne shrugged. "Maybe he didn't make it. Maybe he's back in the Hall of Wonders."

Outside they could hear a commotion, including a lot of singing. Sabrina went to the door and swung it open. There was a sea of little people dressed entirely in green on the lawn. Sabrina recognized them as Munchkins, but that wasn't what shocked her. Right outside the door was a road made entirely of yellow bricks. She and Daphne stepped outside and were greeted like heroes. The Munchkins lifted them onto their tiny shoulders and cheered.

"What do they think we did?" Daphne said.

"You killed the Wicked Witch of the East," one of the Munchkins cried. "You saved us all."

Sabrina turned back to the house and saw the horrible truth—a pair of legs was sticking out from beneath it and they were wearing a pair of shiny silver shoes with a remarkable red tint to them. She suddenly realized they hadn't just entered a story. They had entered one of the most famous stories ever told.

"Daphne, I don't think we're in Ferryport Landing anymore."

To be continued in

THE SISTERS GRIMM

BOOK EIGHT
THE INSIDE STORY

ABOUT THE AUTHOR

Michael Buckley is the *New York Times* bestselling author of the *Sisters Grimm* and *NERDS* series. He has also written and developed television shows for many networks. Michael lives in Brooklyn, New York, with his wife, Alison, and his son, Finn.

This book was designed by Melissa Arnst, and art directed by Chad W. Beckerman. It is set in Adobe Garamond, a typeface that is based on those created in the sixteenth century by Claude Garamond. Garamond modeled his typefaces on those created by Venetian printers at the end of the fifteenth century. The modern version used in this book was designed by Robert Slimbach, who studied Garamond's historic typefaces at the Plantin-Moretus Museum in Antwerp, Belgium.

The capital letters at the beginning of each chapter are set in Daylilies, designed by Judith Sutcliffe. She created the typeface by decorating Goudy Old Style capitals with lilies.

Enjoy this sneak peek at

THE INSIDE STORY

BOOK EIGHT IN THE *SISTERS GRIMM* SERIES

"Call 911!" Daphne cried as she knelt beside the feet.

"There is nothing to be done," the woman in white said in an irritating singsong voice. "She was the Wicked Witch of the East. She held all the Munchkins in bondage for many years, making them slave for her night and day. Now they are all set free and are grateful for the favor."

Daphne ignored her and spoke to the legs. "Don't worry, lady! We'll get you out of there."

One of the Munchkin men stepped forward. "That's not the line."

Sabrina and Daphne eyed each other, confused. "Huh?"

The woman in white looked around and then leaned in close so she could speak in a voice no louder than a mouse's. "You are messing up the story," she said nervously. "You're supposed to ask me if I'm a Munchkin. That's what happens next."

Sabrina scowled and clenched her fists. "What is she talking about? Every person from this nutty place is—"

"Shhhh," Daphne said, and turned to the little woman. "OK, we'll say what you want us to say. Are you a Munchkin?"

The woman sighed with relief and brushed some wrinkles out of her dress. "No, but I am their friend. I live in the land of the North. When they saw the Witch of the East was dead, the Munchkins sent a swift messenger to me, and I came at once. I am the Witch of the North."

"I thought Glinda was the Witch of the North," Sabrina said.

Daphne shook her head. "That's only in the movie. Glinda's the Witch of the South. Haven't you read this story?"

"I skimmed it."

Another of the little men chimed in. "No, you're supposed to say, 'Oh gracious! Are you a real witch?'"

Sabrina fumed and stomped her foot. "Just let me punch one of them out. It will be a lesson for the others."

"Silence your animal, Dorothy!" another Munchkin demanded. "It's altering the story."

"Dorothy?" Sabrina said.

"My name's not—wait! They think I'm Dorothy," Daphne said as a happy smile spread across her face. "The book must have turned us into characters."

"Then who am I?" Sabrina asked. She studied her clothing, but she was wearing the same thing she had had on out in the Hall of Wonders.

Daphne snickered. "Probably Toto."

Sabrina joined in on the laugh, but it quickly faded. She reached under her shirt and found a small leather collar fastened around her neck. On it was a silver tag engraved with the name "Toto." She pulled it off and angrily threw it to the ground. "Of course! *I* have to be the dog."

Daphne laughed so hard she snorted.

"Yes, it's hilarious!" Sabrina steamed. "Don't be surprised if I bite your leg."

Daphne got herself under control. "Well, this is interesting. If the book is turning us into the characters, maybe that's why everyone's being so weird. We're supposed to follow the story. Am I right?"

The crowd regarded them quietly, as if they were afraid to answer. Finally, one of the little old men nodded subtly and whispered, "Please, we beg you. Just say the line."

Sabrina threw up her hands in frustration and turned to her sister. "I feel like I'm trapped in a second-grade play. They're going to have to spoon-feed us every line of dialogue unless you've got this story memorized from beginning to end."

Daphne recited the line the Munchkin had given to her: "Oh gracious! Are you a real witch?"

"Yes indeed," the woman in white said. "But I am a good witch, and the people love me. I am not as powerful as the

Wicked Witch who ruled here, or I would have set the people free myself."

Sabrina groaned. "Enough! We're not here to be part of your story. We're looking for a man who is traveling with a toddler—a little boy. Have you seen them or not?"

The Munchkins stepped back in fright.

"He's short and balding and wearing a black suit," Daphne added.

A rosy-cheeked man in the back of the crowd made his way to the front. "I have seen him."

The rest of the Munchkins broke into excited complaints, begging their friend to be quiet and not change the story. He spat on the ground and refused. "It's best to just get them out of here as soon as possible," he said. "They're just like the last feller. He wouldn't follow the story, either."

"Mirror was here? When?"

"Not long ago," the Munchkin said. "He took off down the Yellow Brick Road in search of one of those magic doors."

"Magic doors?"

"That's right. I've heard rumors they will take you out of this story and into the next."

"Then we have to stop him," Sabrina said. "If he gets to the door, who knows what story he'll step into next."

"Do you know where one of these doors is?" Daphne said.

The Munchkins in the crowd looked at one another nervously. After several moments of heated debate, the woman in white stepped close.

"The doors appear at random and disappear just as quickly. The best way to find one is to follow the story to its ending, where one will appear. Go down the Yellow Brick Road, find your companions, enter the Emerald City, and meet the great and terrible Wizard of Oz. He'll send you to kill the Wicked Witch of the West. Once that's done, a door should appear."

"That will take forever," Sabrina said as she rolled her eyes.

"Isn't there another way?" Daphne asked the witch. "You said they appear at random. Could we find one sooner?"

The old woman shook her head violently. "I've said too much already. I'll anger the Editor."

"The Editor?" Daphne asked.

Everyone shushed her at once. "Don't say his name! You'll call attention to us!"

To be continued . . .

THE SISTERS GRIMM

A Today Show Book Club Pick!

Catch the magic—

read all the books in Michael Buckley's *New York Times* bestselling series!

1 *The Fairy-Tale Detectives*
978-0-8109-5925-5 hardcover
978-0-8109-9322-8 paperback

2 *The Unusual Suspects*
978-0-8109-5926-2 hardcover
978-0-8109-9323-5 paperback

3 *The Problem Child*
978-0-8109-4914-0 hardcover
978-0-8109-9359-4 paperback

4 *Once Upon a Crime*
978-0-8109-1610-4 hardcover
978-0-8109-9549-9 paperback

5 *Magic and Other Misdemeanors*
978-0-8109-9358-7 hardcover
978-0-8109-7263-6 paperback

6 *Tales from the Hood*
978-0-8109-9478-2 hardcover
978-0-8109-8925-2 paperback

7 *The Everafter War*
978-0-8109-8355-7 hardcover
978-0-8109-8429-5paperback

8 *The Inside Story*
978-0-8109-8430-1 hardcover

today!